LAST STAND
ON THE
OCEAN SHORE

Also by Mark Cheverton

Battle for the Nether
Invasion of the Overworld
Confronting the Dragon

Trouble in Zombie-Town
Jungle Temple Oracle
Last Stand on the Ocean Shore

Saving Crafter

MARK CHEVERTON

LAST STAND ON THE OCEAN SHORE

A GAMEKNIGHT999 ADVENTURE

SIMON AND SCHUSTER

First published in Great Britain in 2015
by Simon & Schuster UK Ltd
A CBS company
Originally published in the USA in 2014 by Sky Pony Press

10 9 8 7 6 5 4 3 2 1

Simon & Schuster UK Ltd
1st Floor, 222 Gray's Inn Road
London WC1X 8HB

A CIP catalogue record for this book is available from the British Library

PB ISBN: 978-1-4711-5847-6
Ebook ISBN: 978-1-4711-4440-0

Printed and bound by CPI Group (UK) Ltd, Croydon, CR0 4YY

www.simonandschuster.co.uk

"I saw an angel in the marble and carved until I set him free."

—Michelangelo

CHAPTER 1
THE ORACLE

The speckled creepers flowed out of the jungle like a green, angry flood, the singular thought within their tiny brains echoing over and over again: *explode . . . explode . . . explode.*

Herobrine stood atop the cliff that overlooked the Jungle Temple and watched his creatures move out of the tree line and across the open clearing. Huge gouges torn into the landscape marked where TNT had exploded; the red and white blocks had been detonated by the desperate villagers in their defense against the spider queen and her vicious army of eight-legged monsters. Infant blades of grass were just starting to cover exposed dirt with a fresh velvety green coating, erasing the brown pockmarks that made the terrain around the temple look like the cratered surface of the moon.

The NPCs and Herobrine's arch-nemesis, Gameknight999, were gone. It was Herobrine's plan to pounce on the villagers right after the spiders finished their initial attack, smashing down on them with his army of creepers and zombies. . . . But somehow, yet again they had escaped.

Rage and fury boiled within him, his eyes

glowing bright, but then fading as he regained control.

"I'm done underestimating you, User-that-is-not-a-user," Herobrine grumbled to himself. "Our next encounter will be our last!"

Standing with his arms outstretched, Herobrine yelled down to the black and green spotted creatures.

"Come, my children; give this stone structure your loving embrace."

The massive group of monsters approached the temple. A lone creeper scurried out ahead to the stone side of the structure, its little feet moving in a blur. Stopping right next to the wall, it started to hiss and glow, its body swelling with explosive intent. In an instant, it . . .

BANG!

The creature exploded against the mossy cobblestone wall. It should have been enough to destroy it, but strangely it hardly scratched the rocky partition. Another stepped forward and obeyed Herobrine's command, giving the last measure of its life. . . . Again it exploded, but barely hurt the wall.

Herobrine growled. He could feel the old hag laughing at him from down in her underground chamber.

"So, Oracle, you're using your magic to hold this place together," Herobrine said. "Well, let's see what you do with this."

Reaching his hands up into the sky, fingers curled and extended like a dragon's claw, Herobrine gathered his crafting powers and projected them into the dark clouds overhead. A satisfying rumble echoed across the landscape, followed by another and another until . . .

CRACK!

A bolt of lightning streaked to the ground, striking one of the creepers. Instantly, a sparkling blue charge of electricity surrounded the explosive creature, giving it an almost magical appearance as sparks danced across its green skin. Another bolt slashed down at the monsters, then another and another, creating more of the charged monsters, the electrical energy magnifying their destructive potential.

Three of the super-charged creepers moved silently toward the building, the hissing of their internal fuses filling the air. This time, their horrific explosions tore a gash into the side of the building, the electrical boost from the lightning magnifying their strength. Cobblestone blocks rained down across the landscape, the cubes of stone bouncing off the heads of nearby monsters.

"Excellent!" shouted Herobrine. "The rest of you . . . *ATTACK! LEAVE NOTHING STANDING!*"

A wave of charged creepers scurried forward, each exploding and taking with it another chunk of the jungle temple. Slowly, the upper level disappeared one creeper at a time. The green spotted monsters erupted with hateful fury as they climbed across the structure, looking for any piece of the building they could destroy, satisfying their purpose in life with a violent exclamation point.

Once the surface of the temple was destroyed, the charged creepers moved into the underground passages, blasting away until there was not a single cobblestone left. In minutes, any evidence of the jungle temple's existence was completely erased from the surface of the Overworld.

Teleporting to the now-smoking crater, Herobrine looked down into the hole. A large pool of lava sat off to the left, part of the old hag's traps. But to the right, he could see a set of stairs that plunged down into the depths of Minecraft.

"I know you're down there, old woman, and I'm

coming for you," he said.

Putting his fingers to his mouth, Herobrine whistled. The piercing sound cut through the air like a blade through flesh, making all the creepers cringe. In an instant, moans and growls filled the air as a massive army of zombies stepped out of the tree line and approached the newly formed hollow. Herobrine knew what would be waiting down there at the end of that stairway . . . jaws and fangs ready to tear into flesh. He wanted nothing to do with that fate himself. Instead, he would sacrifice his zombies' lives until it was safe for him.

"Go into that tunnel and secure it," Herobrine said to the mob of zombies, "but leave the old woman alone . . . she belongs to me."

The zombies growled their understanding, then moved down into the crater, around the pool of lava and into the dark stairway. Instantly, Herobrine could hear the growls and barks of wolves, probably a hundred of them. He imagined those snapping jaws tearing into the zombies with reckless abandon, but his monsters continued into the stairway obediently, driven by Herobrine's command and fear of their leader. Wave after wave of decaying green creatures pushed into the passage. Moans and barks echoed out of the underground chamber together. But slowly the zombie growls rose to the front of the cacophony as the barking diminished . . . one wolf perishing for every two or three zombies.

Eventually, the final yelp of pain from the last wolf echoed underground, leaving only the sorrowful moans of the zombies to fill the air. It was now safe for Herobrine to enter. Pushing aside the green creatures, he strode down the stairs like a conquering hero, even though all he did was cruelly sacrifice the lives of others for his own selfish end.

Shoving his way down the stairway, Herobrine pushed zombies out of the way until he finally reached the bottom of the stairs. The passage opened into an elaborately decorated chamber, with blocks of lapis, emerald, and gold spotting the floor. Tall columns of cobblestone stretched up to meet the ceiling, holding the overhead canopy of stone and dirt in place. The walls were ringed with torches spaced four or five blocks apart, their flames casting circles of light that filled the chamber with a golden radiance. The entire scene would be described as beautiful by anyone, except for Herobrine.

"So, you have finally come," a scratchy voice said from the other end of the chamber.

Herobrine moved off the stairs and onto the chamber floor. Looking around him, he could see piles and piles of zombie flesh, many balls of glowing XP floating amidst the carnage. Taking a circuitous path, he stepped carefully away from the XP, not wanting to transform into a wolf or zombie. As he moved across the chamber, he could hear the click of the old woman's cane. She was coming toward him . . . perfect.

"You have caused much trouble, Virus," she said. "Was it necessary to kill all my wolves?"

"I will destroy everything that you cherish, just out of spite," Herobrine answered.

"But you killed many of your zombies as well," the Oracle said. "Have you no respect for any living thing?"

"These zombies are mine to command and mine to sacrifice as needed. They were happy to give their lives for me."

"They didn't look very happy to me," the old woman said.

"You lack vision, old hag, and cannot see what is

really important. A few hundred zombies sacrificed . . . who cares? Your emotions and sentiment cloud your judgment; that is why you will lose and I will win."

"We shall see, Herobrine. But this time, Gameknight999 will be ready for you."

"Like last time?!" he shouted. "Your puny little dogs were all that kept him from being destroyed. That won't work again. The next time I face the User-that-is-not-a-user, I will have a little surprise waiting for him . . . something that even the great Oracle did not foresee." He took a step closer, causing the old NPC to grip her cane firmly. "Did you feel the servers change? I didn't think so. I was ever so careful when I crafted something that seemed so harmless and unimportant that it made it past the ever-watchful gaze of the great Oracle. But this innocuous thing will shift the balance of power for good, and bring the User-that-is-not-a-user to his knees before me."

Herobrine then cackled an evil, maniacal laugh that reverberated throughout the chamber. Taking another step forward, he drew his sword and approached the Oracle.

"Your time is up," he said with a smile on his face, "and now you don't have any of your mutts to protect you. You have been abandoned by all the NPCs and are completely alone. The Oracle is at my mercy."

"You don't know the meaning of the word," the Oracle spat, then lifted her cane and threw it aside.

"What are you doing?" Herobrine asked, confusion showing on his face.

The Oracle then smiled and closed her eyes, linking her arms across her chest.

"What are you doing?"

She said nothing . . . just smiled.

Herobrine could hear the music of Minecraft growing louder, building to a crescendo. He looked about the room nervously, unsure what was happening, then turned back to his prey. Gripping his sword firmly, he raised it high over his head. Taking one last step forward, he swung his weapon down upon the Oracle. But just as the razor-sharp blade was about to reach her gray hair, she vanished, Herobrine's sword slicing harmlessly through thin air.

Turning quickly, Herobrine scanned the room. *What happened? Had she teleported somehow?* He didn't think that she possessed any such powers. As he stood there at a loss for words, the torches mounted on the walls slowly started to extinguish, as if some invisible giant were pinching them between massive transparent fingers. One after another, flames flickered, then died out until the room was bathed in darkness.

Gathering his own teleportation powers, Herobrine disappeared and reappeared on the cliff that overlooked the scene, a gigantic crater now carved into the ground where the majestic temple had once stood. Spinning around, he looked for the Oracle, but she was nowhere to be found. The only hint that something monumental had just occurred came from the music of Minecraft. It had been building, growing louder and louder, but now he realized it was gradually decreasing in volume, almost back to normal, clinking lightly in the background.

With his glowing eyes darting left and right, Herobrine smiled.

"I must have done it. . . . I did it! I destroyed the Oracle!" he exclaimed to himself. "YOU HEAR THAT, GAMEKNIGHT999 . . . I DESTROYED THE OLD HAG, AND NOW I'M COMING FOR YOU!"

He disappeared, then reappeared on the shore of the ocean.

"And this time, User-that-is-not-a-user, I will have

a little surprise for you."

And as Herobrine cackled another of his evil, hateful laughs, he disappeared, leaving behind a smoking, cratered scar in the flesh of Minecraft.

CHAPTER 2

MILKY'S LAND

The collection of boats sailed across the featureless ocean for days. The NPCs had been able to fight off the huge army of spiders back at the jungle temple, with the pitched battle ending when Gameknight999 destroyed the spider queen. But the battle had been close and could have easily gone the other way. With another army of creepers and zombies barreling down on them, a little gift from Herobrine, they were given no choice but to turn and run.

Using boats provided by Gameknight's user-friend, Shawny, they escaped Herobrine's trap by sailing into the unknown; however, many were beginning to question this decision. With no sign of land for days now and their food supplies slowly getting depleted, many of the NPCs were whispering fears that they may never find dry land again. Gameknight could see some of the NPCs with fishing poles out, but the looks of discouragement on their blocky faces told him that few fish were being caught. If they didn't find land soon, they would be in trouble.

On his right, Gameknight could see a collection of squid swimming nearby, their bright red mouths, ringed with sharp white teeth, standing out against the soft blue of the ocean. He always found these creatures interesting. Their toothy mouths always seemed so menacing, especially now that he was within the game; the razor-sharp teeth looked as if they could tear an NPC to shreds in seconds. Yet they were completely harmless; their ink sacks were used as a black dye when crafting. The boxy creatures moved with a peaceful grace through the waters, their long, rectangular tentacles dragging lazily behind; they meant no harm to any creature.

Gameknight999 envied these squid.

Glancing to his left, he found Digger in his own boat moving steadily forward with the flow of wooden vessels. The big NPC turned and looked at Gameknight, his light brown hair glowing in the light of the rising sun just emerging from behind the endless blue horizon, his gray eyes, as always, glowing with hope. Next to him rowed Stonecutter. The stocky NPC moved his boat effortlessly as he scanned the ocean for threats. He was always on watch for monsters.

"I love the colors of sunrise," a voice said to his right.

Gameknight turned and found Monet113, his sister, rowing next to him in her own boat. She was still wearing her iron armor, but had removed her helmet. Bright blue hair streamed down her back, emphasizing her obsession with color and art.

"Me, too," Digger said. "I don't mind saying, even out here, I still feel better when the sun rises."

"Yeah," Gameknight999 answered, "it's been nice not having monsters spawn out here in the ocean. A few days without fighting was just what everyone needed."

The big NPC nodded his head, then moved his boat so that it was right next to Gameknight's, leaving Stonecutter alone.

"You have any idea what we need to do once we

find land?" Digger asked.

Gameknight shrugged his square shoulders.

"Not really," he answered in a low voice. "All I know for sure is that we need to find a village with some food and start recruiting more NPCs. I suspect that Herobrine will be furious when he learns that we escaped his trap back there. He'll likely throw everything he has at us when he finds us again. All the battles that we've faced so far will be nothing compared to the wrath that Herobrine will call down upon us." Gameknight then leaned a little closer to the big NPC and lowered his voice. "I have a feeling that the Last Battle for Minecraft was not what we fought on the steps of the Source, facing Erebus and the monsters of the Overworld and the Nether. The Last Battle will be the conflict that is waiting for us on the horizon, somewhere out there . . . and we have to be ready."

"Maybe we could get Shawny to bring some of the users to help us," Monet said.

Gameknight shook his head.

"The ruling from the Council of Crafters is still in effect," Gameknight replied. "If the users appeared, and the NPCs kept using their hands and weapons, they'd be kicked out of their village . . . and you know what that means."

"They would become the Lost . . . an NPC without a village," Digger said in a low voice, the words sounding like poison on his tongue. "They'd be forced to roam the Overworld without a community or friends or anything . . . completely alone."

"You know how long a villager would survive in Minecraft on their own, Monet?" Gameknight asked.

"Not long," Digger said.

The User-that-is-not-a-user nodded his head.

"So, we're on our own?" she asked.

Gameknight and Digger both nodded their square heads.

"If a villager kept fighting after the users arrived, they'd be sacrificing everything," Gameknight said. "I can't ask anyone to do that. We have to figure out how to defeat Herobrine without the users."

"Well, you should know; everyone has confidence in you to see us through this and defeat Herobrine," Digger added.

I wish I could feel some of that confidence in myself, Gameknight thought. *I don't know what I'm doing. All these NPCs think I'm some kind of great hero, but I'm really a fake, just trying to get by without anyone knowing that I'm clueless.*

He reached into his inventory and pulled out the spotted pink egg, the weapon that would destroy Herobrine, according to the Oracle. Rolling it between his stubby hands, he looked at the surface, trying to figure out what it was . . . but it was a complete mystery.

What am I going to do with this thing?

Thinking back, Gameknight could remember his last conversation with the old woman. She had said, "Look to the lowliest and most insignificant of creatures, for that is where your salvation will lie."

What did she mean? It must be important.

He shuddered as waves of doubt crashed through his mind.

"You have any idea what you're going to do with that thing?" Monet asked.

Gameknight shrugged.

"I'm sure you'll figure it out; just don't sweat it," she advised. "When it's time, you'll know what to do, so don't worry."

"That's fine for you, Monet, but I don't work that way," Gameknight said. "I can't just *wait* for it to happen. There needs to be a plan and preparations, for many lives are relying on me to do the right thing. I can't be like you and just *act first, think later*...that's not the way I work." He looked away from his sister and stared at the rising sun. The blushing sky had now changed to a deep blue, making it hard to see where it ended and the sea began. "Jenny...what if I can't figure it out?" he whispered. "What if I'm not smart enough?"

"What?" she snapped. "Did you say 'what if'?"

Gameknight looked down at the bottom of his boat.

"You know what Dad would say about that, don't you, Tommy?"

He nodded.

"Yeah...he'd say don't focus on the *what ifs*; focus on *the now*," Gameknight recited as if he'd heard this from their father a thousand times. He leaned closer to his sister. "I wish he were here now instead of on the road. We could use his help...with the digitizer... with Herobrine. I bet he'd know what to do if he were home. But he never is, and he has me do his work for him when he's gone...which is always!"

Gameknight's dad was always on the road, trying to sell his inventions, and because of that Gameknight had gotten stuck in Minecraft. When his dad was gone, it was Gameknight's responsibility to take care of his sister and keep her out of trouble. But none of them expected his sister, Jenny, to use the digitizer and go *into* Minecraft. Her *act first, think second* nature put her in trouble all the time, and it seemed that it was always Gameknight's job to fix the situation.

Driving the thoughts of uncertainty and fear from his mind, Gameknight looked at the collection of boats that bobbed about near him. In the distance, he could see a sparkling missile streak up into the sky, then explode in a shower of color—one of Crafter's fireworks. The wise NPC was using them to keep all the boats together, which proved successful through the long nights, but Gameknight was sure that the supply of fireworks must be getting low. Just as he was going to ask Digger about it, he heard Crafter's young voice cry out over the sounds of the ocean.

"I see land!" Crafter yelled. "LAND!"

A cheer erupted from the collection of NPCs, Digger's own exclamations booming across the watery landscape and filling Gameknight's ears. With renewed hope, the villagers drove their individual boats as hard as they could, heading for the salvation that was just starting to peak its earthen head above the horizon.

After a few minutes, Gameknight could see the new land . . . but it was not what he expected. He could see tall red mushrooms standing like silent guardians across the landscape, their crimson sides spotted with small white squares. Intermixed were flat-topped brown mushrooms, their stalks bone-white. The ground itself was a mixture of muted purples and pinks that gave the landscape an almost alien appearance. Gameknight grew excited as he realized that they were approaching a mushroom biome. He'd never been in one of these before, but he had read about them online and watched multiple videos on YouTube.

As Gameknight grounded his boat and climbed out, he could hear the mooing of cattle. Running up a gentle rise, he was greeted by a massive herd of mooshrooms, red and white spotted cows with mushrooms growing out of their heads and backs. Their bright red skin stood out in stark contrast against the lavender mycelium blocks that covered the ground. As Gameknight surveyed the landscape, he could see his sister already standing atop one of the flat mushrooms, her eyes wide. He walked over.

"You like this?" Gameknight asked.

She nodded, then looked down and gave him a wide grin.

"The colors are fantastic," she said. "The blocks that make up the landscape . . ."

"They're called *mycelium*," he said.

"Right, mycelium; they're wonderful. I can count at least six different colors across their tops. And there are tiny spores coming out of them, as if the land itself is trying to grow more mushrooms," Monet said in an almost dreamlike voice. "And the cows—"

"They're called *mooshrooms*."

She laughed when she got the joke.

"But no time for sightseeing right now, Monet; we have work to do."

She looked down at her brother and sighed, then moved down the makeshift steps of dirt that she had made to get onto the mushroom's dome. Gameknight and Monet headed out in search of Crafter. Monet spotted the young NPC first, his black smock standing out against the mauve background. Crafter had his axe out and was heading toward the tall white stalk of a massive flat-topped brown mushroom, the plant standing probably ten blocks high.

Gameknight started to speak: "Crafter, we need to—"

"We need to start harvesting the mushrooms," the young NPC said.

"Right," Gameknight answered, then turned to his sister. "Monet, start getting bowls from anyone who has one. These mushrooms can be used to craft a stew. It takes a brown mushroom and a red mushroom, and of course a wooden bowl. Gather as many bowls as possible so that we can get everyone fed."

He then scanned the sea of faces around him,

looking for a specific NPC.

"Herder!" Gameknight shouted.

"Over here!"

Gameknight turned and saw a tall, skinny boy with long black hair waving at him. He was wearing a smock the color of brown leather, a stripe of white running down the center. The boy ran toward the voice of his idol, the User-that-is-not-a-user, a huge smile on his square face.

"I'm here . . . I'm here," the youth said excitedly as he stopped directly in front of Gameknight999.

"Yes, I can see that," Gameknight answered. "You're almost standing on my feet."

"Oh, sorry," Herder said and took a step back. "What can I do to help?"

"The mooshrooms," Gameknight said.

Herder looked at him confused, then glanced at the red and white creatures.

"I want you to shear them," Gameknight explained. "You can collect the mushrooms; then they'll turn into regular cows. After the shearing, I want you to collect as many as you can. We need a new herd, and everyone knows that herding animals is your job."

"But I don't have any wolves to help," the lanky boy complained.

"Then get some warriors to help. We will need food for later."

Herder cringed when Gameknight mentioned the idea of killing the animals. He knew that this was difficult for Herder, but they both knew the realities of Minecraft. If you ran out of food, you didn't last long.

"I'm relying on you to get this done. Can I count on you?"

Herder looked up at Gameknight and nodded his boxy head, proud that he'd been asked by the User-that-is-not-a-user to do this important task. The boy streaked off with a set of silver shears in his hands. Gameknight gestured for a group of warriors to help Herder. The warriors stopped digging up mushrooms and ran off toward Herder, shouting, "Wolfman! Wolfman!"

Gameknight smiled.

There was been a time when Herder had been a target of ridicule and bullying. His differences had attracted sarcastic and hurtful gibes, with mean-spirited pranks being played on him at nearly every opportunity. His nickname used to be Pigboy because of his work with the animals. The name was meant to hurt, not honor. But the young boy had showed his true courage and strength at the battle for the Source, bringing a giant pack of wolves to push back the monster horde and save hundreds of lives. Now, instead of Pigboy, he was Wolfman, a name given out of respect, his unique strength finally recognized by all. Gameknight was proud of the lanky boy and smiled as he ran off.

Turning back, the User-that-is-not-a-user scanned the landscape. Every NPC was digging up mushrooms, stuffing the small red and brown fungi into their inventory. Some of the NPCs were already starting to make mushroom stew, sipping down the pale liquid, then handing the wooden bowl to the next villager. Gameknight could see Digger standing atop a tall hill, surveying the landscape. Grabbing a bowl of mushroom stew, Gameknight climbed up the block incline until he was at the big NPC's side.

"Digger . . . here," Gameknight said as he extended the bowl.

Reaching out with big muscular arms, Digger accepted the proffered bowl and drank down the stew, then handed back the empty dish.

"Thank you," Digger said in a low voice.

Gameknight nodded, then stood at his side, facing away from the sea. From this height, they could see that the mushroom land was a large island, with only a narrow strip of water separating it from the mainland. In the distance, they could see the land that waited for them: desert. Hot, dry desert.

"There will be little food out there," Digger said without looking at his friend. "We'll need to take every mushroom we can carry."

"Crafter has everyone harvesting them as we speak."

Digger grunted.

"Any idea which way we need to go?" Digger asked.

Gameknight shook his head.

"I figure we keep heading east," the User-that-is-not-a-user answered. "The farther we get from Herobrine, the better. But if we don't find a village soon, we're in trouble. These mushrooms aren't going to last very long."

"We'll need to figure out a strategy when we get to that desert," Digger said. "There weren't any monsters on the ocean, and there are never hostile mobs on mushroom islands, so everyone has been spoiled. But we need to remind everyone that there is still a war going on."

"I'm sure the spiders out there in that desert will remind everyone pretty quickly," Gameknight added.

"I hope not," Digger answered as he pulled out his iron pickaxe and headed down the hill to start collecting his warriors.

Standing on the hill, Gameknight looked out across the mushroom island and toward the vast desert. Closing his eyes, he listened to the music of Minecraft. It was not as strained and dissonant as it had been when the monsters, led by Erebus, had gone to the Source. No, this time it was different. It still flowed as a beautiful background melody, coloring the wonderful scenery of Minecraft with its harmonious hues, but something was wrong. The music lacked its calming presence, and instead left him with a feeling of desperate unease, as if something dangerous was coming their way.

CHAPTER 3

SURPRISE IN THE DESERT

A s Gameknight999 waded across the shallow strip of water, crossing from the mushroom island into the desert biome, he glanced up at the sun. It was at its zenith, staring straight down on them with its square yellow face, bright and pure. But as Gameknight crossed the watery barrier that separated the two habitats, he was surprised to feel the temperature jump up suddenly as his feet met the sandy ground. Looking around, Gameknight could

tell that all the NPCs felt it, the oppressive heat of the desert. It was almost overwhelming, but they all knew that Herobrine and his army of monsters were nipping at their heels, relentlessly hunting them, so they dared not slow their pace. With heads tilted down away from the blazing overhead furnace, Gameknight and the NPCs continued eastward.

"I've never been in a desert before," said a high-pitched voice next to him.

Gameknight looked down and found Topper

staring up at him, the young boy's warm brown eyes sparkling with subtle flecks of gold in the bright sunlight. It was Digger's son, brother to a twin sister, Filler.

"There was one about a day's walk to the south of my village," Topper explained, "but I wasn't allowed to go there. Dad said . . . you know . . . Digger . . ."

"Yes, I know who your dad is," Gameknight said, smiling.

"Anyway, he said it was too far away for someone as young as me."

"Your father is a wise NPC," Gameknight added.

The young boy's smile turned to a frown.

"But when *will* I be old enough?" Topper growled. "We can do things, you know . . . me and Filler . . . but no one believes us. Everyone thinks that because we're small, we're also weak and afraid . . . and that's not right! I want to be treated like a big kid, but everyone treats me like a child. It's not fair."

"Digger is just looking out for your safety, Topper," the User-that-is-not-a-user said. "Besides, when you are older, I'm sure he'll have lots of things for you to do that only big kids can do. You just have to wait a while."

"I don't want to wait!" the young NPC snapped.

"Sometimes our choices and actions define us, Topper," said a voice from behind. Gameknight turned and found Crafter walking behind him, with Stonecutter and Filler at his side. "I've seen young kids make very mature and responsible decisions, and do things that no one ever thought possible."

"Like Fisher?" Gameknight asked.

Crafter nodded his head.

"Our decisions in life show people the kind of individuals we are, Topper," Crafter continued. "Children who make grown-up decisions get treated like big kids, even though they could be among the smallest of NPCs. Age is not the metric by which people are measured; it's what they do and how they do it that matters."

Topper turned and looked at Crafter over his shoulder, then glanced up at Gameknight999, his unibrow furled in concentration.

"Deeds do not make the hero . . ." Gameknight mumbled almost inaudibly to himself.

Glancing over his shoulder, Gameknight could see Crafter smile.

"Well, one day you'll see . . . everyone will see. Topper and Filler are no longer little kids," Topper said proudly.

"That's right," Filler added in a high-pitched voice.

"Well, for now at least you're still small enough for this," Gameknight said.

Reaching out with lightning speed, Gameknight999 grabbed Topper by the waist, then hoisted him up over his head so that the young child sat on his square shoulders. Following his lead, Stonecutter did the same with Filler, the young girl's sandy blond hair flying through the air like a wave of gold. The twins giggled as they sat atop their mounts. Gameknight smiled at Stonecutter and patted the muscular villager on the shoulder.

Looking at the stocky NPC, Gameknight could see that Stonecutter was easily as strong as Digger, if not more so. His arms were like thick tree trunks, the gigantic biceps formed from the countless hours of putting pickaxe to stone. His skin was covered with tiny scars from the many chips of stone that had sliced him over the years. Stonecutter saw those scratches as a badge of honor, a symbol of his hard work and skill. A tangled mop of brown hair, almost the color of the bark on a dark oak tree, covered his blocky head, a sprinkling of gray here and there signaling the coming of middle age. But his eyes were the most notable thing about Stonecutter. They were the color of stone . . . gray, but not sparkling with hope as Digger's or Crafter's eyes did. These gray eyes hid some terrible sadness that sat deep within his soul. Something had happened to the stocky NPC in the past . . . something terrible. Gameknight could see Stonecutter frequently withdraw into himself when he was quiet and contemplative, the painful memories being relived in his mind. At times he seemed incredibly sad, but when around Gameknight999 he seemed to come out of his melancholy and stand up straight and tall. In fact, Gameknight started to notice that Stonecutter was never very far from his side. It was as if he were trying to always protect him . . . curious.

Looking up at the child on his own shoulders, Gameknight could see Topper smile, his short, sandy-blond hair glowing in the sunlight. Next to him, Filler smiled at her brother, then looked down at her mount, Stonecutter. The stocky NPC grinned up at the girl, his stony eyes momentarily filled with happiness.

The two children rode on the men's shoulders as they trudged through the afternoon, walking for what seemed like hours and hours. The oppressive heat of the sun blasted into the NPCs, burning away their strength and in some cases their HP. Gameknight could see many of the villagers pulling out bottles of water to drink, trying to replenish the HP that was slowly being baked out of their already exhausted bodies. As they continued to trudge across the dry wasteland, an uneasy pall seemed to fill the air as the sun approached the horizon; nighttime was coming. Out on the open desert, surrounded only by huge rolling dunes of sand, there was little to use for camouflage or defense. They were totally exposed, and

Gameknight knew that if a large mob caught them out there, it would be difficult to defend themselves.

Climbing a large sand dune, Gameknight looked around, trying to formulate some kind of plan in case they ran into any hostile mobs. He wished they had horses, for in battle speed meant life, but they had left their steeds at the jungle temple because they couldn't bring them in the boats. The cows that Herder had sheared and collected would be of no use in battle, though after a confrontation, the NPCs would need the meat to restore their health.

Gameknight shuddered as he imagined a battle out here on these dunes. It brought back memories of a book he'd once read. He imagined Arrakis and sandworms gliding across the dunes, Fremen standing on the mighty beasts, hanging onto their maker hooks. It brought a smile to his face as he thought about the first time he'd read the legendary book, curled up on his bed, reading into the wee hours of the night, completely absorbed by the story.

Suddenly, a joyous cry pierced the air. Snapping out of the memory, Gameknight looked ahead at the top of the next dune. He could see Digger standing atop the crest, waving his iron pickaxe. Gameknight ran, weaving around other NPCs as he tried to reach the top without jostling Topper too much. When he arrived at the peak, he was shocked at what he saw . . . a desert temple.

The structure was placed in a large flat basin, a ring of sand dunes surrounding the plain. Farther away near the horizon, Gameknight could barely make out the outline of another structure. It looked like a tall stone tower . . . a watchtower.

It was a village . . . still very far away, but now in sight.

Cheers erupted from the NPCs as they reached the

top of the hill. A village meant water, a village meant crops . . . a village meant life. But as soon as it seemed like luck was finally on their side, a cry of terror cut through the air like a razor. Topper was screaming, as if terrified. Gameknight pulled the child off his shoulders and stood him on the ground.

"Topper, what's wrong?" Gameknight asked.

The child's face was white with fear, his brown eyes wide with shock. He slowly pointed off to the north, his stubby rectangular finger shaking with fear.

"Zombies are coming," the young boy said, his voice cracking with fear.

Without realizing it, Gameknight drew his sword as he turned. A chill ran down his spine as he peered across the desert. In the dim light of sunset, he could see the lumbering green forms staggering across the sandy landscape, their rotting arms outstretched. Orange light from the setting sun reflected off their razor-sharp claws, making their pointed fingers sparkle and flash in the distance, as if they were aflame.

"How many are there?" one of the NPCs asked.

"Too many," said another.

Gameknight tried to count, but the fading light coupled with the distance made it difficult. One thing he knew for sure . . . there were a lot of them.

"I think they're heading for the village," Gameknight said.

"We have to do something," his sister replied.

Turning, he could see Monet113 standing next to him, her bow in her hand.

"We can't just let them go down to that village and destroy everything," she said. "They have to be stopped."

Gameknight looked toward the monsters, then glanced back at the village. The angry creatures were clearly heading straight for the desert village, and there was no way the NPCs could get there before the zombies reached their target. But the temple was right along their path. He could see the fear on the faces of the NPCs, fatigue and exhaustion hanging heavily on their tired bodies. If they just ran forward and attacked the mob out in the open desert, many of his friends . . . his family . . . would be destroyed. They couldn't fight that many, not as tired as they all were.

"Gameknight, what do you want to do?" Digger asked.

The sorrowful wails of the zombies wafted on the warm desert breeze and reached their ears. It was a haunting, angry sound that made many of the NPCs start to shake in fear.

"Why are we standing here?" Hunter shouted as she drew her bow and notched an arrow. "Let's go get 'em!"

"No, I don't think that would be wise," Crafter said as he drew his own sword. "User-that-is-not-a-user, what is your plan?"

Gameknight could see concern in Crafter's bright blue eyes. But when he glanced at Hunter, all he saw was someone who wanted to fight. She still sought revenge for the loss of her parents and her village at the hands of monsters.

What do we do?

Indecision raged through him, paralyzing his mind. There were NPCs in that village . . . and they were in danger. But these NPCs with him were his friends; he couldn't just send them into another battle . . . not right now.

If I take care of one, I sacrifice the other, he thought. *I hate this responsibility . . . it makes me want to explode!*

Then the solution started to surface in his head.

Explode . . . yes, that would do it, but what about the zombies? How can we fight that many if we . . . the temple . . . of course.

As everyone around Gameknight asked him question after question, the plan took shape in his mind. It was a good plan, but it was risky.

Life always contains risk, a voice said within his head, a voice definitely not his own.

Gameknight looked around to see if anyone else had heard that voice, but all he saw was confusion and fear. Everyone was talking all at once, each person emphatically shouting out what the group should do. What they needed right now was a direction, a leader . . . the User-that-is-not-a-user.

"*QUIET DOWN!*" Gameknight yelled, then glared at the faces around him, daring anyone to challenge him. Hunter was about to speak up, but Gameknight's scowl instantly silenced her. "OK, here's what we're going to do."

And Gameknight999 explained his plan as the army of monsters moved closer and closer.

CHAPTER 4

THE DESERT TEMPLE

The NPCs sprinted for the temple, their lives depending on it. As they ran, Gameknight could see Crafter ahead of him launching rockets in the air. High overhead, the missiles exploded in a shower of color: a green creeper face, a sparkling orange sphere, a glistening yellow star. In the light of dusk, those in the village would easily see the colorful display.

"I hope the villagers are getting ready for this army," Gameknight said to his sister, Monet, who was running at his side.

"I could run ahead and warn them," she said. "I'm sure I can run faster than the zombies and get there before them."

"NO!" Gameknight snapped. "It's too risky."

"But I could—"

"Absolutely not. I have to keep you safe . . . it's my job. And having you running in front of a zombie army, hoping there will be some place for you to hide until they go away, doesn't sound like a very safe plan."

"But I can do it . . . I know it!" she said, almost yelled.

"Forget about it," Gameknight replied. "We're all heading for the desert temple, and that's the end of it."

Monet113 looked up at her brother. Her unibrow was furled with frustration as she glared at him, her normally soft gray-green eyes burning with anger. He was about to say something when she turned and moved to run at Stitcher's side, an irritated scowl on her face.

As the group ran, Gameknight moved to the edge of the pack and drew his sword. He could start to hear the angry moans and growls from the decaying creatures, their hatred for the living resonating across the desert wasteland.

We have to hurry! he yelled within his mind.

The desert temple was still far away, and the zombies were getting louder.

"Everyone, HURRY!" Gameknight yelled, but he could tell that everyone was already sprinting.

They weren't going to make it to the temple in time;

that meant fighting all these zombies out in the open. Many would die in that battle, and the User-that-is-not-a-user wasn't going to let that happen.

"Woodcutter, Stonecutter, Trimmer, Cobbler, all of you get some TNT and come with me," Gameknight shouted. "Hunter, I'll need you, too."

The four NPCs collected the red and white striped blocks from their friends, taking as many as they could hold, then ran toward Gameknight. Peeling off from the main group, the User-that-is-not-a-user ran at a diagonal, not directly toward the temple and not directly toward the zombies, but somewhere in between. Suddenly, he was surrounded by the NPCs, Hunter at his side, her shimmering bow casting a cerulean glow around the warriors. Running up a tall sand dune, Gameknight could see the approaching mob as they crested their own hill. The monsters saw them and growled, their eyes glowing red with hatred.

"They don't seem very happy. Maybe if we give them a little surprise, it will help with their mood," Hunter said, causing the other warriors to laugh nervously.

Gameknight999 was not laughing, however. He could see that there were more than fifty of them, a sizable number, and now they were shuffling faster. It was no joking matter. Altering his path, he headed straight for that rabble, the other NPCs following. They stopped after cresting the next hill. Gameknight could see the monsters clearly now. They were normal zombies, each with decaying green skin, tattered dark blue pants, and a torn light blue shirt. A sigh of relief came from Gameknight when he could see that there was no zombie king with them. He'd battled Xa-Tul to save his sister, but hadn't killed him. Herobrine had interceded in the conflict and teleported the zombie king away in the last second, saving the creature's life. That always worried Gameknight.

I'm sure you're out there somewhere, Xa-Tul, Gameknight thought.

The idea of facing off against that massive zombie made him shake with fear. He'd barely been able to stop him the last time, but if Herobrine made that monster even stronger, he wouldn't stand a chance.

"Gameknight, what's the plan?" Hunter asked, snapping him back to the here and now.

At the bottom of the sand dune, Gameknight could see the collection of monsters staring up at them, waiting.

"What are they waiting for?" Stonecutter asked.

"Maybe they didn't expect to find NPCs out here in the open desert," Trimmer said.

"We need them to follow us so that the others will have time to get into the temple," Gameknight said. "Hunter, you think you can do something that will make them mad?"

Hunter looked at his friend and smiled, then turned toward the mob, her curly red hair flying in a crimson wave. Drawing a handful of arrows, she stuck them into the sand directly in front of her. Notching one, she fired it at the largest zombie, then quickly grabbed an arrow before her and fired again and again and again. The arrows streaked through the air with a ball of magical blue flame wrapped around their tips. They hit the monster in the chest one after another in quick succession. The creature instantly burst into flames, but then disappeared with a pop when the third arrow struck home, causing his comrades to growl and moan, then charge forward.

"Mission accomplished," Hunter said with a smile as she turned and ran, the other NPCs doing the same.

"Place a block of TNT right below the peak of the sand dune," Gameknight999 ordered.

Stonecutter stopped and placed the block behind a sandy cube, then turned and continued to run, heading back toward the desert temple.

"No, this way," Gameknight yelled as he took off at an angle. "We're going to make the zombies take a zigzag path to the temple. That will slow them down."

The zombie growls grew louder as they crested the peak. Spotting the escaping NPCs, the mob turned and pursued them. But they were not doing the normal zombie shuffle, walking slowly with arms outstretched.

"They're running!" Stonecutter exclaimed, his voice filled with shock and surprise.

"What?" Gameknight asked as he glanced over his shoulder. "I've never seen zombies run before. Herobrine's shadow-crafters must have done something to them . . . giving the monsters this new ability."

"Great, running zombies," Hunter said. "That's all we need."

"Let 'em have it!" Gameknight yelled.

Hunter stopped and spun around, then drew an arrow from her inventory and fired it at the red and white block. The arrow struck the cube right in the center of the N and instantly started to blink. The creatures were so enraged that they didn't notice the ticking bomb.

BOOM!

The block of TNT tore into the mob, flinging green bodies into the air. A few disappeared as they landed, flashing bright red on impact. The decaying monsters howled in anger and ran straight toward the NPCs.

"Here they come," Trimmer yelled. "RUN!"

They all turned and fled, sprinting across the desert with every ounce of speed.

"Head toward those two sand dunes," Gameknight

yelled, pointing with his iridescent, shimmering sword.

The party sprinted forward, not bothering to respond. They headed for the gap between two large hills of sand. When they reached the two mounds, Gameknight stopped to make sure the zombies saw them.

"Hunter, send them a message," Gameknight said.

"Gladly," she replied as she fired a deadly missile toward their pursuers.

The arrow struck one of the zombies in the shoulder, causing it to catch fire for a moment, then went out when the monster dropped to the ground to put out the magical flames. Standing, the wounded zombie roared a bloodcurdling wail, then ran directly at Hunter.

"I think they got the message," Hunter said with a smile, then turned and ran along the narrow pass between the two dunes.

"Quickly, turn this way," Gameknight said as he cut back along their path, heading around the dune and back toward the monsters.

"What are you doing?" Cobbler asked. "You're heading back toward them."

"No, they're behind the dune. They can't see us," Gameknight explained. "We're playing a little game of follow the leader. Put two blocks of TNT right between the two hills."

Cobbler stopped and placed the blocks next to each other, then turned and ran. Hunter laughed as she patted her friend on the back, then also turned and ran, the rest of the NPCs following their leader's direction. As they ran, Gameknight could hear the moans of the pursuing horde as the monsters emerged from between the two sand dunes.

"Hunter," Gameknight said. "Hit 'em NOW!"

With a fluid motion, Hunter pulled out an arrow, notched it to her bowstring, stopped to take careful aim, then released. It flew in a graceful arch, lighting the sand with a soft blue glow as it streaked through the air, then struck the TNT block. Instantly, the red and white cube started to blink. The monsters at the front saw the bombs and tried to turn around and run back, but the mass of zombie bodies surging from behind was too large. They all crashed together, stopping the stampede of decaying creatures.

BOOM . . . BOOM!

More bodies flew into the air. Gameknight didn't stop to count how many; he just turned and ran.

"Come on, we've delayed them enough. Let's get to the temple," he shouted.

The others cheered and ran, heading straight for the temple that was just barely peeking over the top of the sand dune ahead of them. As they crested the hill, Gameknight could see the temple clearly. It looked like some kind of ancient Egyptian pyramid, with sloping sides that narrowed as they stretched up into the sky. Images of the great pyramids of Giza sprang into his mind as Gameknight remembered lessons from school. But those pyramids had been massive. This one before him was but ten blocks high, with an ornate entrance and twin towers standing on either side of the opening. Orange cubes of wool decorated the faces of the towers, giving it an ancient look, as if some kind of great secret lay hidden within its depths.

As they approached the temple, Gameknight could see that most of the villagers were already inside the blocky building. Workers were modifying the structure, adding stone and dirt here and there to form defensive walls and platforms from which archers could fire. As they neared the entrance, Hunter ordered NPCs to distribute the blocks of TNT around the temple. Once they were done, they all ran into the ancient building.

Instantly Gameknight coughed at the dust that filled the air. There were so many people moving around that dust from the sandstone blocks was billowing upward, choking everyone. It seemed that the hard hooves of the cows were the worst offenders.

"Herder . . . where's Herder?" Gameknight yelled.

"I'm here," he replied from across the chamber.

"The cows, they have to go outside," Gameknight said.

"But they won't be safe," Herder complained.

"Zombies don't eat cows," Gameknight replied. "I'm sure they will be OK. Now get them out before we suffocate in here."

Herder nodded his head, then whistled as he moved toward the door. Stepping out of the temple, Herder led the cows onto the open plain.

"Quickly, get back inside," Crafter yelled. "They're coming."

Herder looked at his cows, then turned and glanced at the approaching monsters. Placing a hand affectionately on the nearest cow's neck, he patted the animal, then ran back to the temple doorway. Once inside, Herder turned and placed blocks of dirt in the opening, sealing the entrance.

Moving to one of the side towers, Gameknight climbed the stairs that would let him reach the top of the pyramid. Jumping onto the sloped roof, he positioned himself on the pyramid's peak and watched the monsters approach. They flowed across the desert like a poisonous green tide, knocking over cacti as if they weren't even there and trampling the brown, dried bushes with their clumsy feet. When the horde reached the temple, they stopped and glared up at Gameknight999, their cold, dead eyes filled with hate. By the looks on their decaying faces, he could tell that these creatures wanted nothing more than to tear them all to shreds.

They were completely surrounded, and all the villagers hiding in the temple were exhausted from heat and hunger. There was no way they could go out there and fight off this horde; they were trapped. All the zombies needed to do was wait until Herobrine came here with his main force; then they would all surely die.

"Great . . . what do we do now?" Gameknight said as he looked down on the monsters, waves of uncertainty crashing down on him.

We can't just wait here . . . or we'll be trapped, he thought. *We have to do something, but what?*

CHAPTER 5

BATTLE

The sorrowful moans of the zombies floated up to Gameknight999 from all sides.

"I think they like you," a voice said next to him.

Turning, he could see that it was Hunter, her red curls shining in the moonlight.

"You know, they're harder to get rid of if you name them," she said playfully.

"Stop clowning around," he growled, then turned to stare down at their attackers. "What are they doing?"

"I don't know," Hunter replied. "Maybe they weren't expecting to find us and are a little confused."

"Yeah, well—"Gameknight started to say, but he was cut off by a pain-filled moo from a cow, and then another and another.

"They're killing the cows," Herder yelled from inside the pyramid.

Hunter moved to the side of the roof as she drew back an arrow, then fired.

The projectile streaked through the air and hit a zombie that was swinging at one of the cows with its razor-sharp claws. The arrow struck the monster in the back, but it did not stop the attack. Instead the zombie continued to strike at the cow, ignoring the arrow sticking out of its back. Hunter fired again and again until the creature disappeared.

Gameknight was shocked at what he was seeing.

Why would they want to attack the cows? he thought.

Turning, he ran down the side of the pyramid and into the tower. Taking the steps two at a time, Gameknight sprinted to the front door. Drawing his pickaxe, he broke the top block so that they could shoot at the zombies with their bows.

"Someone shoot at the monsters!" Gameknight yelled. "They're attacking the cows."

"My cows!" Herder exclaimed.

But before anyone could move, Gameknight continued to knock holes in the walls of the temple, creating more spaces from which they could shoot.

"Archers to the top of the temple," the User-that-is-not-a-user commanded. "Shoot at the zombies. We aren't going to let them take our cattle."

NPCs cheered as they pulled out their bows and headed for the stairs that led to the top of the temple.

"Digger, I need more archer slits for the—" but before Gameknight could even finish the sentence, the big NPC was already breaking blocks in the side of the temple, creating places where the warriors could fire on the monsters.

In a matter of minutes, there were holes all the way around the temple. Those with bows fired their arrows at the decaying creatures. When the zombies realized what was happening, they approached the gaps and tried to reach in and attack the NPC with their dark claws.

"Stand back, away from the holes," Gameknight shouted as he drew his sword and stood right next to one of the gaps.

As a zombie reached in to get at the archer, Gameknight hacked at the arms of the monster, causing them to flash bright red. The villagers without bows saw this and instantly lined the perimeter of the temple, standing between the open gaps. Working as a team, the archers drew the monsters close with their pointed barbs, then the swordsmen attacked them with their blades. Soon, the zombies learned to stay away from the edge of the temple. This allowed the archers on the roof of the ancient structure to take their toll.

"*HUNTER!*" Gameknight yelled, hoping his voice could be heard through the sandstone walls. "*LIGHT THE TNT!*"

Gameknight turned and found his sister firing through one of the openings, her enchanted bow lighting the interior of the pyramid.

"Monet, go up and help Hunter and Stitcher . . . quick!" he said.

She flashed him a smile, then streaked for the stairs that led to the roof.

Instantly, the group felt the ground shake as a cube of TNT detonated. Moving away from the wall, Gameknight headed for the stairs as well. He ran to the top of the temple and found Stitcher and Monet there, both firing their bows at the sea of green monsters that were surrounding the structure. Off to the side,

Gameknight could see Hunter firing her enchanted bow at the red and white blocks of TNT.

"Here you go, zombies," Hunter yelled as she fired at another block of TNT.

BOOM!

"Come get some!" she yelled as she ignited another bomb.

BOOM!

The blocks detonated, tearing gashes in the ground and throwing zombie bodies into the air. Running to the other side of the temple, Hunter fired again and again at the explosive cubes. Blasts rippled around the desert temple as the TNT blossomed, enveloping the decaying monsters in their fiery embrace.

Gameknight looked around the temple to assess the situation. There were still at least a dozen zombies still alive, but most of them were now running after the remaining cows and not attacking the temple.

Why would they want cows? he thought.

The cries of the terrified cattle mixed with the growling moans as the zombies fell upon the docile beasts. They attacked the animals, quickly diminishing their HP with vicious intent, multiple monsters falling on the creatures from all sides. But soon the spotted animals were silent . . . the last of them destroyed. With no more cattle to attack, the zombies stopped their moaning wails, turned, and ran back into the desert.

"We can't let them escape!" Gameknight yelled. "If they report our position, Herobrine will be here before we're ready."

Without waiting to see if anyone was following, Gameknight hacked a narrow opening into the temple wall and ran out onto the sand, diamond sword in his right hand, iron in his left. When the villagers in the temple saw this, they all cheered. Suddenly all of them were running across the desert sand in pursuit.

"Where are you zombies going?" Gameknight shouted.

One of the monsters heard the voice and looked over his shoulder. An excited growl came from the monster when he saw the lone user. He turned for Gameknight999, the other monsters following his lead. With a dozen zombies approaching, anyone else would have ran . . . but not the User-that-is-not-a-user. His mind was lost to battle and he was acting without thought, his body moving on pure instinct. Gameknight charged straight toward the zombie leader.

"I'm not gonna let you hurt my friends!" he shouted. *"FOR MINECRAFT!"*

The zombie reached out with its dark claws, swiping at Gameknight's head, but the User-that-is-not-a-user ducked, then spun, his iron sword raking across the zombie's side. The monster flashed red as it howled in pain. Pivoting on one foot, Gameknight returned, striking at the beast with both swords, taking all of its HP.

Not waiting to see it disappear, Gameknight moved to the next creature. Charging straight at it, he leapt high into the air, bringing both swords down onto the monster with all his weight . . . it didn't stand a chance.

Suddenly, moaning sounds came from all around him. Looking to his left and right, Gameknight could see that there were zombies on both sides of him, and a group of three charging straight at him.

How am I going to fight all of these at the same time?

Fear trickled down his spine as he gripped the hilts of his swords. But then a strange whirling noise sounded through the desert air. Out of the corner of his eye, he could see Digger's pickaxe spinning end over end before hitting one of the zombies in the shoulder, knocking it to the ground. Following the pick was a stream of arrows streaking out of the darkness. Their shimmering shafts stuck into the monsters, pushing them back a step and making them flash red again and again. More arrows shot out of the darkness as Gameknight charged the group of three. But before they reached him, he found Stonecutter at his right side, his big iron pickaxe held at the ready, and Hunter and Monet on his left. They fell on the remaining zombies as the villagers ran around the battlefield to close off any possibility of escape. In seconds the battle was over . . . all the monsters were destroyed.

A cheer erupted across the shadowy desert, the villagers joyous that they'd stopped these monsters without losing a single life. But Gameknight was not so happy. There was a puzzle here that he did not understand.

What are you after, Herobrine? Gameknight thought. *Why do you need these cows?*

Surveying the battlefield, Gameknight saw glowing balls of XP everywhere, with chunks of zombie flesh floating on the ground, bobbing up and down as if on an unseen ocean. But on a distant sand dune, at the very edge of his vision, Gameknight thought he saw someone . . . or some*thing* standing there, watching. It looked like a zombie, with dark blue pants and a faded light blue shirt, but there was something different. It looked to Gameknight as if there were something on its chest, something yellow. Straining his eyes, he could almost see the outline of what looked like a . . . sunflower?

Why would a zombie have a sunflower painted on its shirt?

But just as soon as Gameknight noticed the

monster, it disappeared.

Was that real, or did I imagine it? he thought. *I know I'm tired . . . but it looked so real, yet impossible at the same time. A flower . . . on a zombie?*

"Everyone back to the temple," boomed Digger's voice.

A hand slapped Gameknight on the back. Turning, he saw Hunter's smiling face, and his sister, Monet, at her side.

"You really enjoy that two-sword thing, don't you?" Hunter asked. "Maybe you can save some zombies for others."

Hunter laughed, but Gameknight did not respond. He was still staring out at that distant sand dune . . . confused.

"Hey, are you listening?" Hunter asked.

"Ah . . . what?" Gameknight said.

"I said, that two-sword thing," Hunter repeated. "You seem to—"

"*EVERYONE BACK TO THE TEMPLE!*" Digger yelled, his voice almost making the desert sand shake.

"Yeah, we should get back," Monet said, an arrow still notched in her bow. "Come on."

Hunter and Monet turned and headed back to the temple, leaving Gameknight there, staring at that mysterious sand dune. Shaking his head, he turned and followed the NPCs. When he reached the temple, he walked around the perimeter, checking the damage to the structure. There were glowing balls of XP everywhere, which the NPCs picked up. He could see pieces of raw beef floating on the ground, littering the area, but no leather. Moving around the structure, he picked up the meat, careful to avoid the stinking green zombie flesh.

"Why would they do that?" Gameknight said aloud to no one.

"Why would they do what?" asked a voice from behind.

Turning, he found Crafter standing near the temple entrance, his iron sword still in his hand.

"They took the leather, Crafter. Why would they do that?"

Shaking his head, the young NPC surveyed the destruction surrounding the temple.

"I don't know," Crafter answered. "It makes no sense."

"Well, at least we stopped them from getting to the village," Hunter yelled from atop the temple wall.

"Yes, but I'm not sure they were even heading for the village," Crafter said. "Maybe they were attracted to our cattle and not the village at all."

"That's ridiculous," Hunter said as she moved near the entrance. "All zombies want to do is destroy, be it cattle or villagers . . . it's in their nature. They should be exterminated."

"Hunter!" Stitcher snapped. "Violence is not always the answer."

"It is when it comes to monsters," the older sister replied. She then turned and faced Gameknight999. "Let's get to that village out there."

"No, not at night," he replied. "We'll rest up here for the night then go in the morning."

"A wise plan," Crafter added.

Everyone moved back into the temple; Gameknight stayed out until he was sure that everyone was accounted for. As he headed for the doorway, he found Herder on his knees, looking at the spot where his cattle had been. Gameknight could see tiny square tears flowing down the lanky youth's cheeks. Putting a reassuring hand on the boy's shoulder, Gameknight knelt next to him.

"Why would they do this?" Herder asked as he

turned to look at Gameknight999. "They were just innocent animals. They had nothing to do with this insane war."

"I don't know, Herder," Gameknight answered. "But rest assured, we're going to find out. Now, come on; we have to get into the temple and get some sleep."

As they stood, Herder looked at his idol, then wiped his cheeks with a dirty sleeve. With eyes cast to the ground, he walked back into the temple, Gameknight999 following right behind. After closing in the doorway with blocks of dirt, Gameknight moved to one of the archer holes and looked one last time at the sand dune where he'd seen that lone zombie.

I'm sure I saw something yellow on its shirt, but why would it be yellow, unless . . .

A maelstrom of possibilities spun through his head as he contemplated what he'd seen. He wanted to think about every one of these possibilities, but he was too tired. Yawning, he found a bed that someone had put out and sat down. On the other side of the temple he could see Digger and motioned the big NPC to come near.

"What does the User-that-is-not-a-user need?" Digger asked.

"There is a chamber beneath this floor," Gameknight explained. "If you make another of your spiral staircases, you can get down to it. There is a pressure plate that is wired to blocks of TNT. If you break the redstone circuit, you can take the plate and all the TNT."

"We will take care of it," Digger said as he pulled out his mighty pickaxe.

"There's more," Gameknight said as he put a hand on Digger's muscular arm. "There are four chests with treasure. Be careful and look for traps, but we should be able to get some diamonds from there. You should have a diamond pick . . . and use the enchantments for Crafter's sword."

"I'll get it done," Digger said, then rushed off to give orders.

Gameknight laid his head back on the pillow as he listened to the sounds of digging, his eyes becoming heavy.

I wish we were back home and not stuck in here, he thought. *If only Dad were home. He'd know how to help us and get us out of here without letting Herobrine escape. If only he were home . . . if only he were home.*

Then, finally, Gameknight999 lost his battle with fatigue and fell asleep.

CHAPTER 6
WINGED SPIES

Herobrine materialized in a large underground chamber. His glowing eyes lit his surroundings with an eerie illumination, casting strange shadows on the rocky walls. He could see that this was not the cavern he sought. The evil shadow-crafter transported to another large cave. Instantly, he could tell that this was the right place.

All around him, Herobrine could hear the squeaks and splashes of bats. Allowing his eyes to flare bright, he lit the cave with his evil glare. The cavern was not as big as a zombie-town, nor a spider lair, but it was still a sizeable enclosure. With a span of about fifty blocks across, despite its immense width, it felt like a cramped space. The ceiling was only a dozen blocks high, and compared to the extent of the cavern, the stony roof felt low, making Herobrine want to stoop.

A stream of water poured out of a hole in the wall and fell to the cave floor, forming a pool that stretched across half the cavern. All around the pool flew bats, maybe a hundred of them. They flitted about throughout the cave, then periodically plunged into the water, checking on their precious treasure lying at the bottom of the shallow pond.

Teleporting to the edge of the pool, Herobrine peered into the cool waters. He could see the bottom lined with brown eggs, each spattered with tiny black spots. There were probably a thousand of them, some bigger than others, the largest ready to hatch. This cave was one of the main hatcheries for the bats on this server. As the tiny creatures emerged from their oval cocoons, they fluttered through the tunnels and underground passages until they spread out all across the digital landscape. With the lifespan of bats naturally being short, it was important for the species to have this collection of eggs. These speckled seeds would generate a consistent trickle of bats throughout the server, maintaining a balance of creatures for the species.

But Herobrine didn't need balance . . . he needed numbers.

Plunging his hands into the cool water, Herobrine gathered his crafting powers. As his hand started to glow a pale, sickly yellow, the water in the pool became peppered with magical yellow bubbles. In the depths, he could see the eggs begin to hatch. The bats in the cave squeaked with agitation as tiny newborn creatures struggled to get out of the water and fly into the air. Those that were too weak from the premature hatching simply sank to the bottom, their bodies flashing red. Many of the adult bats plunged into the pool, trying to help the weaker ones get to the surface, but only those that were strong enough to take to the air survived.

Many of the tiny creatures died, but Herobrine did not care. He needed these creatures now, and refused to wait. As the last of the eggs hatched, Herobrine stood and looked at the massive collection of bats. It was as if the cave had suddenly filled with a black, fluttering fog of beady eyes and flailing wings. There was barely room enough for all of them to be airborne at the same time. Some settled on the walls and ceiling, giving the impression that the entire cavern was carpeted with living, breathing creatures, but even with all the crowding, none would go near Herobrine. They all feared him, which made the shadow-crafter smile.

"Come, my children . . . to the surface," Herobrine said, his voice filling the chamber with echoes, eyes glowing bright.

Herobrine teleported to the tunnel entrance that led to the deep underground hatchery and stood near the opening. As he waited, his eyes glowed brighter and brighter, thoughts about his enemy, Gameknight999, flowing through his head.

Soon, the bats started to emerge. Their tiny red eyes watched Herobrine warily as they flew out of the opening, staying in a tight fluttering sphere. They formed a giant undulating ball of tiny wings and beady eyes that grew in size as the rest of the colony shot up into the night sky.

"You will be my eyes and ears on this server," Herobrine shouted to the bats. "I command you to find my enemy and his friends. You will continue to seek them out and not stop while you can still draw breath." His eyes then glowed bright. "If you fail me, all the creatures of the dark will be at risk."

The bats gave off agitated squeaks as they flew

even faster, their tiny eyes glowing red with anger.

"Gameknight999 did this to you . . . he is your enemy, as he is mine," Herobrine lied. "He seeks to destroy all the creatures of the shadows and save Minecraft only for the NPCs. You can help me defend our lives against this threat. If you fail, the User-that-is-not-a-user will destroy you all. Your children and your children's children will be destroyed if you do not succeed. Spare nothing, not even your lives in this mission. *NOW GO!*"

Bats squeaked loudly, then flew off in all directions. To Herobrine, it looked like a massive dark cloud flowing across the landscape. The cloud thinned as tiny wings beat furiously, the bats spreading out in all directions. Herobrine could see their bright hateful red eyes inspecting every crevasse and shadowy knoll, looking for his enemy . . . good!

Herobrine held up his hands and cackled a maniacal, evil laugh as the bats disappeared into the distance.

"This is just one hatchery," he said aloud to no one. "When I've gone to all of them, I will have bats everywhere looking for you, my friend. There is nowhere you can hide from me, User-that-is-not-a-user."

He then laughed again as he teleported to the next bat hatchery, his evil, glowing eyes slowly fading away in the darkness.

CHAPTER 7
DREAMS

Gameknight suddenly sat up in his bed. He thought he'd heard something, but he could see that he was alone. Around him swirled a silvery mist, its embrace cool and damp. Instantly he knew where he was . . . the Land of Dreams. Peering deep into the billowing fog, he could see his friends around him, asleep on beds. They were all curled up under red blankets, their boxy heads lying on crisp white pillows.

Standing, Gameknight faced the wall of the desert temple. He could see that it was nearly transparent. Moving up to the sandstone blocks, the User-that-is-not-a-user extended his hand. It passed through the block as if it were not there. Stepping forward, he passed through the side of the temple and was out on the open desert . . . but something in the silvery mist was different. He could see tiny blue bubbles floating through the gray fog.

What's this? he thought. Bubbles . . . something is wrong!

Before he could make any sense of the bubbles, a voice percolated through the silvery mist, as if it were riding on these bubbles.

"You can accomplish only what you can imagine," an aged, scratchy voice said.

"Oracle . . . you're here!" Gameknight said.

"Yes, User-that-is-not-a-user, I am here . . . I have always been here."

The music of Minecraft then sounded through the

Land of Dreams, filling the misty scene with beautiful tones that eased Gameknight's fears. And in that moment, Gameknight999 realized that the Oracle was always present in the back of his mind. She was the music of Minecraft. With all his experience in the game, he knew that you didn't always hear the music; it came and went. Now he realized that the Oracle had always been there in the background somehow . . . watching.

"That is correct, User-that-is-not-a-user," the Oracle said, her voice coming to Gameknight from all directions. "I check on all the users while they play the game, making sure that Herobrine does not infect any of them. In the past, when you heard my music, it meant that Herobrine was near. I was designed to keep him in the game and not allow his escape, but also to protect those he could harm."

Moving forward, Gameknight walked through the desert. He could see that it was empty. The only inhabitants being lonely green cacti; the spiny plants kept vigil over the barren wasteland. Trying to find the Oracle, Gameknight999 moved at the speed of thought through the Land of Dreams. In an instant he was in a grasslands biome, then a birch forest, then an ice plains biome, then wading through a dense swamp with a witch's hut visible in the distance. Everywhere he traveled, he could hear the music of Minecraft enveloping him . . . it was everywhere, yet the Oracle was nowhere.

"Where are you now?" Gameknight asked as he moved to an orange and brown mesa biome.

Looking around, the User-that-is-not-a-user marveled at the pillars of banded dirt that stood tall and silent throughout this beautiful mesa biome. The stripes of sun-burnt brown and soft tan and rich orange tones gave the landscape a particularly calming appearance, as if these muted hues could somehow stop the violence that was surging across Minecraft.

"Are you alright?" Gameknight asked the Oracle. "What happened when Herobrine returned?"

"The spoiled child finally figured out how to break into my temple. He destroyed my beloved home . . . flattened it to the ground and left a smoking crater where it once stood."

"That happened to me once; I know how hard that can be. I'm sorry, but at least you escaped."

"I did not escape," the oracle said in a calm, scratchy voice. "I stood before Herobrine once again, and he used his diamond sword on me."

"You mean he killed you?"

"No, child, he does not understand what I am. He thinks that the body that stood before him was the Oracle, but that was just an extension of my being. I am the antivirus program that was designed to keep him within the game and slowly destroy him. I am much larger than he realizes."

"Why not just destroy him all at once?" Gameknight asked.

"He is too well entrenched in the game to be directly attacked," the Oracle explained. "That would have risked destroying all of Minecraft. No, my purpose was to slow his spread and watch over the users and NPCs. The Oracle was just the smallest piece of my being. I am the music that you hear during the game. That is my true self . . . the computer code that watches over the workings of Minecraft. That spoiled child, Herobrine, thinks he destroyed me, but he understands little . . . other than violence and destruction."

"But how am I supposed to stop him?" Gameknight asked as he moved from the dream-like mesa to a mysterious roofed forest biome.

Looking up at the overhead canopy, he teleported to the top of the trees. All around him, the leafy treetops stretched out in all directions, the occasional giant red mushroom peeking its crimson face through the flowing green carpet. Reaching into his inventory, he pulled out the pink egg and held it in his hands.

"I still don't know how to use this weapon . . . please tell me what to do," Gameknight pleaded. "Everyone's lives are depending on me to do the right thing. You have to help me!"

"Gameknight, you must figure this out on your own so that you can make the correct decision at the correct time. If I tell too much, I will alter what might be. It has taken a hundred years to get the right sequence of events in line so that Herobrine can finally be stopped. If I say too much, I will change everything, and there is too much at stake for that. All I can do is help you find the courage and wisdom you will need to do what is necessary."

"Courage," Gameknight scoffed as he moved from the roofed forest to a jungle biome. He could see ocelots around him and felt at ease; there were no creepers nearby. "I don't remember the last time I felt brave. I fight because I have no choice, not because I'm brave. In fact, I'm afraid all the time."

"Do not confuse fear with weakness," the Oracle said. "Only a fool is not afraid in battle. It is how we deal with that fear that is important. A coward allows himself to be consumed by his fear and let others suffer because of it. A hero faces his fear, acknowledges it, then does what he must to protect those around him."

"That's great, but tell me how to find the strength and wisdom that I'll need to face Herobrine again."

"Find the ancient Book of Wisdom," the Oracle explained. "At one time, it was within my temple, but Herobrine was able to steal it many years ago. I can still feel its presence, but it will be up to you to find it . . . and survive. It will likely be guarded by the most vile and dangerous of creatures."

"Where is this book?" Gameknight asked.

"It is held in the most ancient of buildings, older than the temple in which we met."

"Where is this place?"

"I cannot say for sure. But there is only one biome where I haven't looked, so it must be there," the Oracle explained.

"Where . . . what kind of biome are we looking for?"

"Deep Ocean," the Oracle stated.

"Ocean . . . how can the temple be in the ocean? I thought it would be a jungle temple or maybe a desert temple."

"No, this temple, though only recently made visible to users, has been hidden in Minecraft since its creation. The temple you seek is an Ocean Monument, and it lies deep underwater. But you must go with care, for terrible beasts guard the Monument, and the worst of them, the Elder Guardian, will be protecting the Book of Wisdom."

Gameknight had heard something about the Ocean Monuments. They'd been in the 14w25a snapshot, but he hadn't bothered to look at it, only reading a few scant details online.

"No one, user nor NPC, has survived an encounter with the Elder Guardian. You must be clever and brave, for the slightest doubt will bring your downfall. And if that happens, woe to us all."

"Can you tell me anything more?" Gameknight asked. "How do I destroy the Elder Guardian?"

"You must be creative and do what Herobrine does not expect you to do," the Oracle said, "for the Elder Guardian is waiting. And when you go into the Guardian's Monument, you will be in his domain, and he will have every advantage. But you must hurry. Herobrine is bringing monsters here from the other *servers. He is destabilizing the pyramid of servers and threatening the existence of all. Only the User-that-is-not-a-user can solve this puzzle and survive; if you cannot . . . everyone is doomed . . . doomed . . . doomed . . ."*

Her last word echoed throughout the Land of Dreams like the cold beat of a funeral drum. Gameknight started to ask the Oracle one last question when someone grabbed his shoulder and shook him, slowly drawing him out of the Land of Dreams and back into the waking world. As the silvery fog thinned, Gameknight thought he saw something in the mist. It was a tall, brown rectangle, with ten individual sections to it, four of the top sections empty.

Slowly, he recognized the object . . . but didn't understand. Was this a hint from the Oracle, or something from his past experiences in Minecraft? He couldn't be sure, but as the Land of Dreams faded and the waking world became solid, he knew what he needed, though he didn't know why . . . yet.

"Gameknight, are you awake?" a voice said.

Opening his eyes, he could see it was his sister, Monet113, her fluorescent blue hair framing her square face and adding a bright accent to her colorful armor.

"Gameknight, are you—"

"Yeah, I'm awake," he said.

"It's morning; we're heading to the village," she said.

Gameknight stood and stretched his arms. He could see the orange light of dawn trickling in through the holes they'd put in the temple walls.

As he walked, he suddenly realized that the shape he'd seen in the mist was a door. But he still didn't understand what it meant.

Doors . . . why would we need doors? he thought to himself.

Then the music of Minecraft swelled within his mind and he laughed. Looking at the other NPCs, he could tell that they all heard it, for a satisfied smile came across all their faces.

OK, he thought to the Oracle. *I'll get doors, even if I don't really understand how they could help us.*

But then another image materialized in his mind. It was a large, pale yellow cube, the blocky structure covered with razor-sharp purple spines. At its rear, Gameknight could see a long, segmented tail with a wide fin on the end. It was some kind of frightening sea creature. He could see a single evil-looking eye on one side of its huge body, its center colored bright red. It reminded him of a mythical Cyclops, like the one that fought Ulysses.

He shuddered.

The creature was massive, far bigger than Gameknight999, and looked more dangerous than any of the monstrous creatures Herobrine had thrown at him so far. Was the Oracle telling him that he would have to face this monstrosity? Or perhaps this beast would be his ally and would help him in his quest?

Which one is it? Gameknight thought to the Oracle, but he received only silence for an answer.

Sighing, he put aside his uncertainties and followed his friends to the village.

CHAPTER 8
XA-TUL

Herobrine appeared in a cavern deep underground. Instantly, heat, smoke, and ash from lava assaulted his senses. Taking in a huge breath, he smiled. Hanging from the ceiling in front of him was the massive, hulking body of a zombie wrapped in chainmail. The zombie's feet were firmly entrenched in a spider's web that was attached to the stony roof. The huge monster hung over a small pit of lava, its heat slowly driving the HP from the hulking creature. A shimmering green HP fountain jutted out of a nearby wall, spraying emerald-green splashes of life just out of reach of the tortured monster.

Moving around the upside-down body, Herobrine inspected his creation. As he stepped to the front, Xa-Tul saw his Maker and replaced the look of helplessness on his face with one of grim determination

"The Maker returns to release Xa-Tul?" the zombie king asked.

Herobrine walked slowly toward the pit of lava; the heat and smoke from the molten stone was delicious. The golden helm of Xa-Tul, his crown of claws, was balanced precariously on the edge of a block. The slightest bump or smallest vibration would send the golden crown into the boiling mass of stone.

"You disappointed me when you fought the User-that-is-not-a-user," Herobrine said. "You allowed yourself to be defeated, and failure will not be tolerated. I need to make sure that you have sufficiently learned your lesson."

Herobrine walked around the zombie king and could see that the monster was just barely alive. He was on the brink of disappearing into the void; the only thing keeping him alive was the occasional splatter of green sparks from the nearby HP fountain. There is nothing more torturous than having salvation just out of reach. It made Herobrine smile.

"Have you learned your lesson, zombie?" Herobrine asked, his eyes glowing dangerously bright.

Xa-Tul nodded his head vigorously, though the spider web made any movement difficult.

"If I had not appeared at the end of that battle, the User-that-is-not-a-user would have destroyed you. This is an embarrassment that I will not tolerate again . . . is that understood?"

Xa-Tul again nodded his head, his red eyes filled with sincerity. "Xa-Tul will do as the Maker commands and will not fail."

"Very well," Herobrine said.

Reaching into his inventory, he pulled out a pail of water and poured it on the bubbling pool of lava. Instantly, the glowing orange liquid solidified, forming dark obsidian. Herobrine then pulled out his diamond sword and cut through the webs that held the zombie king in the air. With the last bit of gossamer sliced away, Xa-Tul fell to the ground in a heap and flashed red, his HP precariously close to zero. He crawled to the nearby HP fountain, then lay on the ground as the green sparks fell across his body and rejuvenated him, drawing him back from the brink of destruction. As his HP returned to full, the zombie king stood up straight, then moved toward the obsidian blocks. His chain mail clinked as he walked, his steps thundering across the purple and black stone. Leaning down, the zombie king picked up his crown of claws. Placing the hot piece of metal on his head, he turned and faced his master.

"Xa-Tul is ready for the Maker's commands," the zombie king said in a guttural, animal-like voice.

Herobrine paced back and forth before the huge monster. Looking up at his creation, he knew that Gameknight999 would defeat Xa-Tul if they faced each other in battle, especially now that his enemy had learned how to wield two swords at the same time, just like that blacksmith had done those many years ago. He needed something to help his zombie king, but knew that he could not make him stronger . . . and certainly not smarter. And then an idea came to Herobrine.

"Xa-Tul, I will give you allies to help you defeat our enemies," Herobrine said. "I will create three other kings over which you will have command. You will be my four kings . . . the four horsemen of the apocalypse, who will deliver destruction to the NPC army."

"Xa-Tul does not need a horse," grumbled the zombie king.

Herobrine's eyes flared bright with anger, causing Xa-Tul to lower his head.

"War is an art, you fool, and needs to be done with style," Herobrine said. "This will add to the User-that-is-not-a-user's fear, and make him easier to deal with when the Last Battle lands on his doorstep."

"Forgive Xa-Tul," the zombie said.

"Just shut up."

Herobrine disappeared from the cave, then reappeared with a gray horse on a line. He placed a fencepost in the ground far from the HP fountain, tied the horse in place, then teleported across the chamber. Grabbing a zombie, he reappeared next to the horse.

"Thank you for volunteering," Herobrine said to

the zombie, then struck him with his diamond sword.

Instantly, the zombie fell to the ground, his HP nearly consumed. Herobrine did the same to the horse, bringing it to the brink of death. He pulled the two creatures together and used his crafting powers to combine them into one. As he worked, Herobrine's hands glowed a pale, sickly yellow that seemed to seep into the bodies on which he worked. Slowly, the two forms merged into a new shape, one that was bigger and greener that before.

When he finished his work, Herobrine dragged the creation to the HP fountain. As glowing sparks of HP danced across the body and rejuvenated its life force, the new creature slowly stood on its four strong legs. Before him now stood a huge zombie-horse, its eyes black as pitch, red pupils burning within. Its skin shared the same sickly green look that all zombies possessed, with flaps of decaying flesh hanging off here and there. Grabbing the lead that was still wrapped around its neck, Herobrine pulled the beast toward Xa-Tul.

"This is your mount," Herobrine explained. "You will make sure that the NPCs of the Overworld see you on it, for it will strike fear in their hearts."

"As the Maker commands," Xa-Tul said while mounting the beast.

Turning, Herobrine could see zombies approaching from the nearby zombie-town that was housed in this massive chamber, their sad moans echoing off the stone walls. They sensed Herobrine's presence and came, ready to hear their master's commands. He waited for the collection of decaying creatures to gather near, then placed a block of stone on the ground, then another, so that he was standing high above them all. With his eyes glowing bright, he turned and faced the mob, speaking to Xa-Tul, but also to the masses.

"Here is your task, zombie king," Herobrine explained. "Gather all zombies here in this zombie-town. Expand the walls using creepers so that the size of the cavern can be increased tenfold. Use as many creepers as you need, for we will not be using them in the Last Battle for Minecraft. Go to the other servers and bring all their zombies here as well. The greatest zombie army of all time will be gathered. Once they are here, and my little friends have found the User-that-is-not-a-user, I will take all of you to our enemy. We will destroy all of his NPC friends, and then I will destroy him myself." He then leaned closer to the zombie king. "My winged messengers are out looking for the User-that-is-not-a-user and his rabble. When they find them, the bats will report to you. I want you to punish him a little, by destroying some of his friends." Herobrine then glared at Xa-Tul, his evil eyes glowing bright. "There will be no mistakes this time. It this understood?"

The zombie king nodded his head.

"There is a second task as well. Zombies, I command you go to out and gather all the leather you can find. I have already given this message to many zombie-towns on this server, but more must be collected. Search the land for cows and collect their leather, for we will need as much as we can get. Use the zombie portals and command the other zombie-towns to do the same; we must collect every bit of leather we can find." He paused for a moment and allowed his eyes to flare bright, letting them know that failure to follow his commands meant death. "Now, go . . . I have others to gather. But soon the world of NPCs will quake in fear of the army that I will form. And with the old hag gone, I can move about with impunity, and there is nothing to stop me. The Four Horsemen and their armies will vanquish the

NPCs in the Last Battle for Minecraft, and I will have my revenge on the User-that-is-not-a-user and those in the physical world."

He laughed an evil, maniacal laugh that made all the zombies cringe in fear, then teleported away, his glowing eyes the last thing to disappear.

CHAPTER 9

STONECUTTER

The NPCs walked through most of the morning in silence, the heat hammering them into silent submission. But as the sun rose, so did their spirits. Gameknight walked with Filler on his shoulders, her small body being more of a joy to bear than a burden. Next to him strode Stonecutter, Topper sitting tall and proud on his stocky shoulders. The young brother and sister made it their job to serve as lookouts for the community, and they took their responsibility seriously. They scanned the sunbaked landscape as the group walked the pale empty desert, watching for threats.

Putting the temple to their backs, they headed for the distant village, its tall watchtower just barely visible through the desert haze.

"I've never been in a desert village before," Gameknight said. "Only ones on the plains or in the savannah. This is the first desert village I've actually explored."

"It won't be that exciting," Stonecutter explained. "It's like every other village. I should know; mine was a desert village until it was destroyed."

"What?" exclaimed Monet, who was walking right behind.

"Your village was destroyed?" Crafter asked as he walked next to the stocky NPC.

Stonecutter nodded solemnly, then raised his hand, fingers stretched out wide. Slowly he clenched his hand into a massive fist, squeezing it tight, performing the salute for the dead, then lowered it back down and grabbed hold of Topper's slim leg again.

"Please, tell us what happened," Crafter said.

Stonecutter sighed.

"It is difficult," the stocky stonecutter said, his voice cracking with emotion. "You see, it was my fault . . . it was *all* my fault."

"That can't be true," Monet said. "One person can't be responsible for an entire village. Tell us what happened."

He sighed again, then slowly nodded his head.

"I was out working on a nearby jungle temple when they came. We heard distant rumbling and thought it was thunder, but noticed that there weren't any clouds in the sky . . . so I kept working. Then the rumbling got louder and started to happen more frequently . . . it was strange. The warriors who were with me at the jungle temple went to investigate. One of them, Woodcutter, tried to get me to go with him.

"'Come on,' Woodcutter said. 'There's something wrong; we have to go check it out and make sure the village is safe.'

"But I refused, because I knew that nothing could hurt my village."

"How did you know your village was safe if you couldn't see it?" Monet asked.

"Because I built the wall that surrounded it," Stonecutter answered. "I cut each stone by hand, shaping every block so that they all fit perfectly together. The sides were perfectly vertical, the tops perfectly flat. Every piece fit together so tight that not even a bat could have squeezed through. And, just to be safe, I made it two layers thick. Not even a creeper could have punched a hole through it."

A look of pride came across Stonecutter's face as he thought about his wall—his work of art—but then a sad look filled his eyes.

"So, instead of making sure that my village was safe, I stayed at the temple, to work on my *art!*" He spat the word as if it were poison. "You see, I was trying to make the greatest jungle temple ever seen in Minecraft. It would be a work of such magnificence that no one, user nor NPC, would dare set foot in it, for it would be too spectacular for mere mortals to enter. And after I finished," he paused to wipe a tear from his eye, "everyone would know that Stonecutter had built this magnificent structure and that I was the greatest stonecutter in Minecraft." He sniffled as more tears ran down his square cheeks. "How pathetic I was."

"There's nothing wrong with wanting to be the best, Stonecutter," Topper said from the big NPC's shoulders.

"There is when ego gets in the way of responsibility!" he snapped.

"What do you mean?" Gameknight asked.

Stonecutter turned and looked at Gameknight999. His tears dripped off his chin and landed on his gray smock, creating wet spots that collected dust from the desert. His stone-gray eyes bore into Gameknight with a sad intensity that made the User-that-is-not-user look away.

"At that moment, all I wanted to do was work on my temple, not because I was doing it for Minecraft, but because I was doing it for me . . . for me!" Stonecutter turned his head and looked at everyone around him, then looked at the village in the distance. It was getting closer, and they would reach their destination soon. "I let my desire to be famous get in the way of my responsibility."

"What was your responsibility?" Gameknight asked.

"To keep my village safe," Stonecutter said in a loud voice, as if he were stating some kind of universal truth. "To keep my wife and son safe . . . to keep everyone's wife and son safe! I built a wall that was supposed to protect everyone in my village, but instead of being there to make sure that it did its job, I was out trying to build a stupid temple . . . just to satisfy my ego."

"Stonecutter . . . what happened?" Crafter asked.

"My wall failed," he said in a soft voice, almost a whimper. "The monsters were able to break through and get into the village. The thunder that I heard wasn't thunder at all . . . it was creepers, lots of them."

"But you can't be blamed for that," Monet said, putting a reassuring hand on the NPC's shoulder. "A wall can only do so much. I'm sure there were other defenses to help stop the monsters."

"You don't get it!" he snapped. "I was so arrogant and confident about my wall that I convinced our crafter to forget about building other defenses. I told him that nothing could get through my wall, not even a creeper."

"But you didn't plan on twenty creepers, did you?" Hunter asked.

Stonecutter spun his head to glare at her, angry at her accusation . . . but instantly saw in her eyes that she was not accusing, but rather commiserating.

"I too lost my village to the monsters," Hunter said. "And I was not there to protect them with my bow. I was out hunting instead of being home. But the thing was, we didn't need the food. There was enough for a while, so I could have been home with my family, but instead I was out in the forest, testing my skill." She paused as a tear trickled down her cheek, only to get trapped in one of the crimson curls that hung next to her face. "I too failed my friends and family."

She moved forward and walked next to Stonecutter, letting her arm brush against the big NPC, her touch lending support. Stonecutter looked down at her and nodded his head.

"Hunter is right, I didn't plan on twenty creepers," Stonecutter continued. "When I finished working for the day, I headed back to my village. But when I reached the edge of the jungle, I expected to be greeted by the sight of my fabulous wall . . . but all I saw was smoke and a huge crater where my village had once stood. They destroyed everything except my wall! I could see where they broke through, but once inside the perimeter, there was nothing to stop them.

"Sprinting as fast as I could, I went down to see if there were any survivors . . . but I found only one. It was Woodcutter, the warrior who had been with me at the temple. I found him propped up against my wall, in pain. He was badly wounded, and I could tell that he would not survive the night.

"He said that he saw the whole thing from the edge of the jungle. A huge army of monsters came to our village—creepers, zombies, spiders, but also monsters from the Nether as well. The creepers went in first. But since there were no archer towers . . . because of me . . . they were able to just walk up to the wall and detonate. Some warriors fired from the top of my wall, but the blazes kept most of the archers from being very effective. First, two of the green beasts would scurry up to the wall and explode, then two more, then two more. Slowly, they tore through the wall until it crumbled. Then the rest of the monsters streamed into the village and destroyed everything. The blazes burned all the homes to the ground. Fortunately, the majority were empty; most of the NPCs evacuated to the crafting chamber, my family among them.

"But when they were done destroying the homes, the creepers went to work on the watchtower. They blew it to bits, leaving a massive crater in the ground, exposing the secret tunnel. Woodcutter said that was when the ghast showed up. He said it was the biggest thing he'd ever seen, a huge bone-white creature with long tentacles and blazing red eyes. Woodcutter ran down to the village with his axe in hand, hoping to stop some of them, but once he got into the village, blazes fell on him. They blasted him with fireballs, and left him for dead . . . but he wasn't. With just enough HP to stay alive, but not enough to stand, all he could do was sit there and watch the nightmare."

Stonecutter stopped to sniffle and wipe more tears away from his eyes.

"Woodcutter told me the ghast went down into the crafting chamber, then after a few minutes came out with someone trapped within its tentacles."

"Malacoda," Gameknight hissed, his voice filled with anger.

Crafter placed a hand on his shoulder to calm the User-that-is-not-a-user.

"He cannot hurt NPCs anymore," Crafter said, trying to ease the User-that-is-not-a-user's rage.

Gameknight nodded and relaxed a little, then stopped to readjust Filler on his shoulders.

"That was the ghast's name . . . Malacoda?" Stonecutter asked.

Gameknight nodded as he continued to walk.

"He isn't around anymore," Gameknight said.

"You took care of him?" Stonecutter asked.

Gameknight shook his head. "Someone else ended his miserable life."

"Good," Stonecutter said, then breathed a deep sigh and continued. "Woodcutter said he tried to get up and stop the ghast, but he didn't have the strength to stand, so he just sat there and watched as they sent creepers down into the crafting chamber. My family was down there. My wife, Baker, would have grabbed our son, Weaver, and gone down to the crafting chamber as soon as she heard the first creeper. She probably took as many kids with her as she could. That was always the plan if there was danger.

"Weaver . . . he was your age, Topper. He was the greatest son a father could ever want. His little hands could weave incredible designs into carpets . . . better than anyone else in the village. Whenever he finished a new one, he would bring it to me so that I would be the first to see his newest creation. Each one was better than the last, and it was my greatest joy in life so see his face light up when he was showing his work. That morning, before heading to the temple, he showed me his newest carpet. It showed my wall around the edge of the rug, and then, somehow, he'd woven pictures of himself, his mother, and me into the fabric. It represented my wall protecting all of us . . . what a joke!"

He paused to wipe another tear from his square cheek.

"I'll never get a chance to see that look in Weaver's eyes ever again."

He grew silent for a moment, and Gameknight could tell from the look in his eyes that Stonecutter was likely reliving some wonderful memory of his family. But then the bright light in his stone-gray eyes dimmed and his face was again covered with sadness.

"Woodcutter said that he could hear the explosions underground, and knew that they were destroying all the survivors. My wife and son, Woodcutter's family . . . everyone's family perished in that underground tomb. And it was all because of me!

"I left Woodcutter for a moment to search our home . . . maybe Weaver or Baker was there, hiding. But the only thing that I found was . . ."

He paused for a moment to regain control of his emotions.

"What was it?" Topper asked. "What did you find?"

"It was the most ironic thing of all," Stonecutter said. "I found Weaver's last rug. It was in perfect condition, as if nothing had ever happened. The image of my wall in the fabric looked impeccable and unflawed, and our happy faces ringed within the barricade looked safe and content. I sat there with the rug in my hands and wept for I don't know how long. And when all the tears were gone and my emotions were wrung out, I knew that I couldn't bear to look at that rug ever again, so I buried it there among the ashes of our home."

He grew silent again.

"Stonecutter, this isn't your fault," Crafter said. "We can only be responsible for today. Our decisions and actions have ramifications for tomorrow, but we can't know for sure what those ramifications will be. All we can do is our best each day, work our hardest, and make the best decisions we can make. You made the best wall you could make . . . that was your job. Perhaps the fault lies with your crafter."

"Our crafter was the best!" the stocky NPC snapped.

"I'm sure he was," Crafter answered, "but he was responsible for your community as well. And your blacksmith, he was responsible for making weapons to protect your village . . . does he not share some of the responsibility?"

"Well . . . I guess . . ."

"In a community, everyone is responsible for the health and safety of everyone," Crafter explained. "No single individual carries the weight for all. Everybody does their share . . . that's what it means to be part of a community."

Crafter glanced at Gameknight999. They made eye contact for a brief second, then the User-that-is-not-a-user looked away.

"So, how did you end up in our village?" Topper asked from Stonecutter's shoulders.

"I heard Crafter's call for the defense of Minecraft, so I came . . . and I fought." He turned and faced Gameknight999, his stone-gray eyes now streaked with red from crying. "I followed you to the Nether and then to the Source. I fought by your side on the steps to the Source and watched your back during that terrible battle. While you fought Erebus in the Land of Dreams, I kept the zombies and skeletons from reaching your sleeping bodies."

He pointed to a long, jagged scar along his arm.

"I got this from a wither skeleton that was trying to get to you and your friends," Stonecutter said. "But I stopped him with my pickaxe."

Gameknight reached out and touched the long scar with his blocky fingers, and realized how painful it must have been. He looked up into the gray eyes and was about to speak, but Stonecutter interrupted him before he could start.

"I vowed that day, when Woodcutter finally died, that I will never forsake my responsibility to protect Minecraft and everyone on the servers. And the best way I could do that is to protect the User-that-is-not-a-user, even if it means sacrificing myself for him."

"Stonecutter, I won't allow that," Gameknight said sternly.

"You have no say in the matter," the stocky NPC snapped. "This is my debt to repay for causing the deaths of everyone in my village . . . Baker and Weaver." He paused for a moment to take a deep breath to stop more tears from flowing, then continued. "I will never stop watching your back, or being at your side to lend my pickaxe to your sword, even if it means my very destruction. It will be, and that's the end of it."

Gameknight was about to object, but Crafter placed a calming hand on his shoulder.

"This is Stonecutter's responsibility to bear, and we must respect that," the wise NPC said.

Gameknight looked into Crafter's bright blue eyes and wanted to complain, but he could tell that it would do no good. Glancing up at Stonecutter, he could see the look of absolute conviction in his eyes and realized that resistance was futile. Reaching up, Gameknight placed a hand on Stonecutter's big shoulder and patted him affectionately, then turned and faced the village that was just over the next dune. He thought that maybe having Stonecutter there to cover his back would be reassuring, but all it did was make him responsible for another life.

I can't take all this responsibility, he thought. *I don't want to be a hero . . . I just want to be a kid.*

Then an ancient voice filled his mind, echoing through the music of Minecraft as if were coming to him from very far away.

Those who have the ability to help others are obligated to do so, no matter how difficult it may be, the Oracle said.

But I didn't ask for this, he complained, *and you know that, Oracle. I don't know if I can do all this.*

You can accomplish only what you can imagine,

the Oracle replied.

But how do I imagine being brave, or imagine not being afraid to fail . . . how do I do that?

But the Oracle was gone, the music of Minecraft having gone silent for the moment. Glancing around, Gameknight noticed that all eyes were focused on him.

"You OK?" Crafter asked.

The User-that-is-not-a-user nodded.

"You had a serious look on your face all of a sudden," Crafter said. "What's going on?"

"I was talking with the Oracle," Gameknight said, as if it were something that he did every day.

"What?" Hunter asked.

"I can hear her in my mind," he replied. "We talked last night in the Land of Dreams."

"Did she tell you what's been happening with Herobrine?" Crafter asked.

Gameknight nodded.

"He destroyed the jungle temple and all the wolves . . . don't anyone tell Herder." Gameknight looked at his friends to make sure they would comply, then continued. "He sort of killed her. I mean, he destroyed her body, but she isn't dead. The Oracle is part of the music of Minecraft and is watching over us."

"So you mean she's OK?" Crafter asked.

Gameknight nodded. "But she told me where we need to go, so that I can figure out how to work this weapon."

"Are you going to share . . . or keep this to yourself?" Hunter asked.

Gameknight looked at Hunter and smiled, causing her impatience to build, then explained.

"We have to find an Ocean Monument. In that Monument, we'll find the Book of Wisdom. This book will tell me how to use the weapon, but it's guarded by one of Herobrine's creations."

"Of course it is," Hunter said with a sarcastic tone.

"Well, at least we know where we need to go," Crafter said. "Let's hurry up and get to the village so that we can start our search."

The User-that-is-not-a-user nodded, then shifted from walking to running, holding onto Filler's legs tightly. As he ran, Gameknight thought about the Elder Guardian from his dream, those long, razor-sharp spines waiting for him. Somehow, Gameknight999 could feel those spines getting closer and closer . . . and he was sure that when they were close enough . . . they would strike.

CHAPTER 10

DESERT VILLAGE

The NPCs ran down the sand dune toward the desert village, their voices raised high in celebration. Villagers from the desert community came out to greet the visitors, many of them with pails of water and loaves of bread for the newcomers.

As Gameknight crested the dune, he saw that the village looked like every other one he'd ever seen, with the exception that everything was constructed out of sandstone. The pale yellow walls of the homes and buildings merged into the sandy background of the desert, making the entire community blend into the landscape . . . all expect for the crops. They were planted in dark brown soil, a cool strip of blue water flowing between lush green beds of wheat. Green cacti stood as silent sentinels on the outskirts of the community, bright against the pale background. As with the fields of crops, the cacti seemed even greener than normal against the sandy backdrop, their prickly spines reaching out to anyone who dared come too close.

The smell of lush, fertile soil greeted Gameknight's nose as he moved into the village, the crops driving the dusty, dry smell of the desert from his nostrils. He smiled as he pulled in the aroma . . . it was wonderful.

High overhead, Gameknight could see the watchtower that loomed above the village. It was made of the same sandstone as all the buildings; stone was a difficult thing to get in the desert. Watchers, NPCs with the best eyesight, stood atop the watchtower, their keen eyes always scanning the surroundings for monsters; that was good. It always paid to be careful in Minecraft.

As he approached the field of crops, Gameknight realized how dry his mouth had become. Since the telling of Stonecutter's story, he'd been lost in thought and had forgotten to drink. Reaching into his inventory, Gameknight could see that he didn't have any water. He carefully pulled Filler to the ground, then knelt down. Brushing his hands clean on his pants, Gameknight dipped his hands into the flowing water that moved between the two fields and cupped them together. Bringing his hands to his mouth, he let the water spill over his face; some managed to make it past his lips, but much of the liquid spilled down his shirt, cooling him for a brief instant. It felt good. Reaching in for another handful, he brought it to his face again, but at the last second threw it on Filler. She laughed as her long sandy-blond hair caught most of the water, rivulets of cool moisture running down her square face.

Feeling rejuvenated by the cool drink, the User-that-is-not-a-user stood and surveyed the area. The village was spread out over a large area; a few sand dunes surrounded the community but were not tall enough to be used for defense. The village was completely exposed on all sides; how were the NPCs going to defend the settlement if monsters came?

Suddenly, a flicker of motion caught Gameknight's attention off to the right. Turning his head, he thought he saw something peeking over a large sand dune that was far from the village. It looked like some kind of creature, maybe an NPC or a user, but it looked strange. It had red across its chest, and its arms were covered with blue and white stripes. The colored creature stood out in stark contrast to the pale, sandy surroundings, but it disappeared behind the dune just as quickly as it had appeared.

Was it really there, or was I just seeing things? Could it have been another . . . no, that's crazy. Why would they be following us?

Looking up at the sun, Gameknight could see that they still had a few hours until nightfall . . . they had to work fast.

"Digger, let's get some defenses set up," Gameknight said as he stepped forward and took Topper from Stonecutter's shoulders. "Filler, Topper, I need you two to go up to the watchtower and help the watcher. Stay there until I tell you to come down . . . you got it?"

The twins nodded their heads excitedly, then took off running. Gameknight smiled at Stonecutter, then glanced around, looking for Hunter.

"You looking for me?" said a voice from behind.

He spun and found Hunter, her bow in her hand. The sun was positioned directly behind her, making her red hair light up like a scarlet halo.

"Yes," Gameknight answered. "I need you to set up some defenses. We're totally exposed on all sides, so we need to be able to defend everywhere around the perimeter of the village until we know where the attack is coming from. Get people building archer towers, then lay some traps out there in the sand."

"I'm on it," Hunter replied as she turned and started gathering NPCs.

Looking about the village, Gameknight999 could see that the inhabitants of this village looked confused.

They probably feel like they are being taken over by us, he thought. *We need to explain things to them.*

"Where's Crafter?" he yelled.

"Here," came a voice from the other side of the village.

Sprinting toward the sound, he found Crafter talking to some of the village elders. The town's blacksmith appeared to be angry, yelling at some of the other NPCs, gesturing wildly with his hands. But as Gameknight neared, the argument stopped abruptly.

"What's going on?" Gameknight asked.

"I was explaining to these villagers that the User-that-is-not-a-user was here, and that you were going to take over for a while," Crafter explained. "They didn't completely believe me until . . ."

Gameknight looked at the village elders. They were all staring above his head, their mouths hanging open in shock. He could tell that the NPCs saw the white letters of his name floating in the air above him, but some of them looked high up into the sky. Their eyes grew wide with astonishment as they noticed the absence of the server thread that a normal user would have.

"Hey . . . look at me," Gameknight said to the elders. "You need to get over this. Yes I'm the

User-that-is-not-a-user, so get used to it and get to work."

Just then, Monet113 walked up and stood next to her brother. The NPCs glanced at her name, their mouths agape as they saw her server thread missing as well.

"Yeah . . . yeah, there are two of us. Get over it; we don't have time for this," Gameknight said.

"Be nice," Monet chided.

Gameknight looked at her and shrugged, then turned back to the villagers.

"We have to fortify this village in case an attack comes," the User-that-is-not-a-user explained, "and it seems that there are always monsters attacking us, so we need to be prepared."

This brought the villagers back to their senses.

"What is it you need?" the blacksmith asked.

"You see that big NPC over there?" Gameknight said. "That's Digger. He's setting up the defenses, and he knows what he's doing. Go help him. We need every NPC to be working and doing what he says."

"OK," the elders replied, then set off toward Digger.

"Crafter, you and I need to have a discussion with this village's crafter."

"What about me?" Monet asked.

"Come with us to the crafting chamber," Gameknight said.

"Yippee!" she squealed, clapping her hands together.

Gameknight frowned at her, then headed for the watchtower, Crafter and Monet right on his heels. Using the secret tunnel, they moved through the underground passages until they reached the crafting chamber.

When they entered the subterranean cavern, all activity instantly stopped, and all eyes swiveled toward the visitors. Not waiting to be invited, Gameknight streaked down the stone steps and headed directly for the village's crafter. He was easy to spot in the crowd; his black smock with gray stripe was identical to Crafter's.

Without waiting for any questions, Gameknight explained the situation, describing the battles with Herobrine and Herobrine's desire to destroy Minecraft. The villagers all knew of the legendary creature, but few actually believed his existed. But with the User-that-is-not-a-user standing before them, his sister at his side, they were all instantly convinced.

"So, above us, everyone is building defenses in case Herobrine finds us tonight," Gameknight explained. "What we need you to craft are minecarts . . . as many as you can make."

"And weapons," Crafter added. "We need weapons for your own villagers."

"My villagers are not warriors. This is a peaceful community," the villager crafter explained, a look of disgust on his face.

"So was mine, until an army of monsters attacked," Crafter answered. "Gameknight999 here taught us how to fight back, and you are part of this war, whether you like it or not."

"But violence doesn't solve anything," the gray-haired crafter said. "It only breeds more violence. We aren't part of your fight . . . just leave us alone."

"Listen to me!" Gameknight shouted. "Herobrine and his horde don't care if you believe in fighting or not. He'll destroy everyone here if it suits his purpose; he's done it to hundreds of villages, and the names of all those who have fallen to his wicked desires are too numerous to count." Pausing for a moment, the User-that-is-not-a-user raised his hand, fingers spread wide, then clenched it into a fist . . .the salute to the dead. He squeezed his hand hard, trying the crush the memory of so many that had perished because of him. Everyone in the chamber could hear his knuckles crack as he squeezed and could see the look of rage in his eyes. "Everyone is part of this war. The Last Battle is coming like a freight train with no brakes."

"What's a freight train?" Crafter asked.

"Yeah, and what are brakes?" the villager crafter asked.

"It's not important right now, but what is important is that we are prepared," Gameknight explained. "We aren't staying here in the desert; this is not where the Last Battle will be, and all of you must go with us."

"We aren't going to leave our village," the crafter said. "This is our home. You can't expect us to just pack up and leave."

"I know I'm new to Minecraft," Monet said, "but I've come to learn that a home is not defined by the walls that surround you; it is defined by the people who surround you." She took a step forward and put a soft hand on the crafter's arm. "If you don't do as my brother says, all those around you will be destroyed, without mercy." She looked up into the crafter's brown eyes and spoke softly. "Nobody likes this war, but all of Minecraft is in it, whether they know it or not. You have a chance to help *stop* the violence and bring peace back to the land. If you don't help, more NPCs will perish. Do you want to live with that? *Can* you live with that?"

The crafter paused to consider her words, then turned and looked at his friends in the crafting chamber. Their dark eyes were all looking to their crafter, expecting him to keep them safe. Slowly, he brought his gaze back to the User-that-is-not-a-user and sighed.

"If you don't come with us, you'll get overrun by monsters," Gameknight explained. "Eventually Herobrine will figure out that we're here, and then he'll send everything he has against us. Our defenses are not strong enough here, and this location cannot be defended well; it's too exposed. We need a place where we can use the environment to our advantage. If you don't leave with us, you will die."

Suddenly, a burst of glaring bright light filled the crafting chamber, then faded away, revealing Gameknight's user friend, Shawny, standing before him. All the NPCs saw the server thread shining bright, stretching from Shawny's head and piercing the rocky ceiling overhead. Instantly, they all stood up straight, dropped their tools, and linked their hands across their chests.

"Hi, Gameknight; hi, Monet," Shawny said with a goofy smile. "What's new?" He then glanced around at the NPCs, then turned back to Gameknight. "I hoped they wouldn't be doing that anymore."

"They can't be seen talking or using their hands in front of any users . . . you know that!" Gameknight answered, a frown on his square face. "What are you doing here?"

"We need to talk, and I didn't want to do it through chat," Shawny answered, then turned and faced Crafter. "Hi, Crafter; good to see you again. The last time I saw you, we were battling to save Minecraft on the steps of the Source. I know you can't reply, but it is good to see you again. You should listen to what I have to say."

"Come on, Shawny, get to it," Gameknight insisted.

"OK, OK," his friend answered. "Here's the deal. None of the users can get on any of the servers across Minecraft. They're still blocked by that thing that Herobrine did a while back. But I've been talking with some friends, Impafra, Kuwagata498, and AttackMoose52, and I think we came up with something."

"What is it?"

"Well, we figured out how to reroute some of the other Minecraft servers through your dad's computer to connect up with Mojang. We then reconfigured the router to—"

"What are you talking about?" Gameknight asked. "You know that I know nothing about computer networks."

"What I'm saying is, it might be possible for some users to come online onto this server," Shawny explained. "I don't know if your router can handle all the traffic, and I don't know how many people we can contact . . . but it's possible."

"This is great . . . but . . ." Gameknight faced Crafter, then turned back to Shawny. "If it's only a handful of people, it will do more harm than good . . . you understand?"

"Yeah," Shawny answered, glancing to the linked arms across the NPC chests. "The big question is . . . how much traffic can your connection to the Internet take? If we blow the network, I don't know what might happen. You might get disconnected from Mojang, or the server might crash, or . . . who knows. It's a big risk, but I thought you should know."

"What about the digitizer? Is it working?"

"Nope . . . I've pretty much given up," Shawny said as he looked to the ground. "Sorry, but I just can't find the parts in your basement. Your dad must have a supply of components somewhere, but I have no idea where to look. If he were here, it would be a different story."

"Maybe he'll be back soon," Monet said, an insincere smile on her face.

"Yeah, well, that's not too likely, is it?" Gameknight replied. "I've learned to do things on my own over the last couple of years. Shawny, you'll just need to do the same. Do what you can . . . but for now, you should go so that we can get back to work in here."

"OK, but don't do anything stupid," Shawny said with a smile.

"You sound like Hunter," he replied just as his friend disappeared.

Once Shawny was gone, the NPCs bent down and picked up their tools and continued their work.

"Sorry about that, everyone," Gameknight shouted. "I wasn't exactly expecting him to just appear."

"A little warning next time would be helpful," Crafter said with a scowl.

"I'll give you as much warning as I can. But now let's go check out the defenses." Gameknight moved up next to Crafter and whispered in his ear. "I have a bad feeling that something is gonna happen soon."

"What was that?" Monet asked.

"Nothing," Gameknight replied. "Let's go."

Crafter nodded and placed a reassuring hand on his square shoulder, then turned and headed up the stairs, Monet following close behind.

"Keep making minecarts," Gameknight said to the village crafter. "I bet many lives will depend on these minecarts. Also, set up TNT around all the minecart tunnels. We many need to seal them quickly."

The crafter stared at Gameknight, then glanced at the letters over his head, then up to the server thread that was not there. Sighing, the crafter nodded his head and turned to give commands to his workers.

Gameknight headed back up the steps that led to the secret tunnels and the surface. When he reached the two iron doors at the top of the stairway, the User-that-is-not-a-user looked down at the crafting chamber. Half of the workers were crafting minecarts, while the other half were banging out armor and weapons. The cacophony was nearly deafening.

Satisfied, he turned and opened the iron doors at the top of the stairs. As he stepped into the next chamber, he found Monet at his side.

"You know, you said something earlier, back while we were on the ocean, and it didn't sit very well with me," she said.

"What did I say?"

"You said something about Dad," Monet said, "and that he's never around."

"Yeah . . . so?"

"You know he's traveling because he's trying to sell his inventions," she explained.

"Of course I know that," Gameknight answered as he stepped away from the iron doors and headed across the circular chamber.

"Don't walk away from me!" she snapped.

"Now you sound like Mom," he replied, but stopped in the center of the chamber.

Monet scowled at her brother. "Listen, Dad is doing what he has to do to take care of our family," she said. "I know he hates being away . . . flying to different cities . . . living out of a suitcase. But he's doing it for us."

"Is he?" Gameknight asked as he turned and faced his sister. He took a step closer so that he was looking down at her. "Is he really doing it for us, or is he doing this invention thing so that he can be famous? You know just as well as I do that he really wants people to know how great he is. He worked at the big company for a long time, working on airplane engines and lasers and stuff, but nobody paid any attention to him. Now he's trying to get noticed with his inventions, and we're the ones who end up suffering!"

"NO!" she snapped. "That's not true. Dad would never do that."

"Really? Then why has he been secretive about what he's trying to sell?" Gameknight replied. "If you look around at his creations in our basement, do you see any of them that are worth buying? The only thing he's made that does what it's supposed to do is the digitizer, but you know just as well as I do that it's too dangerous to be sold. If it got into the wrong hands, people could do some really bad things with it, and you know it."

Gameknight turned away from his sister to stare at the wall. All the anger and frustration with his father had been building up for a long time, and now the feelings were boiling over. He could hear Crafter walking softly through the chamber and heading for the tunnels. Obviously his friend did not want to intrude on this sibling discussion.

"I don't believe any of that rubbish," Monet said. "Dad loves us more than any of his inventions, and he's just trying to do what he can to provide for us."

"And being away is how he does it?"

Monet stepped up to her brother and put a hand on his shoulder.

"He's doing what he must and needs our support and understanding," she said.

"I'm tired of being supportive and understanding. I just want him home. Is that too much to ask for?"

He sighed and looked down at the ground.

"I don't want to be the man of the house anymore," Gameknight continued in a soft voice. "I just want to be a kid. But, no, I have to take care of you and pretend I'm happy so that Mom won't get worried. I'm tired of acting out a lie. I just want to be me."

"But don't you see? If he makes his big sale, he'll be home all the time," Monet said. "We won't have to share him with the airports and train stations. It will just be us . . . together."

"I hope so, Jenny. I really hope so . . . but when?"

Gameknight faced his sister. He could see that she had a tiny square tear in the corner of her eye. This made him choke with emotion, drawing the same square tear from his own eye. Reaching out, he wrapped his hands around his sister and hugged her tight.

"I hope you're right Jenny, I really do."

"Me, too, Tommy."

"Come on, Monet," he said as he released his sister and wiped his eye on his sleeve. "We have a village to defend and a massive army of monsters to defeat."

"And don't forget Herobrine," she added with a smile.

"Oh, yeah, Herobrine, too," Gameknight said with a laugh. "Come on."

They turned and headed through the tunnels and up the long vertical ladder.

When they reached the bottom floor of the watchtower, Gameknight could hear the chaos before he saw anything. It sounded as if every pair of hands in the village were building something. As he exited the sandstone tower, he could see a beautiful four-block-high wall surrounding their position. Archer towers were interspersed all throughout the village, their platforms standing at least ten blocks high. Outside the wall, Gameknight could hear NPCs yelling and digging, likely planting some little surprises for the monsters.

Suddenly, a jubilant shout came from the watchtower. Glancing to the top, Gameknight could see Hunter with her bow, her wild red hair blowing in the wind.

"I hit another one," she shouted.

Notching an arrow, she fired up into the air, shooting at who knows what. She fired again and again, but finally gave up.

"What are you shooting at?" Gameknight shouted.

"Bats," she yelled down to him. "I hate those filthy creatures."

"Well, quit goofing off and get down here!"

In seconds, she was standing at his side, a huge smile on her face.

"What are you so happy about?" Gameknight asked.

"I've been shooting down bats," she said. "You can't believe how many are flying around. I don't trust them after going to the Nether. They're just as bad as the monsters and should be destroyed."

Gameknight gave Crafter a worried look, then turned back to Hunter.

"What would bats be doing out here on the desert instead of underground?" Crafter asked.

"I don't know, but I got all of them except for the last one," Hunter said. "That one was just too far away, and I missed it."

"One got away?" Gameknight asked.

Hunter nodded her head. "But I'd say getting twelve out of thirteen is still OK."

"I don't like this," Gameknight said as he glanced around the village. "They're coming . . . I can feel it. Hunter, post guards all around and get everyone inside the walls. Have everyone get some rest, but keep the guards watching the desert."

"Monet, I want you up in that archer tower over there." He pointed to a tall column of wood and stone. "Have Stitcher up there with you and keep your eyes open."

His sister nodded her head, then turned and ran off, her bright blue hair flinging in a wide arc like an ocean wave.

The User-that-is-not-a-user headed for one of the beds that had been placed on the ground near the crops. Sitting down, Gameknight looked at his hands. They were shaking. He needed rest, but that was not why they were shaking.

Will he be here tonight? Will I have to face Herobrine here in this village?

Glancing around at all the villagers, he could see parents getting their children ready for bed, a look of apprehension on their boxy faces. Innocent shopkeepers, bakers, farmers, and craftsmen moving to stand on the wall that surrounded their once-peaceful village, a look of confused fear on their faces. He'd brought this to their doorstep, and it was his responsibility to keep them safe . . . but could he?

Laying back, Gameknight tried to reach for the puzzle pieces that would help him if the monsters came, but there was nothing, only silence.

How can I keep all these people safe if Herobrine arrives with his army? We barely have a hundred NPCs within the walls.

You can accomplish only what you can imagine, an ancient voice said in Gameknight's mind. *You can accomplish only what you can imagine . . . you can accomplish only what you can imagine. . . .* The Oracle's voice, mixed with the music of Minecraft, gradually lulled him into a restful sleep. But just before he fell asleep, Gameknight thought he heard a hint of desperate uncertainty within the harmonious melody, as if the Oracle herself were afraid.

CHAPTER II

REAPER

Herobrine cackled evilly as he materialized in the narrow tunnel. His red woodcutter's smock, the apparel from his last victim, was barely visible in the darkness.

The tunnel in which he stood was long and straight, though the walls and floor were uneven. Herobrine could see that the passage extended for probably twenty blocks, if not more, and though the walls undulated with the length, the center of the tunnel seemed laser-beam straight. Teleporting as far as his vision would let him, the shadow-crafter quickly found the end of the corridor. It seemed to stop at a blank wall of gravel with a single cube of rock sticking out in the middle. Pushing gently on the lone block, Herobrine could hear stones moving, their rough surfaces scraping against each other as the barrier of gravel slowly slid to the side, revealing a new passage. The secret tunnel had smooth walls and floors, as if meticulously carved by a group of expert diggers.

Herobrine knew that this was the place.

Stepping into the new corridor, the music of Minecraft swelled, and Herobrine smiled. He could sense an apprehensive, almost terrified feel to the music. Baring an eerie, toothy grin, Herobrine stretched out his arm, as if embracing the world with his suffocating touch. He could feel Gameknight999's fear through the music of Minecraft, and it brought him such joy that he wanted to destroy something.

"Why aren't there monsters around when I feel the need to destroy one?" he said to the empty passage.

He's probably sleeping, and his emotions are leaking through into the Land of Dreams and the music of Minecraft, Herobrine thought as his eyes brightened with evil intent. *I should go torture him in his dreams . . . give him a little nightmare.*

But just as he was about to move into the Land of Dreams, a noise echoed through the tunnel. It sounded like a collection of sticks clattering together . . . and Herobrine knew that he was close to his destination.

"Another time, User-that-is-not-a-user," he sneered, then headed down the tunnel.

The narrow tunnel pierced through the foundation of Minecraft, going straight for a bit, then turning to the left, then to the right, then sloping downward steeply. Herobrine followed the serpentine passage, teleporting when he could see the end of a straight portion, walking when he had no other choice. It wasn't possible for him to teleport directly to his destination without having been there before. Any miscalculation could cause him to materialize within solid stone, and Herobrine wasn't sure what would happen to him in that situation. So, to be safe, he used his teleportation powers only when he could see his destination, or when he'd been there before.

The clattering sound grew louder . . . he was getting closer.

Herobrine moved faster through the twisting tunnels. As he walked, the temperature in the passage began to rise; he was getting close to lava. A smile grew on his boxy face at the warm feeling; lava always reminded him of comfort and safety . . . of home. But this was not his home; it was theirs. And it would stay theirs as long as they did his bidding.

Teleporting to the end of another long, straight passage, Herobrine came across a collection of bones lying on the tunnel floor; only his eyes could have picked them out of the darkness. It was likely some poor skeleton that didn't make it back in time . . . some fool. As he continued on, he saw a few arrows scattered on the ground here and there.

"Careless idiots," he said to the darkness.

Ahead, Herobrine could see a faint red glow . . . he was there. Teleporting to the feeble burgundy light, he materialized at the end of a long, straight tunnel. He could see redstone torches placed on the roughhewn walls every dozen blocks or so, causing them to cast a circle of rosy light that filled a small section of the tunnel. On either side of the lit sections, dark stretches spanned half a dozen blocks until the next circle of light was reached. The pattern of torch-lit tunnel followed by darkness stretched off into the distance as far as Herobrine's glowing eyes could see. Sparkling white fountains were interspersed among the redstone torches. A nearly constant flow of glittering white HP flowed from the fountains, the tiny glowing sparks throwing splashes of light on the stone walls.

Connected to this tunnel were perpendicular passages, each with its own torches and HP fountains. They intersected in the dark sections so that the adjacent passages were not visible unless you were standing directly in the shadowy section.

Skeletons filled the passage, their pale white bodies clustered around the white twinkling HP fountains, drinking in the life-preserving sparks of HP. This was the skeletons' joy . . . and curse. They fed off these HP fountains every day, but it kept them shackled to these underground passages, for they could not last long away from skeleton-town.

Gathering his crafting powers, Herobrine allowed his eyes to flare brilliantly white, lighting the entire length of the tunnel and those that intersected as well. Knowing the layout of skeleton-towns well, he teleported to the gathering chamber that sat at the center of the crisscrossing tunnel system. He materialized at the far end of the large circular chamber. It had a low ceiling, only five or six blocks high, but it spanned fifty blocks across, its wide expanse making the roof seem even lower by comparison. Shimmering white HP fountains dotted the perimeter of the chamber, casting their faint glow throughout the room.

"Come, my children," Herobrine said in a loud voice that echoed through all the tunnels. "We have much to discuss."

Slowly, the skeletons trickled into the chamber, but not fast enough to suit him.

"COME...NOW!" he screamed, his booming voice thundering through the passageways.

The skeletons scurried faster, the sound of their clattering bones echoing off the stone walls. Herobrine motioned for a half-dozen of the creatures to come closer, his eyes glowing dangerously bright. They moved forward, a look of fear on their bony faces, for they knew they had no choice. When they were close enough, he drew his sword and cut through their HP, bringing them to the brink of destruction. Gathering the barely connected bones together, he knelt and started to craft. As he worked, his hands glowed a sickly, pale yellow, giving them an infected and diseased look. The insipid glow lit his face, giving the dark shadow-crafter a washed-out look that almost matched the color of the skeletons, his red woodcutter's smock now a faded dirty orange.

As he crafted, the skeleton bones slowly merged

together, forming an unrecognizable shape of twisted parts and jagged edges. Herobrine's hands glowed brighter as he pulled two large bones together, forming the spine. Adding curved parts, he crafted ribs that arced around the spine like the ancient buttresses of some medieval cathedral. Gradually, the monstrous shape morphed into a blocky torso, then thick muscular arms and legs sprouted out, then at last, a terrifying skeletal head appeared. When he finished, the new creation dragged itself to the sparkling HP fountain that glowed nearby. As the life-giving embers melted into the white bones, the creature slowly stood. It was a head taller than the rest of the skeletons in the room, its arms thicker and stronger. As more HP flowed into the bony monster, it stood even taller. And when its HP was full, the creature's eyes started to glow a deep red that made all the other skeletons step back.

Herobrine placed a block on the ground, stood on it, and addressed the skeleton-town.

"Behold, my latest creation, the king of the skeletons. He will command you in the Last Battle and finally bring the race of skeletons back to the surface of Minecraft."

The skeletons in the room started to murmur at the sound of this promise.

"I know how long you have suffered in these passageways, forced to stay close to your precious HP fountains," Herobrine said in a softer voice, forcing the creatures to draw nearer. "That was your punishment after the first great zombie invasion. The skeleton race chose to help their monster neighbors in their just cause to overthrow the NPCs, but the inhabitants of the Overworld punished you for your dedication to your green brothers. Now you live in squalor in these dark caves, unable to go to the surface during the day."

The skeletons started to grumble, some of them issuing curses toward the vile NPCs.

"But you will again live under the blue sky of daylight," he said in a loud, clear voice.

"The sky . . . the sky . . . the sky," the monsters chanted, their ancestral memory yearning to stand under the clear blue dome of the digital heavens once again.

"You have been punished for far too long, and it is now time for you to take back what is yours." Herobrine pointed to the skeleton king. "Your commander will lead you and the skeletons from across all the servers in the Last Battle that will finally exterminate the NPCs from Minecraft!"

The skeletons cheered, their hoarse shouts echoing off the chamber walls. Many held their bows high over their heads, shaking their pale white fists at the NPCs that lived far above them.

Herobrine held his hands over his head to calm the rabble, then continued.

"But before we begin, there are some tasks you must all complete. First and foremost, you must collect as much leather as possible. Spare nothing in this task, not even your lives. Everything depends on leather." He then turned to the skeleton king. "Second, your king will collect all the skeletons and have them ready when I call. You must be prepared when I signal for the Last Battle; any delay will be dealt with severely."

"But, master, how will I be able to travel to the other skeleton-towns without burning under the cursed sun?" the skeleton king asked. "They are too far away for me to walk to them."

Herobrine's eyes flared bright for just a moment, then he disappeared. In a second, he reappeared with a skeleton horse at his side.

"You will wear a helmet specially designed by me," Herobrine said, "and ride this skeleton horse."

He reached into his inventory and dumped some items onto the ground. Pieces of armor from his many victims clattered to the ground: gold, iron, and leather all mixed together in a heap. Herobrine picked up a gold helmet and held it high in the air. Gathering his crafting powers, he made the golden helm glow in his hands, becoming brighter and brighter until the skeletons had to look away. When the intense light faded, the skeletons looked back to the Maker. A cheer rang out as Herobrine placed the helmet on the skeleton king's bare head. Instead of a normal, square helmet, it now became a collection of golden bones intricately woven together into a king's crown.

"Your golden crown of bones will protect you from the burning rays of the sun, and your skeleton horse will let you travel quickly from skeleton-town to skeleton-town," Herobrine said, his eyes glowing bright and evilly. "You will strike fear into our enemy's hearts when they see you on your mighty steed, wearing your crown of golden bones. No one will dare defy you!"

The skeletons cheered as their king looked down on them, the golden bones reflecting the sparks from the HP fountains.

Herobrine then turned and stepped toward the wall. He pulled out a diamond pickaxe and dug a three-block-wide by four-block-high rectangle into the wall. After putting his tool back in his inventory, he pressed his glowing hands against the stone wall. Slowly, a shimmering light formed within the recession. It started out as a faint glow, but grew in strength, gradually pushing back the light from the HP fountains. When Herobrine stepped back, all in the chamber could see a sparkling undulating portal filling the rectangle, the shining surface pulsing as if alive. The new teleportation portal lit the gathering chamber with a flickering pale yellow glow.

Herobrine smiled as he stepped away from the newly created portal. He felt weak, his crafting powers taxed to the limit, but it had been important, and he knew that the skeleton king would need these portals to gather his troops.

Herobrine faced the skeletons. "This portal will take you to the other skeleton-towns," he explained. "I have just modified the code of all skeleton-towns using my shadow-crafting abilities so that one of these portals is present in each."

The skeletons cheered loudly.

"When I signal, these portals will bring all of you to the Last Battle," Herobrine yelled, then drew his diamond sword and held it high over his head. "And when we meet our enemies in the Last Battle, we will vanquish them and take back the Overworld."

The skeletons were cheering nearly out of control.

"Now, go to the surface and collect the leather!"

The skeletons surged out of the gathering chamber and headed through the twisting tunnels to the surface. As the bony creatures moved out, the skeleton king moved to Herobrine's side, a bony hand holding onto the horse's rope lead.

"Master, I have one question," the skeleton king said.

Herobrine could see that there was fear in those red eyes, fear of the Maker . . . good.

"What is it?"

"What am I to be called?" the tall skeleton asked.

Herobrine looked at the creature and considered for a moment, then drew on what he'd gleaned from listening to the delicious information on the user's

Internet.

"I shall call you Reaper," Herobrine said in a slow, booming voice. "You shall be my second horseman."

Reaper nodded his glowing skull of a head, then mounted his skeleton horse and guided it toward the portal.

"Prepare your troops, Reaper, but remember . . . failure will not be tolerated. Is that understood?"

"Of course, Master."

"Then go and gather your troops."

Reaper led his horse through the pale yellow portal and disappeared. Once Herobrine was completely alone, he cackled a wicked laugh that resonated into the very fabric of Minecraft.

"Soon, Gameknight999, you will meet my four horsemen, and then we'll see how clever you are."

He let out a short, harsh laugh that stabbed at the music of Minecraft, then disappeared, his glowing, hate-filled eyes the last things to fade away.

CHAPTER 12

THE REUNION

Gameknight999 woke with a start, his heart pounding, his breathing heavy. Sitting up quickly, he scrutinized his surroundings to see if anything was wrong. The sky sparkled with a thousand brilliant stars as the moon's square face slowly moved overhead. He could see sentries patrolling the newly constructed wall that ringed the village, their armor clinking softly as they walked along the parapet.

Archers stood atop the many towers that had been built across the village, their prickly weapons ready to pour steel-tipped rain down upon any monsters that approached. Everything seemed fine.

So, what jolted me awake?

At that moment when he crossed over from being asleep to being awake, it felt as if something evil had been making an eerie growling or howling noise in his ears. But the strange thing was that the sound came from inside his head. It was an evil, cackling sound— some kind of terrible beast laughing and growling at the same time—but the noise had come through the music that played in the background, through the very fabric of Minecraft . . . *but how was that possible?*

Standing, Gameknight drew his diamond sword and walked to the stairs that led to the top of the barricade. Climbing the rocky steps, he stood on the wall and gazed out into the desert. There was nothing out there in the dark midnight landscape . . . just cactus and sand.

It still didn't feel right.

Running along the wall, he did a lap around the perimeter of the village, the NPCs on guard duty looking at him as if he were crazy. Everything seemed calm, but he knew that it wasn't right. What he'd felt through the music of Minecraft meant something . . . he just wasn't sure what.

"HUNTER . . . *WHERE'S HUNTER?!*" Gameknight yelled.

"She's asleep in the blacksmith's house," one of the villagers said.

"Get her up . . . *NOW!*" Gameknight999 commanded. "And get Stitcher as well. I need them both."

Three NPCs ran off to find the sisters, happy to be away from the agitated User-that-is-not-a-user.

Suddenly, Stonecutter was at his side; the NPC's

gray smock was almost invisible in the darkness of the desert night.

"What's happening?" Stonecutter asked.

"I don't know, but something doesn't feel right." Gameknight walked a few steps away from the stocky NPC then came back, pacing back and forth. "Maybe I'm just going crazy, but I think there's something out there in the darkness."

"Maybe you should trust your instincts," Stonecutter said. "My brother, Saddler, used to have a special instinct for the weather. Nobody believed him except for me. You see, he could tell when it was about to rain, but, more importantly, he could tell when there would be lightning. When we were kids . . ." he stopped for a minute to laugh at some image in his head, a smile growing across his square face, his stone-gray eyes bright with the happy memory, then continued.

"When we were kids, he used to steal an iron sword when he felt a lightning storm coming. We'd go out into the fields and stick the sword in the ground, then back up and watch. The lightning used to hit the sword and make it glow bright orange, showering the area with sparks." He laughed again, then closed his eyes to enjoy the moment in his mind.

Slowly, he opened his eyes again, still filled with joy. "The first time, he ran out to the field to pull the sword out of the ground after it stopped glowing, but it was still hot. It burned his right hand when he pulled up on the hilt. He then dropped the sword on his right foot and burned that as well." He stopped to smile, then laughed again. "He had to hop all the way back to the village, but by that time, everyone had come out to see the lightning. All the NPCs saw him coming back and started to hop as we entered the village, making fun of him. Oh . . . we laughed for a day . . . well, except for Saddler. After that day, everyone called him Lefty for a while . . . he hated it. Even as adults, we used to do the sword thing every time a storm came near. It was one of our favorite things to do . . . I guess not anymore."

Stonecutter became silent as he looked out into the darkness. The joyful look in his gray eyes faded, leaving behind cold stone pupils filled with sadness and regret.

"He was in the village that day . . . when the monsters came."

The stocky NPC took a few steps away from the User-that-is-not-a-user and stared out into the darkness, his entire body tense.

He carries such a burden, Gameknight thought.

Just then, Hunter ran up the steps and stood before the User-that-is-not-a-user, her younger sister at her side.

"I hear you're causing some kind of fuss and felt it necessary to wake me from my glorious dream," Hunter said. "Believe it or not, I was dreaming about destroying monsters."

"That's shocking," Stitcher said with a smile as she rubbed her tired eyes. "Now what's going on, Gameknight?"

"I'm not sure," he answered.

"That's great!" Hunter replied. "Thanks for waking us up."

"Something's going on," Gameknight continued. "Herobrine is up to something, I can feel it, but it's too dark out there in the desert to see anything. I need you two to go up to the watchtower and shoot your arrows all around the village. With the Flame enchantment on your bows, your arrows will give us some light. Now, *GO!*"

Hunter rolled her eyes at Gameknight999, then

spun around quickly so that her crimson locks splashed across his face. Laughing, she ran down the steps and toward the watchtower.

"Come, Stitcher . . . let's light up the desert," Hunter yelled over her shoulder as she ran.

The younger sister stepped up to Gameknight999, gave him a smile, then spun around and splashed him with her long red curls as well, laughing as she followed her older sibling.

"What's going on?" said a voice behind Gameknight.

Turning, Gameknight found his sister staring up at him, her sleepy eyes still filled with fatigue.

"I don't know," Gameknight answered. "Hunter and Stitcher are going to shoot some arrows out in the desert so that we can see what's out there."

"What do you need me to do?"

Gameknight could tell that she was anxious to help.

"Go up into the watchtower and be a lookout," he explained. "I need your eyes to tell us what's out there."

"Got it," she said as she smiled, then turned and splashed him with her blue locks.

"I hate that!" he exclaimed.

Monet laughed.

Gameknight smiled as he watched her streak to the sandstone tower. In seconds, Monet and the sisters appeared at the top, their iridescent bows shimmering in the darkness, lighting the tower with a blue glow. Hunter and Stitcher drew back their arrows and fired. Instantly, the tips of the arrows erupted with magical fire as they streaked through the darkness like two tiny meteors coming down from the heavens. When they landed, the arrows impaled themselves into the pale yellow sand but continued to burn, casting a circle of light.

Slowly, the sisters fired more arrows into the darkness, Hunter to the left, and Stitcher to the right. They painted a burning arc of light along one side of the village. Gameknight stood on the wall and peered into the lit desert, looking for Herobrine and his monsters of destruction, but all he saw was brown scrub brush and green cacti, the only inhabitants in this dry wasteland.

The sisters continued to launch their arrows, competing to see who could shoot the farthest. As they fired, Gameknight followed Hunter's glowing trail, while Stonecutter followed Stitcher's. With their burning projectiles stuck into the sand, the two sisters slowly painted great flaming arcs around the entire village, the landscape lit with magical flickering light . . . but still only empty desert showed within the burning glow.

Gradually, the two blazing arcs started to come together as Hunter and Stitcher almost completed the circle of flame. Gameknight peered at the dark gap that still lay hidden in gloom as the shadowy section grew smaller and smaller. In the distance, Gameknight could just barely make out the outline of the desert temple, the spot where they'd fought the zombies.

Maybe there's a zombie-town out there somewhere?

The dark gap became narrower and narrower as Hunter and Stitcher filled in the darkness with their fiery arrows.

Did I see something move out there? Was that a flicker of gold? I must be going crazy.

Another pair of arrows streaked into the air and landed into a sand dune, casting more light into the surroundings; the circle of fire was almost complete.

Still nothing . . . I must be going crazy . . . wait . . . what was that?

He thought for sure that he saw something out

there, a dark form moving slowly through the shadows, but it looked too big to be a monster . . . it had to be his imagination.

The sisters fired the last two arrows into the air. Gameknight watched them carve a gentle arc through the air then land. One of them hit a tall cactus, causing it to burst into flames.

But no one noticed the burning cactus.

"Out there!" Monet screamed. "I see something!"

One of the villagers screamed, then ran from the wall to find her children.

Gameknight was shocked and numb with fear.

"It can't be," Gameknight said. "No . . ."

"Ah . . . I see the Fool stands before me once again," a deep voice grumbled from the desert. "Why don't you come down here and face me, Fool? This time, the outcome will be different, that can be assured."

Gameknight stared at the monster and was overcome with panic.

"How can he be here . . . how did he find us?" Gameknight asked, but the village was in a panic and no one heard him except for Stonecutter, who stood at his side.

"The User-that-is-not-a-user looks afraid . . . this is not a surprise," growled the monster.

Now everyone could see a massive army of zombies approaching the burning circle of light, their dark claws sparkling in the fiery glow.

The monster then moved forward so that he was completely lit by the glow of the burning arrows: Xa-Tul on his massive zombie horse. The steed's eyes glowed blood red, as did the rider's, the zombie's shining chainmail sparkling in the moonlight, giving him an almost magical appearance.

Urging his mount forward another step, the zombie king glared up at Gameknight999, then pointed at him with his massive golden broadsword.

"ZOMBIES . . . *ATTACK!*" bellowed Xa-Tul, his voice making the desert itself shake with fear.

Stepping off his mount, he moved forward another step and looked straight up at Gameknight999.

"The last time, the User-that-is-not-a-user won, but this time will be different." Xa-Tul took another step forward and brought his sword down on a sandstone block, crushing it into dust. He smiled and spoke in a loud, gravelly voice for all to hear: "Come on, user . . . let's dance."

CHAPTER 13

CHANGING THE GAME

The zombies ran forward, flowing around Xa-Tul as if he were a large stone in the middle of a raging river. Archers opened fire on the approaching horde, and nearly all hit their mark; there were so many zombies that it was difficult to miss. Flaming arrows streaked down from the watchtower and ignited the TNT that was buried in the sand. The red and white blocks started to blink, then detonated, tearing deep gashes in the desert landscape. Zombies flew through the air in all directions as the flashing cubes exploded, but the creatures continued to charge forward out of the darkness, ignoring the fiery blasts.

Gameknight stared at the massive flood of zombies—there must have been hundreds of them. The sound of their moans stretched out into the darkness and beyond, causing little square goosebumps to form down Gameknight's spine.

"There are too many," the User-that-is-not-a-user mumbled as he stared at the attacking army in disbelief. "How did he get so many zombies? Where did they all come from?"

Gameknight stood there and stared down at the mob, a look of despair on his square face.

"How can we fight this many?" he mumbled to no one.

Looking around, he could see that all the villagers had their bows out, firing down on the monsters, but their arrows were not slowing the tidal wave of destruction that was crashing down upon them. Gameknight could hear the claws of the zombies scratching at the stone walls that protected the defenders. Their angry growls filled the air with such hatred that Gameknight had the urge to cover his ears. Dismissing the thought, he peered over the edge of the wall to look down on his attackers. In their fury, the zombies were starting to climb on top of one another in an attempt to gain purchase on the ramparts and attack the defenders.

Suddenly, a zombie head poked up in front of Gameknight. Before he could react, Stonecutter was there with his pickaxe, crashing down on the monster and obliterating it quickly. Moving along the wall, the stocky NPC smashed at the zombies that neared the wall's edge, rending their HP from them with vicious strokes of his pick. More swordsmen were coming to the wall, following Stonecutter's example . . . but, still, the defenders were too few. Eventually, the zombie wave would flow over the wall and gain access to the village.

Water, said a familiar voice in Gameknight's head. It was Shawny.

What? he asked.

Use water to slow down the zombies, Shawny said through the chat, the words forming in Gameknight's mind.

"Of course!" he said.

Sheathing his sword, Gameknight999 pulled out a bucket and ran toward the crops.

"Gameknight, what are you doing?" Crafter yelled from the defensive wall.

The young NPC had his iron sword in his hand, the normally dull blade now shimmered with magical power. He was trimming back the zombies that were popping up over the edge of the wall, sending them back into the void, their XP lying on the ground.

"Grab a bucket and follow me!" Gameknight yelled back, then streaked to the garden.

He dipped his bucket into the water and ran back to the wall, passing Crafter on the way. Rushing up the steps, the User-that-is-not-a-user carefully poured the water on the outer face of the wall, forming a flowing stream of liquid that gushed down on the attacking zombies. The instant waterfall made it impossible for the zombies to attack that part of the wall, forcing them to separate and move to a new section.

Smiling, Gameknight999 looked up at the star-filled sky and mouthed "thank you" to his friend.

NPCs, seeing what the User-that-is-not-a-user had done, grabbed their own pails and ran for the water that fed the crops. Scooping up bucketful after bucketful, the watery source was quickly consumed as the precious liquid was taken to the wall in the defense of Minecraft.

"Ha, ha, ha!" bellowed Xa-Tul. "Does the User-that-is-not-a-user think that Xa-Tul's army can be stopped with a few buckets of water? HA! Come out here, Fool, and face the king of the zombies. The outcome will be different this time!"

Gameknight looked at the monster and shook with fear.

I barely survived the last time I faced him, he thought. *I don't know if I can defeat him again.*

Closing his eyes, he tried to imagine himself battling the zombie king, but all he could see in his mind was that massive golden sword smashing down onto him.

"Zombies, move away from the water and attack a new section," Xa-Tul commanded.

The decaying creatures heard their king's command and shifted, picking a new section of wall that was dry. Many of the NPCs ran back to the fields with their empty buckets, but found the stream completely dry. They had no more water . . . their only choice was to fight.

"Gameknight, what do we do?" an anxious voice said to his right.

Turning, he found Crafter looking up at him, his bright blue eyes filled with fear.

"How do we stop all these monsters?" Crafter continued. "We need you to think up one of your famous tricks, and hurry!"

"User-that-is-not-a-user, what are your orders?" This time it was Digger.

Gameknight looked up at the big NPC and could see that his shiny iron pickaxe was dented and cracked . . . it had seen a lot of use in the last ten minutes.

"Gameknight, how about some fancy strategy to help us before we're all dead?" Hunter yelled from atop the watchtower.

He looked up at her. She was firing down on the monsters as fast as she could, Stitcher and Monet at her side. Gameknight then looked at the walls and could see NPCs flashing red as zombie claws reached up and swiped at exposed legs. One of the zombies extended an arm and grabbed the leg of a defender, then pulled him off the wall. The doomed soul fell among the zombie horde and disappeared almost instantly.

"What's wrong, User-that-is-not-a-user—have nothing to say this time?" Xa-Tul yelled. "Maybe this will help."

The king of the zombies then yelled a piercing, bone-rattling howl that was echoed by more monsters in the darkness. Another massive wave of zombies charged forward, intent on destroying this village and all its inhabitants. Now the monsters had doubled their numbers, and they were attacking all sides of the village.

"Think of this as a little gift from Herobrine," Xa-Tul yelled to his enemy. "But don't worry—there are more where this came from . . . many more. Ha, ha, ha."

The zombie king's maniacal laughter made the decaying monsters around the wall moan in anticipation of their impending victory. The sound made Gameknight999 drop his sword and cup his hands to his ears.

"User-that-is-not-a-user . . . what do we do . . ."

"What are your commands . . ."

"How should we fight this . . ."

"Where do we go . . ."

All the questions smashed into Gameknight's courage like a giant's hammer.

I don't know what to do. I hate this responsibility . . . I HATE IT!

He bent down and picked up his sword, then looked at the faces that were staring at him, expecting some kind of miracle to come out of him and save them all.

I don't want to fail all these people and lead them to their deaths, but I'm afraid to do anything or make any decision . . . what should I do?

And then a voice came to him from very far away. It floated on a gentle wave of music that slowly washed over him, driving back his panic and buoying his spirits.

You can accomplish only what you can image, the Oracle said.

But I can't imagine anything . . . only failure! he shouted back at her.

Failure comes only when one refuses to try. You cannot fight these monsters; there are too many. If you try to stand up against this flood, you and all your friends will be washed away.

Thanks for pointing that out, Gameknight snapped. *It was really helpful.*

If you cannot fight, don't . . . choose another path, the Oracle said. *If you always do what Herobrine wants you to do, he will be victorious. He sends his servant here to goad you into battle, but you must not dance to his tune. Instead, you must make your own choices and stay true to your friends, for they are all counting on you, both in Minecraft and in the physical world. All hope rests on the User-that-is-not-a-user . . . may you find the wisdom to know when to fight and when not to fight.*

And then the music of Minecraft flowed away, carrying with it some of his fear and uncertainty.

I have to figure out what to do . . . but we can't fight.

But then he remembered something a friend, Impafra, had taught him; if you don't have room to retreat, you attack. Maybe the opposite was true as well.

If you can't attack, you should retreat . . . that's what we should do.

Looking up, Gameknight glanced at all the faces that were looking expectantly at him.

"Everyone, to the crafting chamber!" he yelled. "We'll all take the same tunnel to the next village. *RUN!*"

The NPCs didn't wait for a second invitation. They all sprinted for the watchtower and the secret tunnel that sat under its foundation. Gameknight walked slowly, allowing all the villagers to go first.

"Gameknight, you must get into the crafting chamber," Stonecutter said, pushing him gently in the back.

"No, I'll go last," the User-that-is-not-a-user said.

"Someone has to trigger the TNT so that the monsters cannot follow, and that's my job."

He could hear the moans of the zombies getting louder as they neared the top of the wall.

"Stonecutter, I need you to look after my sister," Gameknight said, pointing to Monet, who still stood at the top of the watchtower with Hunter and Stitcher. "Please . . . go get her and take her to a minecart. Carry her if you must, but make her safe."

The stocky NPC nodded his head, his stone-gray eyes staring back at Gameknight999 with confidence and strength. Turning, he sprinted into the watchtower and shot up the ladder. At the top, he could hear Monet arguing with Stonecutter; she then grew quiet as she followed him down the ladder and into the crafting chamber.

Growls echoed off a building wall . . . the zombies were in the village.

"Gameknight, come on," Hunter yelled from the watchtower door. "Everyone's in the—"

She stopped talking as she pulled back an arrow and fired it at a zombie that was charging toward them. Another arrow streaked from the window of the structure, striking the monster in the chest and consuming its HP. It disappeared with a pop. Stitcher leaned out of the window and smiled at Gameknight, then disappeared, taking the tunnel down to the underground chamber.

"Come on," Hunter shouted. "Everyone is down in the chamber."

"OK, we'll—"

Suddenly, the ground shook as a crashing sound filled the air. Another crash sounded, then another and another, until part of the wall fell away, a golden sword smashing it to pieces. As the dust cleared, Gameknight could see Xa-Tul standing over the collapsed wall, his mighty golden sword in his hand. Zombies surged through the opening and flowed throughout the village, looking for victims.

The zombie king pointed his sword at Gameknight and bared an eerie, toothy smile.

"Where is Herobrine's plaything going?" Xa-Tul bellowed, then laughed maniacally.

Fear coursed through every nerve as Gameknight watched the monster approach. But then someone grabbed him by the back of his chest plate and yanked him backward. Landing in a heap, he found Hunter standing over him, her brown eyes filled with rage.

"Let's go, you idiot!" she shouted, then dropped down the tunnel.

Gameknight scrambled to his feet and followed her down the ladder. When he reached the bottom, he sprinted through the tunnel system and into the crafting chamber. The last of the villagers were loading into minecarts and disappearing down the rails, leaving only Stonecutter and Hunter.

"Go!" Gameknight yelled as he ran down the steps that led to the chamber floor.

Not waiting to discuss the issue, Hunter jumped into a minecart and shot down into the darkened tunnel.

"Stonecutter . . . go!"

"I will follow the User-that-is-not-a-user," the stocky NPC said, his big pickaxe in his muscular hands.

"Stonecutter . . . this is something I *must* do. I have to face the zombie king before I go, or I will continue to be afraid of him. He must see me standing here, unafraid, so that I can plant a seed of doubt in his peanut-sized mind. Do you understand?"

"I understand most of what you say, but I have one question."

"What is it?" Gameknight asked.

"What is a peanut?"

Gameknight laughed, then shoved Stonecutter into a minecart and pushed him down the track. As he disappeared, the doors at the cavern entrance boomed with a massive blow. Looking up to the entrance, Gameknight could see Xa-Tul's blade tear the iron doors to shreds. The zombie king stepped into the crafting chamber and looked down on his prey.

"Xa-Tul has found the User-that-is-not-a-user at last. It is time to meet in battle. Come . . . face the destiny that was meant for Gameknight999."

"I know that Herobrine won't let you kill me, so stop with your pathetic threats."

"Xa-Tul didn't say that the Fool would be killed, only made to suffer," the zombie king said as he waved his sword in front of him.

Gameknight looked at that blade and could remember it smashing into him in their last battle. Waves of fear started to bubble up from within his soul, forcing feelings of doubt and uncertainty into his mind.

NO! I won't be afraid . . . that's the tune Herobrine wants me to dance to. I REFUSE to be afraid!

Closing his eyes, Gameknight imagined the rage on Xa-Tul's face when he disappeared down the minecart tunnel, and he started to laugh.

"What is the Fool laughing at?"

"I'm laughing at you . . . now who's the fool?"

"What?" Xa-Tul asked.

Gameknight climbed into a minecart and stood, glaring at the monster.

"I'm won't be afraid of you this time, Xa-Tul," Gameknight shouted. "I am Gameknight999, the User-that-is-not-a-user and I won't let you hurt my friends."

Courage cleared the fog of fear that shrouded

his mind—courage that he could stand up against Herobrine and his monsters. He drew his diamond sword and pointed it at the zombie king.

"Next time we meet, I'll finish what I started in front of Crafter's village . . . and it will end with your destruction, and the destruction of Herobrine," Gameknight shouted.

He reached down and flipped a lever, activating a redstone circuit. Instantly, the trail of crimson powder that snaked around the room lit up bright red; repeaters glowed bright and added a delay for his escape. He could see the redstone signal moving past the repeaters and finally reaching the blocks of TNT that ringed each minecart tunnel.

"NOOOOO!" Xa-Tul screamed.

Pushing his minecart forward, Gameknight999 sat down and smiled at the monster as he disappeared down the tunnel. Seconds later, the ground shook with the explosion of TNT, the bombs closing off all the tunnels, denying the zombies access. And through the booming echoes, the User-that-is-not-a-user could hear Xa-Tul yelling out in frustration.

Gameknight smiled.

"I'm done being afraid!" Gameknight999 said to no one . . . to everyone. "I'm tired of being fearful of this responsibility because I *might* fail. Those days are over. I'm done playing your game, Herobrine!" Gameknight999 shouted with all his might. "It's time we played mine!"

CHAPTER 14

THE NETHER

Herobrine materialized on a jagged outcropping that overlooked a massive ocean of lava. The ground around him was made of the rust-colored netherrack, with patches of shining nether quartz placed here and there. Looking up at the rocky ceiling, he could see clusters of glowstone clinging to the roof as if cemented in place, their yellow glow adding to the orange radiance of the lava.

Herobrine took in a slow breath, filling his lungs with blazing hot air mixed with smoke and ash . . . it was wonderful.

Turning to take in the scene, he could see the dim-witted zombie-pigmen walking about, their golden swords held before them. In the distance, he could see the large, bone-white ghasts floating over the boiling sea. Many of them dragged their nine long tentacles through the molten stone as they drifted across the burning ocean of lava, their baby-like cries filling the air.

Closing his eyes, Herobrine teleported to the far shore of the ocean, then turned and looked at his surroundings. It was still much the same, with streams of lava falling from great heights, forming massive pools of molten stone that eventually flowed down hill to the ocean. Everywhere, he could see the zombie-pigmen and ghasts, but they were not what he wanted.

Then he spotted what he was looking for: a lone

pillar of dark stone jutting up from the lava shore. He teleported to the structure and found that there were more pillars nearby, each of them constructed from dark burgundy nether bricks. Above the pillars, Herobrine could see a walkway suspended over the tall supports. Teleporting upward, he materialized above an enclosed causeway that extended off into the distance. Moving along the walkway, he could see that it stopped at the side of a mountain of netherrack and soul sand.

Herobrine laughed.

Most users figured that the building ended right there, at the side of the rusty mount of netherrack, but that was his little joke. A century ago, Herobrine had altered the code that governed the nether fortresses so that some of it would be obscured by the netherrack, keeping the users from seeing what was there. Stepping up to the blocky barrier, Herobrine closed his eyes and gathered his crafting powers. As his hand started to glow the sickly yellow that he'd come to expect, he plunged his hands into the mountainside, then concentrated with all his might. Slowly, as if being gradually erased, the netherrack mountain faded from view, disappearing as if it never existed. But it was not just the mountain that stood before him that disintegrated; it was all the blocks that obscured the nether fortress.

In an instant, the entire fortress was exposed to Herobrine . . . every raised walkway and balcony and treasure room and spawning chamber. The structure stretched out in all directions; it was far bigger than any user or NPC had ever suspected. Long raised walkways spanned the landscape, with tall pillars of nether brick holding them aloft. They loomed high above the Nether, some of them intersection through boxy chambers while others stretched straight out into the distance, disappearing in the haze and smoke. At the center of the complex of passages sat a huge rectangular structure; all the raised corridors slowly snaked their way to this massive building. As Herobrine gazed at the entire fortress, he realized that it reminded him of some kind of massive dark spider. The elevated walkways looked like spiny legs, all connected to the central bulbous body and reaching out across the landscape. The titanic creature looked ready to strike some unsuspecting prey.

The comparison made Herobrine smile. Closing his eyes, he drank in the feelings around him, the heat, the smoke . . . everything.

It was wonderful.

He was surrounded by the sounds of the Nether: the cat-like purring of the ghasts, the sorrowful moans of the zombie-pigmen, the clattering of the wither skeletons, the sticky bouncing sounds of the magma cubes, and the mechanical wheezing sounds of the blazes. They had all sensed him now and were unsure if they should move toward him, or flee.

Herobrine looked up at a huge group of ghasts that was approaching and frowned. His last attempt to destroy the Source and escape these pathetic servers had failed miserably because of that fool of a ghast, Malacoda, the King of the Nether. That floating gasbag had built a fortress as big as this one . . . maybe even bigger. But that idiotic ghast had built it out of greed, not strategy. He wanted the biggest army and the grandest fortress just to satisfy his own image of himself. But his greed and conceit had led to his downfall and the failure of Herobrine's plan. He would not make that mistake again . . . ghasts are too selfish . . . too focused on their overinflated egos. Herobrine knew the floating giants had too much to prove because of the shameful act that had gotten them sentenced to this burning world, their faces forever scarred with the tears that never came. No, this time he needed something sensible and vicious.

The robot-like breathing of a blaze sounded directly behind him. Spinning, Herobrine drew his sword and faced the burning monster. It floated there, staring at him with its dark, coal-black eyes, a glowing blaze rod revolving about its interior, bathed in a body of flame.

"Blazes . . . that's what I need," Herobrine said to the creature of fire, then teleported away.

Instantly, he materialized in the huge square structure that sat at the center of the fortress. It was a massive gathering chamber with a tall pedestal at the center from which he could address the creatures of the Nether. But today he wasn't here to talk . . . today he was here to create. He teleported toward a group of approaching blazes. Drawing his diamond sword he attacked them as he had done with the skeletons and zombies to create his previous kings. As with the others, the blazes fell to the floor, their HP nearly consumed. Drawing on his crafting powers, he pulled the creatures together and formed a new blaze, this one bigger and stronger than any others.

As the new creature's life force stabilized, Herobrine disappeared, then reappeared an instant later with a bucket full of lava. The dark shadow-crafter poured the molten stone next to the creature. The new blaze leaned forward and drank in the burning liquid, the molten stone causing its internal flame to grow brighter and hotter, restoring its fiery health. As the large blaze became stronger, it stood up and floated over the small pool, continuing to draw live-giving HP from the lava's heat, its eyes glowing blood red.

By now, the massive chamber had filled with the creatures of the Nether. Blazes crowded forward to see the new creation standing tall next to the Maker. The elemental creatures of fire knew that their position in the pecking order of the Nether had just been significantly improved.

As more monsters moved into the huge chamber, Herobrine teleported to the pedestal that stood at the center.

"Friends, the time of our retribution is at hand," he shouted to the multitudes. "The Last Battle draws near, and this time we will not rely on a ghast to lead us."

Zombie-pigmen moaned, skeletons clattered, blazes wheezed, and magma cubes bounced, all the creatures staring up at the ghasts that floated high overhead.

"This time, we will destroy the NPCs of the Overworld, and you will get to watch me destroy the User-that-is-not-a-user."

The monsters all cheered in their own way. It was a strange sound that didn't sound like jubilation, but Herobrine understood the intent.

"You have been banished from the land of *sky* for too long."

That word triggered a solemn response from the monsters; their eyes drifted upward, not toward the ghasts or the overhead rocky ceiling, but to the imaginary blue sky that had been denied them so long ago.

"And now it is time to take your revenge on the NPCs and their leader. Your new blaze king will lead you to victory, but you must gather your people and bring them here, for we will launch the assault on the Overworld from this fortress!"

More cheering.

Moving to a doorway, Herobrine extended his hands and allowed his crafting powers to build. As they glowed, a portal started to form in the doorway, its purple teleportation field growing brighter and brighter. Soon, an undulating surface stabilized as sparkling lavender particles floated around the edge of the field, making its perimeter sparkle and shine.

Walking through the portal, Herobrine disappeared for an instant, then returned, pulling a chestnut-colored mare behind him. The horse looked terrified at being in the Nether; the heat was intolerable for the beast. It did not matter; it would soon be something else.

Pulling Herobrine pulled the horse toward some blazes, he then struck at it with his sword, drawing its HP from the animal. Herobrine then reached into the center of some blazes and pulled their glowing blaze rods out of the creatures. Without the rods to hold their elemental flames together, they burst outward, showering the nearby flaming creatures with fire, which they happily drank up. Crafting the blaze rods into what was left of the horse, Herobrine created a new kind of horse. It was an animal of flame and smoke, of fire and ash. As the creature stood, the shadow-crafter stepped back and admired his handiwork. The horse now looked something akin to a skeleton horse, only its body was not composed of bone—rather, it was composed of blaze rods. Flames encapsulated the beast, its body formed of fire, the blaze rods glowing bright orange from within.

Herobrine brought the fire horse to the blaze king and motioned for the new ruler to mount. Climbing atop the fiery steed, the blaze king looked down on his new subjects.

"Behold, I give you my third horseman, Charybdis, king of the blazes. He will lead the creatures of the Nether in glorious battle to destroy the NPCs of the Overworld and take back what was stolen from you . . . the sky!"

The monsters cheered . . . even the ghasts.

Moving close to Charybdis, Herobrine spoke in a low voice.

"Gather all your blazes and bring them here," the Maker commanded. "Use the other creatures of the Nether for this task. When I signal, you will come through this portal and will be at my side for the Last Battle. Do you understand?"

"Charybdis understands," the blaze king said, his voice wheezy and mechanical.

"Excellent," Herobrine answered, then allowed his eyes to glow bright. "Failure will not be tolerated . . . is that understood?"

Charybdis nodded.

"Then prepare and do not fail me."

The king of the blazes nodded again, then turned and began to give orders. The monsters of the Nether listened to their commands, then left the gathering chamber and to pursue their tasks.

Herobrine closed his eyes and imagined the look on Gameknight999's face when hundreds of blazes emerged out of this portal and into the Overworld. He started to laugh, first with the faintest of evil giggles, but then it built to a raucous, gut-splitting roar that filled the chamber with echoes.

"One more horseman," Herobrine shouted to the wall of the chamber, "then I'm coming for you, User-that-is-not-a-user."

With his eyes blazing bright, he disappeared from the Nether and headed for his last king . . . the one who would make his enemy's blood run cold and destroy all hope from the NPCs of the Overworld.

CHAPTER 15
SQUID

Gameknight emerged from the minecart tunnel to sounds of confusion. The tunnel had led them to another village, which was not a surprise, but a hundred minecarts suddenly appearing was likely a huge shock to the community they were invading.

Gameknight stepped out of the minecart, moved to the center of the chamber, then jumped into the air and placed a block of stone under his feet. He did this again and again, continuing the process until everyone stopped talking and looked up at him. Once the commotion finally stopped, Gameknight999 was standing seven blocks into the air.

"Everyone stop talking and listen," he said to the NPCs. "Where's the village's crafter?"

"Here," said a voice from the crowd.

An old, gray-haired NPC stepped forward, his body bent with age. As expected, his smock was black with a gray stripe running down the center.

"What is the meaning of all this?" the crafter asked, his voice gravelly and coarse.

"We'll explain in a minute," Gameknight replied. "But, first, answer me one question . . . is this village on the coast?"

"No—we're in the middle of grasslands with a birch forest biome on one side and a mega taiga on the other. Why?"

"We need to find an Ocean Monument, fast," Gameknight said, then turned to scan the crowd.

"Where's Crafter?"

"Here, Gameknight," said a young voice, a small hand sprouting out of the crowd.

"Come closer," Gameknight said as he carefully dug away the blocks under his feet with his pick. When he reached the ground, Crafter was standing before him. "We need riders going out to look for a village on the ocean shore. Herobrine knows where we are and will be coming fast."

"But we aren't there anymore," Digger said as he pushed his way through the closely packed bodies.

"Yes, but he knows that we're close," Gameknight added. "We have to move fast now or be destroyed." He then turned and faced Crafter. "I have to find the Ocean Monument and the Book of Wisdom so that I can figure out how to defeat Herobrine."

"But where do we look?" his young friend asked.

"I don't know, but we do know that it will be in the ocean, so we need to find a village on the ocean shore. That will be the first place to look. Send out riders on all the minecart tracks. We need to search everywhere as quickly as possible. All our lives depend on this."

Crafter nodded, then turned and spoke to some of the NPCs from his village. They quickly pulled out minecarts and jumped on the tracks, shooting down the tunnels. As they disappeared, more people grabbed minecarts and followed, thirty riders searching Minecraft for the survival of everyone.

"Now tell me what is going on," the old crafter asked.

Gameknight explained what was happening; he did not try to comfort the aged NPC or ease his fears . . . there was no time for that. As Gameknight spoke, the crafter kept glancing up at the letters that floated above Gameknight's head, noticing the conspicuously absent server thread.

Pausing for a moment, Gameknight turned and faced Digger.

"Go check the surroundings for monsters, and quietly bring everyone from the village down here," Gameknight explained. "Take whomever you need to help, but keep it quiet. There could be eyes watching from the forest or even closer."

"Got it," the big NPC replied, then took off running, taking four others with him.

"Hold on," the old crafter said, then pointed to some of his villagers. "Runner, Planter, Smithy, go with them and help."

The NPCs sprinted up the steps and headed to the tunnels that led to the surface.

"OK, continue," the old crafter said.

"You're pretty much caught up," Gameknight said.

Reaching into his inventory, he pulled out the spotted pink egg and held it in his hands.

"The Oracle told me that this could be used to defeat Herobrine," Gameknight explained. "She also said, 'Look to the lowliest and most insignificant of creatures, for that is where your salvation will lie.' I still have no idea what that is supposed to mean, but one problem at a time. We need to find the Ocean Monument before Herobrine gets here, or we're all dead."

"You're a lot of fun to have around," Hunter said from behind.

"I'm just telling it like it is," Gameknight replied.

"What do we do while we're waiting for the NPCs to come back from their search?" Monet113 asked.

The old crafter turned to see who was speaking, and his green eyes grew wide with amazement. He stared at the letters over her head, then glanced up in the air, noting the lack of a server thread.

"There are two of them?" he stammered.

"Yeah," Hunter answered. "If you thought one of them can cause trouble, just imagine what two of them can do."

Everyone in the crafting chamber burst into laughter as Hunter slapped Gameknight on the back. Once they calmed down, Gameknight spoke.

"We should be preparing while we wait," the User-that-is-not-a-user said. "Armor needs repairing, bows need to be restrung, swords sharpened . . . let's all get to work. We can't waste any time; I'm sure Herobrine isn't."

The name of their foe snapped everyone into action. The crafting chamber suddenly became a beehive of activity, with the village's NPCs banging out armor and weapons while Crafter and his people set up their own crafting benches. As they worked, a gradual trickle of people slowly came down into the crafting chamber from the village overhead. Some of the village diggers went to work on one of the walls, slowly expanding the crafting chamber so that there would be enough room for everyone.

"Everyone, quiet!" an NPC yelled by the minecart rails. "One of the minecarts is coming back."

All activity ceased as they waited for the rider to return. When the minecart rolled into the crafting chamber, the rider was shocked to find all eyes on him.

"Well?" someone asked. "Did you find it?"

The rider shook his head while he stepped out of the cart. One of the NPCs from Crafter's village took the minecart from his hands and chose another tunnel. Placing it on the track, he shot down the rails, followed by two more volunteers. As they sped away, activity in the crafting chamber continued.

Three more riders returned with discouraging reports that made some of the villagers shake their heads, looks of fear beginning to fill their eyes. They all knew that everything depended on finding the Ocean Monument, and every fruitless search brought them and Minecraft one step closer to the brink.

"Do not be discouraged," Gameknight shouted, his voice echoing off the cavern walls, ringing with confidence and hope. "The only failure here is giving up, and that's not gonna happen. We will continue to search until we've covered all of Minecraft. And when that happens, we'll start over and keep trying until we are successful."

His words made the discouraged NPCs stand a little taller, their eyes shining a little brighter. But just as Gameknight was about to add to his words, he heard a scream coming from one of the minecart tunnels.

Are there monsters coming? Gameknight thought.

Drawing his sword, he moved to the tunnel to face the oncoming threat, but before he could get to the dark opening, he found Stonecutter's hulking form already there, his pickaxe out and ready.

"Archers, stand on some blocks," Hunter shouted as she built a small pillar on which she could stand.

"Swordsmen, to the front," Crafter shouted. "Children to the back of the cavern."

Gameknight turned and watched the NPCs prepare for the unknown threat; he was impressed. They didn't know what was coming, or how many. It could be all of Herobrine's army coming through that tunnel, or maybe the monsters from the Nether . . . or both; but you couldn't tell from the looks of the NPCs' faces. Staring at the dark tunnel, they all held grim, determined looks, a refusal to back down showing in their eyes.

The screams echoed through the tunnel, this time louder.

Gameknight gripped his diamond sword firmly in his hand, then drew his iron sword with his left. Many of the new villagers gasped when they saw him with two swords, but the User-that-is-not-a-user didn't bother to turn and look at them. He was ready for battle, and all that mattered right now was keeping those around him safe.

The scream sounded again, this time even louder. It was almost at the entrance.

Gameknight could hear bowstrings creak as they were pulled taut, arrows aimed at the dark tunnel.

"Whatever comes out of that tunnel . . . show no fear!" Gameknight shouted. "This is our land, and everyone around you is family. Nobody is going to take this from you . . . WE REFUSE TO YIELD!"

A cheer rang out through the crafting chamber, but was then cut short as another scream sounded from a different tunnel . . . and then another and another. The shouts were coming from four different tunnels.

Are we being invaded? Gameknight thought.

As the NPCs positioned themselves around the other tunnels, a minecart shot out of the darkness, an NPC sitting within.

"Yahoo . . . I found it!" the rider screamed.

"Was that what you were screaming?" Hunter asked with an angry glare.

The NPC nodded, then looked around and saw all the arrows pointed at him. He swallowed nervously.

"Sorry," the rider said as he lowered his head.

Before anyone could respond, more minecarts shot out of the tunnels, with more cries of exuberance filling the chamber.

"I found it . . ." a rider said.

"I found the ocean village!" another cried.

"The village on the ocean shore . . . I know where

it is!" the last yelled.

Gameknight sheathed his swords, then raised his hands to get everyone to relax and put away their weapons.

"All of you should be a little more careful when you scream in a dark tunnel," Hunter chided. "You almost got shot full of holes."

But the NPCs were too excited to be abashed. They pushed their way through the crowd to get to the User-that-is-not-a-user. As they neared, the cavern grew quiet with a nervous silence. Their survival depended on what the riders had to report, and every NPC knew it.

"OK, what did you find?" Gameknight asked each.

"I found a village right on the shore of a huge ocean," the first reported.

"So did I," said the second.

"Me, too."

"And me."

"Great," Hunter said as she stepped off her stone pillar. "First we can't find a village on the ocean shore; now we have too many."

"Hunter . . . shush!" Stitcher said to her sister, then turned and faced Gameknight999. "Go on."

"Did any of them know about the Ocean Monument?"

They all shook their heads.

"None of them had ever heard of it nor the Book of Wisdom," the first rider said. "They said they used the ocean for fishing, and that's about it."

"That's what the crafter said at the village that I found as well," the second rider said.

"Mine, too," the third added.

But the fourth rider remained quiet, silently contemplating the information that he had in his blocky head.

"What about you?" Gameknight asked the fourth rider.

"Well, the crafter of this village didn't know anything about the Ocean Monument, either," the rider said.

"This is great!" Hunter said, her voice dripping with sarcasm.

"But . . ." the rider added.

"But what?" Crafter asked as he moved next to the NPC.

"But the crafter at this village said that they don't fish in the ocean because of all the ink sacks," the rider explained.

"Ink sacks?" Crafter asked. "What do you mean?"

"The crafter told me that they keep finding ink sacks all over the ocean floor or washed up on the shoreline," the NPC said. "They never go into the ocean because of this. In fact, all the NPCs are afraid of the ocean because it looks lifeless and empty . . . nothing but ink sacks."

"Great," Hunter said again. "This is really helpful, but we need—"

"That's it!" Gameknight exclaimed.

"What are you talking about?" Crafter asked.

"The squid . . . they're being attacked by the guardians of the Ocean Monument," Gameknight explained. "That's the village we need."

"But how can you be sure?" Hunter asked. "This could mean anything. It could be—"

Gameknight silenced her by raising his hand . . . he was actually surprised that it worked.

"That's where we're all going . . . now!" Gameknight said, then turned and looked at the NPCs in the crafting chamber. "Everyone grab a minecart; we're going to that village. Rider, show us the way."

The NPC grabbed a minecart and shot down the tracks, Gameknight999 right behind him. And for the first time, he felt excited rather than afraid. Instead of running from Herobrine, they were getting ready to take the fight to him. Gameknight could feel all the pieces of the puzzle start to line up; he knew this village was going to be the location of the Last Battle for Minecraft, and for some reason that made him feel calm and at peace.

As he sat in the minecart, one of the sayings on his teacher Mr. Planck's wall popped into his head: *Those skilled in war bring the enemy to the field of battle and are not brought there by him.* It was a quote from Sun Tzu, a Chinese military general from 500 BC, and likely one of the greatest military strategists in history.

"It's time you danced to my tune, Herobrine!" Gameknight said to the darkness.

Closing his eyes, he imagined what he was going to accomplish at this village, and the pieces of the puzzle started to tumble around in his head . . . hidden defenses . . . traps . . . surprises for Herobrine and his monsters. As images of the preparations popped into his head, the music of Minecraft swelled in volume and filled his being. For the first time in a long time, the music lacked a desperate feel, and instead was filled with hope.

CHAPTER 16

THE END

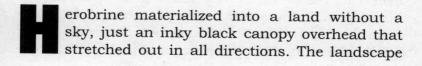erobrine materialized into a land without a sky, just an inky black canopy overhead that stretched out in all directions. The landscape

lacked any vegetation—no grass, no trees, no bushes . . . nothing. It was a bare wasteland made of pale yellow cubes, each spotted with the same pattern as cobblestone. Tall pillars of purple obsidian stood out against the yellow blocks that made up the ground, but nearly disappeared as they stretched high up into the starless sky. Herobrine would have had a difficult time finding the summit of the obsidian monoliths were it not for the burning crystal that sat atop each. Purple ender crystals floated within a ball of flame on top of each pillar, the intricately carved cubes bobbing and spinning about, showing their disdain for gravity.

Herobrine was in The End.

Around him, he could see endermen standing in small groups, some of them teleporting across The End, their bodies always enveloped by the sparkling purple teleportation particles. Their smaller cousins, endermites, scurried about near the clusters of the endermen, their small, rat-like bodies making a scraping sound across the pale yellow End Stone as they scurried about.

Suddenly, a thunderous roar echoed across the pale landscape, drawing the attention of all the endermen. The dark creatures stopped what they were doing and looked up into the featureless sky.

And then Herobrine saw it.

Two bright purple eyes shone in the overhead darkness. They first looked like two small pinpoints of violet light moving about through the air, but then the broad wings began to emerge through the darkness as the creature approached. The monster flapped its wings once, then banked gracefully over the tallest of the obsidian pillars. Instantly, an iridescent blue-gray beam of light reached out from the top of the pillar and struck the dragon, the healing beam from the ender crystal replenishing the monster's HP. Roaring again, the dragon flapped its wings, then turned its head and glared at Herobrine, its eyes glowing bright and angry.

The massive creature flew straight toward him, the dragon probably seeing the NPC woodcutter and thinking it had a new victim. With its shining claws outstretched and its purple eyes blazing, it swooped down to attack. Drawing on his crafting powers, Herobrine allowed his eyes to flare bright white, causing the flying demon to suddenly stop in midair, hover, then slowly settle to the ground. The dragon had recognized the Maker, and bowed its giant head low to the ground.

"You dragons always did know how to show me the proper respect," Herobrine said as he petted the mighty beast between the eyes.

Turning, he motioned for a group of endermen to come near. A half-dozen of the lanky creatures teleported across the landscape and appeared right near him. Drawing his sword, he quickly reduced their HP to nearly zero, allowing the monsters to fall to the ground in a heap. As with his other creations, he kneaded their bodies with his crafting powers, drawing them together and reshaping them into something bigger and stronger than before. His eyes glowed bright with his evil intent, drawing the endermites to his side.

Shoving aside the annoying little creatures, he continued his work, finishing the body and legs, then forming the muscular, quick arms. But before he finished, Herobrine reached into his inventory and pulled out a handful of red flowers and ink sacks. Dropping them into his creation, he let the colors flow across its body, staining it a dark, dark red, almost the color of dried blood.

"The color has to be just right to strike fear into

my enemy's heart," Herobrine said aloud, to no one.

Pouring all his hatred and malice into this new monster, Herobrine slowly finished the dark red creature, then added an extra bit of vile disgust for the User-that-is-not-a-user just for good measure.

It was complete.

Stepping back, he let his creation stand slowly, its HP still dangerously low . . . too low for it to teleport. Pulling out a stack of obsidian blocks from his inventory, Herobrine quickly made a portal and lit it with flint and steel. The purple gateway writhed and undulated as if it were alive. Purple teleportation particles floated out of the glowing field and away from the structure, only to be drawn back into its lavender surface.

Herobrine's creation sensed the portal and moved close to it, drinking in the teleportation particles as if they were mother's milk. Gradually, the shining particles added to the creature's HP, though it was a slow process. This was how an enderman fed, by teleporting and drinking in the particles that surrounded its dark body, though it only worked in The End.

Once the new enderman had enough HP, it teleported across the landscape, jumping from place to place to place as it consumed the particles and grew stronger. It took many teleportation jumps, but eventually its HP was full, and it returned to the Maker.

"Welcome, king of the endermen!" Herobrine yelled so that all the creatures of The End could hear him.

The dark creature looked about The End as if seeing it for the first time, then stared down at Herobrine.

"Master, what is your command?"

Herobrine smiled. "Just wait here for a moment,"

the shadow-crafter said, disappearing for an instant, then reappearing with a dark horse in tow.

Releasing the animal, Herobrine commanded two endermen to come to his side. The dark creatures instantly appeared. Drawing his sword again, he cut through the two endermen and horse until their HP was nearly depleted, then crafted them together, making a new kind of horse never seen before in Minecraft. When he was complete, the horse stood on its four dark legs, a black saddle across its back, its eyes softly glowing with an evil purple light, small teleportation particles dancing about.

The ender-horse moved next to the portal and drank up all the teleportation particles that leaked out of the glowing lavender field. As its HP grew, its eyes glowed brighter and brighter until they rivaled the intensity of the Ender Dragon. Breathing heavily, Herobrine could see streams of teleportation particles flowing out of the horse's nostrils, as if they were purple flames. This creature was nearly overwhelmed with a hatred for the NPCs of the Overworld, its mind almost drowning in a need for destruction.

It's perfect, the Maker thought, then showed an eerie, toothy grin that made the endermen take a step back in fear.

"You are my fourth horseman, and here is your mount," Herobrine said. "Come, get on your steed."

The king of the endermen moved next to the gigantic horse, then stepped up onto its back.

"I name you Feyd, king of the endermen."

Feyd nodded his dark head in understanding. "What are your commands?" Feyd asked.

"You are to assemble all endermen you can find and bring them here. Send a few out to scare the NPCs, but do not engage in battle. Your job is to bring all your brothers here, and then come when I signal you."

"How will we recognize your signal?" Feyd asked.

"That will not be a problem . . . you will know it when it comes."

"What will happen next?" the king of the endermen asked.

"The Last Battle will finally arrive, and unlike your predecessor, Erebus, you will not fall victim to greed or ego. I have made you only to hate and destroy those who oppose me. When it is time, you will bring your enderman army and join Charybdis, the blaze king, Reaper, the skeleton king, and Xa-Tul, the zombie king, in battle. We will not underestimate our enemy, Gameknight999, again!"

At the sound of Gameknight's name, Feyd's eyes glowed bright red, an evil scowl coming across his shadowy, crimson face.

"Yes, my child, you will get a chance to exact revenge on the User-that-is-not-a-user. Gameknight999 and his NPC friends have infected Minecraft for long enough. It is time that we cure these lands of this disease, forever."

An evil smile spread across Feyd's dark face.

"Now, go; send out your endermen and bring all your brothers here."

Feyd looked down from his mount at Herobrine and nodded his head, then disappeared, materializing across The End amid a large collection of endermen. After talking for a moment, they all disappeared, leaving behind a sparkling cloud of purple particles.

Smiling, Herobrine turned and faced the dragon that still sat nearby.

"This time my plans will be successful. When my four horsemen arrive with their armies, we will overwhelm the NPCs. And when they see the little surprise I have waiting for the User-that-is-not-a-user, all hope will leave them, and the NPCs will know it is truly the end of their days." He patted the dragon on its massive snout. "After I have destroyed all his friends, I will focus my rage on the User-that-is-not-a-user. But this time, if he refuses me, I will destroy him and then use the little girl instead. I have no doubt that she will bend to my will, but it would be more satisfying to have the User-that-is-not-a-user surrender and release me from this prison." Herobrine cackled. "Now, go, my dragon; fly about and guard your domain."

The dragon nodded its huge head, then leapt into the air and flew away on its dark wings. As Herobrine watched the monster soar into the dark sky, he gathered his crafting powers, his entire body glowing an insipid pale yellow. Looking at the ground, he could see that the sickly glow leaked into the blocks at his feet. This made Herobrine chuckle so maliciously that the sound seeped through his body and flowed into the fabric of Minecraft, making the very world around him cringe.

"Your time is almost up, Gameknight999!" he said to no one . . . to everyone. "When I find where you are hiding, I will squash you and all your friends! And this time, you don't have the hag or her dogs to protect you. My little surprise will take care of anything you have waiting for me!" He paused as he listened to his words echoing throughout The End. "THE LAST BATTLE HAS COME TO MINECRAFT" Herobrine screamed, "*AND YOUR END DRAWS NEAR!*"

CHAPTER 17
THE OCEAN VILLAGE

Gameknight's minecart emerged from the tunnel and into the new crafting chamber. He leapt out of the cart, pulled it off the tracks, and set it on the ground, allowing the next to arrive. Glancing around the chamber, he could see that it was like every other crafting chamber in Minecraft. About a dozen crafting benches were scattered across the floor of the cavern, a worker at each banging out what Minecraft needed. Snaking between the benches was an intricate series of minecart tracks that moved the crafted materials to one of the many tunnels that pierced the side of the cavern. On one wall was a flight of steps that climbed up to a pair of iron doors. Gameknight knew that these doors opened to tunnels that led to the surface, the secret tunnel emerging from within the cobblestone watchtower that sat on the surface high overhead.

He expected to hear the banging of tools, but instead he heard silence. Looking at the surprised faces, Gameknight could see the NPCs and village crafter staring at the letters over his head, then glancing above to look for the server thread that was not there. By the awe on their faces, Gameknight knew that they recognized him as the User-that-is-not-a-user.

Suddenly, Crafter shot out of the tunnel, followed by Digger and Hunter, with Monet and Stitcher following close behind.

Before Gameknight could say anything, Crafter

sprinted to the village's crafter and started to explain the situation. As they spoke, Gameknight could see the village crafter continually looking at him, glancing up at the letters that floated above his head.

While they spoke, Digger took a contingent of workers and started expanding the crafting chamber. If this *was* going to be the location of the Last Battle, lots more people would be coming here, and this chamber would need to be much, much bigger.

As Gameknight stood there, more minecarts emerged from the tunnels. Like a well-oiled machine, the villagers hopped off the tracks as soon as their cart stopped and put the minecart into their inventory, making room for the next arrival. Without being told, the NPCs pulled out pickaxes and shovels and went to work on the crafting chamber. But when Smithy arrived, Gameknight999 called the NPC to his side.

"Smithy, we need more NPCs for the Last Battle," Gameknight said in a quiet voice.

Smithy looked at the User-that-is-not-a-user and nodded his head.

"We can't do what we did last time, and have Crafter use his powers to call NPCs to this village," Gameknight explained. "That would tell Herobrine right where we are. Instead, we need to send riders to all the villages and bring them here quickly and quietly."

Smithy smiled, then patted his dark apron, causing gray dust to fall to the ground.

"Smithy knows what to do," the NPC said.

He grabbed a handful of villagers who were just arriving and pulled them aside. Explaining what was needed, the NPCs looked at Gameknight and nodded their boxy heads, then disappeared into different tunnels, their minecarts clattering down the tracks at high speed. Turning to give the User-that-is-not-a-user a smile, Smithy also disappeared down one of the tracks.

"Good . . . it's begun . . . the call for the Last Battle," the User-that-is-not-a-user said to himself.

Gameknight looked at the progress that was being made on the crafting chamber. The wall had been moved back by ten blocks and was progressing quickly. A group of diggers was starting to carve tunnels above the level of the minecarts, heading straight into the stone. Gameknight knew that these tunnels would serve as makeshift homes for the many families that would hopefully arrive.

If Smithy fails on his task and nobody comes to help, we're doomed, Gameknight thought. *He must succeed!*

Images of the Last Battle with only a handful of NPCs on his side started to surface in his mind . . . images of what *might be* filled him with fear.

NO! I won't focus on the what ifs; *I'll focus only on the NOW!*

Shaking off the thoughts, Gameknight moved to Digger's side and put a cautious hand on his shoulder, careful to stay far from the huge pickaxe that was tearing through stone as if it were sand.

"Digger, let's go up top and look around," Gameknight said.

Digger nodded as he put away his pick. He gave instructions to the other workers and followed Gameknight to the stairs that led to the tunnels and the surface.

"Hunter, Stitcher, Monet . . . follow us," Gameknight shouted over the sounds of pickaxes splitting stone.

Not looking to see if they were following, Gameknight streaked up the steps and through the tunnels that led to the surface. While he waited for his friends in the watchtower, he peered out of the building's windows. He could see the bright yellow face of the sun just starting to rise in the east, the warm rays of sunlight shining down on the land and lighting it with a golden hue. Seeing the sun made him relax a little.

He turned and smiled at Digger, who had just emerged from the secret tunnel.

"I love the sunrise in Minecraft," Gameknight said. "It looks so much more spectacular from inside the game than on a computer monitor."

"I can assure you, NPCs love it as well," Digger replied. "Nighttime might be monster time, but the daylight belongs to us, and we plan to keep it." He moved closer to the window and looked up at the sun's radiant square face. "If Herobrine's monsters want a fight, I say let them come in the light of day so that the sun can burn them. But, alas, I'm sure we can't be that lucky."

"You're probably right, Digger," Gameknight agreed. "You're probably right."

As his friends climbed out of the secret tunnel, Gameknight stepped out of the cobblestone building and into the village. Instantly, he could smell salt in the air; the ocean breeze made everything seem fresh and clean.

Stepping out into the morning sunlight, he could see the sparkling blue ocean stretching off into the distance. On the other side of the village, a birch forest filled his view, the white bark of the trees standing out against the dark foliage. The village sat on a narrow strip of grasslands, with the ocean on one side and the forest on the other.

Large fields of crops stood near the center of the village, some filled with tall stalks of wheat, others with boxy melons, while some showed the leafy ends of carrots sticking out of the ground. Every shade of green was visible in the fields, with the beautifully colored striped melon cubes mixing with the bright green of the wheat, creating a visual feast for the eyes. By the look of them, Gameknight could tell that most were ready for harvesting. Good—they'd need the food when more NPCs started to arrive . . . *if* they arrived.

Beyond the fields, Gameknight could see a large pen filled with cows and another pen with pigs, lots of them . . . likely the recipients of the carrots. The pink animals milled about in the fenced yard, their oinks filling the air, the moos from their neighbors adding to the symphony. It was a beautiful scene to behold, but it made Gameknight sad thinking about what was going to happen here soon.

And then the pigs reminded the User-that-is-not-a-user of something.

"Monet, call down for Herder," Gameknight said over his shoulder.

He could hear her footsteps shuffling back to the tunnel, then her voice echoing through the stone underground passages. In a minute, Herder was standing at Gameknight's side.

Gameknight pointed toward the forest.

"Herder . . . we'll need wolves, lots of them," the User-that-is-not-a-user said. "You know why we need them, right?"

Herder nodded his head.

"I'm counting on you to be ready when I need them," Gameknight explained. "Do you understand?"

"They'll be ready," Herder said confidently.

"Good," the User-that-is-not-a-user said. "Monet, go help him collect 'em."

"I can do this better on my own," the lanky youth said, then spun and sprinted toward the forest, his long, stringy black hair bobbing up and down as he ran.

Pulling a bone from his inventory, Herder shot into the forest and disappeared as he wove his way around the birch trees, looking for his friends.

"I'll get to work on the defenses," Digger said as he turned to start mapping out where he would build the walls and archer towers.

"No, that's what Herobrine will expect," Gameknight said.

This stopped Digger in his tracks.

"Is it your thought that no defenses might confuse him?" Hunter asked. "I'm not sure that's your best plan."

"We will have defenses," Gameknight replied, "but just not what Herobrine will expect."

Closing his eyes, he imagined that he was at his keyboard, typing in the chat.

Shawny, are you there?

Yep.

Good, Gameknight said. *We need defenses that will surprise Herobrine, something that he won't expect and cannot see, at least not right away. You have any ideas?*

I have a few, Shawny said. *But how can I build them? It will make all the NPCs stop what they're doing and freeze up.*

I want to you draw the plans on the ground, so that Digger can see them. Explain them to him, then go away so that he can build them, Gameknight explained. *You got it?*

I got it, Shawny answered. *Have him meet me by the edge of the forest.*

And then his friend's voice was gone from his mind.

"Digger, you and Monet go to the edge of the forest," Gameknight explained. "My friend Shawny will tell you what you need to do. Listen to him . . . he's an expert at strategy. He can help us.

"Monet, I need you to help Digger. You can ask questions if you think something isn't clear . . . he won't be able to. This is important—I'm relying on you to get this done. Can you do it?"

"I'm all over it," Monet113 said with a smile.

She followed Digger, who was already heading for the forest. When they reached the tree line, Gameknight could see Shawny suddenly appear. Digger instantly went rigid and linked his hands across his chest, but his head followed Shawny as he spoke. Pulling out his own diamond sword, Shawny started sketching something on the ground; Digger looked down at the drawing intently. As Shawny explained, Gameknight could see Monet interrupt to ask questions, then nod her head, allowing Shawny to finish.

"What about us?" Hunter asked, Stitcher standing impatiently at her side.

"Let's go down to the ocean," Gameknight said. "I want to look for that Ocean Monument."

The trio sprinted down to the waterline, then placed boats in the water and got in.

"Which way?" Stitcher asked.

"Maybe we should separate?" Hunter suggested.

"No, we need to stay together," Gameknight said. "Follow me."

Moving his boat off to the left, the User-that-is-not-a-user peered into the cool blue water. As his boat glided across the surface, Gameknight could hear the music of Minecraft playing in the back of his head, but it was getting fainter and fainter. Turning his boat to the right, he found the music growing in volume, filling his mind with its melodious tones. The farther they moved to the right, the louder the music became.

You're helping us, aren't you, Oracle? he thought, but he received no reply in return.

"There . . . you see that?" Stitcher yelled.

"What?" Gameknight asked.

"I saw a squid suddenly flash red, as if it were being attacked," Stitcher explained. "It flashed red once, then again, then just disappeared. Look, there, I can see its ink sack."

Gameknight steered his boat where Stitcher was pointing. Peering down into the dark waters, he could see a black ink sack slowly settling down into the depths. The ocean was deep here, and getting down there and back up to get air was going to be difficult.

Just then, one of the puzzle pieces fell into place; an image of a door filled his mind . . . *yes, of course.*

Suddenly, pain erupted throughout his body, a strange buzzing sound filling his ears.

"Look out," Hunter yelled as she stood up in her boat and fired arrows into the ocean.

The pain slowly faded away.

"What was that?" Gameknight said.

"I don't know," Hunter answered. "All I saw was one giant eye staring up at you. It looked like it was shooting something at you, with rays of light coming from the center of that eye."

"It must have been one of the guardians," Gameknight said. "I think we'll have to—"

Suddenly, Stitcher cried out in pain.

Turning, Gameknight could see a shaft of golden, searing light shooting up out of the ocean and striking Stitcher in the shoulder. He steered his boat over to her, moving his craft so that he could block the beam with his body. Instantly, Gameknight999 was filled with agonizing pain as the beam of light struck him in the chest. Gameknight was almost doubled over in pain, but he was able to steer his boat away from the monster and head back to the village. As he moved his craft across the calm water, he looked back and saw a blue crystalline structure in the watery depths, its tall pillars and graceful arches lit up by strange white cubes of light.

"Thanks," Stitcher said.

Gameknight smiled.

"I saw the thing," Stitcher continued. "It has just one huge eye, and orange spines all over its body . . . big spines, like the kind that could go right through armor. It was terrible."

"Well, we knew we weren't expecting teddy bears," Gameknight said.

"What?" Stitcher asked. "Teddy bears? What are teddy bears?"

"Never mind," Gameknight replied. "At least we know our destination now. That building down there was the Ocean Monument, and that's our next objective."

"This sounds like a really great idea," Hunter said mockingly, with a nervous smile. "Crazed one-eyed spiny fish with deadly vision and needle-sharp spikes guarding an ancient building at the bottom of the ocean . . . this might be one of your best ideas yet!"

"Yeah . . . I'm scared, too," he replied as he looked back at the underwater structure.

I know what's waiting for me inside the Monument . . . another monster. I don't know how I'm going to do this without seeing all my friends destroyed.

As Gameknight landed his boat on the ocean shore, he tried to imagine destroying the creature that lay waiting for him in that underground temple. But all he could see in his mind was the monster that waited in the depths—a huge beast with long purple spikes and a single hateful eye. Instead of visualizing the monster's destruction, he could see only a shaft of intense light blasting him from that angry eye and filling his body with pain . . . and fear.

CHAPTER 18

DOORS

Running back to the village, Gameknight knew what he needed in order to go back to the Ocean Monument: doors . . . they needed lots of doors. But, first, they needed more doors in the village, for one of the pieces of the puzzle was still missing. Running a circuitous path around the buildings, Gameknight counted the number of doors . . . sixteen . . . not enough.

"Stitcher, go down and tell the crafters that I need doors, lots of doors," Gameknight said. "We need as many as they can make."

"Doors . . . why?"

"No time to explain," Gameknight replied. "Just trust me."

Nodding her head, the young girl spun and headed back to the crafting chamber.

"Hunter, follow me."

Without waiting for her to answer, Gameknight headed for the forest. He could still see Shawny talking with Digger at the far end of the village, so he headed in the opposite direction so that Hunter would not seize up and stop helping. When he reached the tree line, the User-that-is-not-a-user pulled out his axe and started cutting down the trees.

"Get wood, as much as you can," Gameknight said as he hacked at a huge birch tree.

The pair cut down tree after tree, putting the blocks of wood into their inventory until they had twenty blocks each.

"That should be enough," Gameknight said. "Follow me."

"Are you going to tell me what this is all about?" Hunter asked, her voice sounding frustrated.

"No," Gameknight replied, then smiled at his friend.

They headed back to the village, quickly changing the blocks of wood into planks.

"Make a crafting bench, then start crafting doors out of the wooden planks," Gameknight instructed.

In the distance, he could see that Shawny had disappeared and Digger had his hands separated again. He and Monet were looking at the diagram that had been drawn on the ground. Carefully, they pulled out their own swords and started to scratch their own lines around the village, marking where Shawny's contraptions would be built.

Focusing on his own task, Gameknight made a crafting bench using four planks and placed it on the ground. Then, using more wood, he started to craft as many doors as he could with the planks that he still hand in his inventory. In total, he was able to make thirty-six doors from his twenty blocks of wood.

"That will be enough for now," Gameknight said. "Come on."

"Any time you want to clue me in on what you're doing, it would be great," Hunter said.

"Well, it's kinda fun seeing you confused," Gameknight said. "But I'm trying to get an iron golem to spawn here in this village."

"We could just craft one," Hunter insisted.

"I don't think it's the same," Gameknight replied. "You ever wonder where the golems come from when they spawn in a village?"

"Of course not. Why do I care where they come

from?"

"Well, I think this time it matters," Gameknight said. "Come on, start placing your doors on the ground."

They placed about ten doors on the ground, then stepped back and waited.

"Why is nothing happening?" Gameknight asked. "All you need is twenty-one doors and then an iron golem should spawn. One should have spawned by now."

"No it shouldn't have," Hunter stated with an exasperated sigh. "Users know nothing."

"What do you mean?" Gameknight asked.

Hunter ignored his question and ran to the watchtower, Gameknight following close behind.

"Are you going to tell me what you're doing?" the User-that-is-not-a-user asked.

She stopped and gave him a smile.

"No," Hunter answered, then continued into the watchtower.

She burst through the door and started down the secret tunnel that lead to the crafting chamber, but suddenly stopped and looked up at Gameknight999 from the hidden ladder.

"You stay here," she said in a stern voice.

"Why . . . what are you doing?"

"You're right," she said with a smile. "It is kinda fun seeing you confused."

Before he could respond, she disappeared down the ladder. After a long minute, she shot back up, followed by a dozen villagers. The NPCs moved out into the village and stood around the well at the center of town.

"Golems don't spawn to protect houses," Hunter instructed. "They spawn to protect villagers. There must be at least ten NPCs in the village in order for the iron golem to appear."

A rumbling sound, just barely audible, began to fill the air. It first started out faintly, like a storm brewing on the horizon, but then it grew louder and louder as the ground pulsed and shuddered. Stepping out of the watchtower, Gameknight could see a tall iron golem approaching the villagers, its huge feet smashing the ground with every step.

The metal giant looked like all the other golems he'd seen save one . . . the king of the golems. This one before him had shining silver skin, with green stringy vines hanging down the right side of its body as well as down its left arm, tiny yellow flowers interspersed between the leaves. It had long, muscular arms that seemed impossibly thick and nearly dragged on the ground. A large, bulbous nose covered half its face and sat below two sad dark eyes, a long unibrow spanning its forehead. The creature lumbered about the village looking for threats, and when it saw Gameknight999, the golem headed straight for him.

Careful to put away all his weapons, Gameknight reached down and grabbed a handful of flowers and held them out before him. He wasn't sure if the giant was going to attack him or just pass him by, but he had to hold his ground . . . they needed this creature. As it approached, Gameknight could see the golem's eyes darting about, first looking at the User-that-is-not-a-user, then Hunter, then the other villagers. Apparently, it was convinced that all was safe, for it stopped directly in front of Gameknight999 and held out its massive fist. Extending his arm out, Gameknight handed the golem the flowers, then moved closer and spoke to it.

"Golem, we need your help," Gameknight said, keeping his voice low so that no one else could hear. "Herobrine is bringing his army to this village, and there will be a great battle." He could see the metal giant's eyes start to dart about, looking for monsters. "They aren't here now, but they will be soon, and we don't have enough villagers to fight them off. Herobrine seeks to destroy Minecraft and all the NPCs in every village, but I don't know if we can stop him with the people we have here. We need your help. Go and tell your king that we need his help—without it, I fear that we may fail to save Minecraft. Do you understand?"

The golem looked down at Gameknight999; he thought he saw a subtle nod, but he wasn't sure. The creature then looked up into the sky and closed its eyes, its body frozen in place. After a moment, it opened them again and proceeded to move about the village, ignoring Gameknight999 and all the villagers.

"That was really helpful," Hunter said sarcastically.

Gameknight gave her a smile and a shrug.

"Well, at least we tried," he said. "Come on, let's get back to the crafting chamber. There are still things that need to be done."

Hunter nodded, then turned and headed for the watchtower, with Gameknight right on her heels. As Hunter descended down the ladder, the User-that-is-not-a-user stepped toward the window and looked out at the peaceful village. It was an idyllic scene, with this small cluster of buildings nestled on the grassy plain, a beautiful birch forest on one side and the expanse of a great ocean on the other. Glancing up at the sky, he could see the rectangular white clouds drifting across the blue sky. It was all so perfect, and now Gameknight999 was about to bring Herobrine and his monster horde to this place. And everywhere Herobrine went, death and destruction followed.

Closing his eyes, he tried to imagine himself defeating Herobrine, but the image would not form in his mind.

Focusing with all his strength, he tried to force the scene to materialize, but he just couldn't do it.

"Well, one problem at a time," he said to himself. "First, the Ocean Monument, then Herobrine."

Shuddering, he tried to force away the feeling of fear that trickled down his spine, but pretending it wasn't there didn't make him feel any braver . . . it just felt ridiculous.

"Are you done talking to the wall?" a voice said from behind.

Turning, he saw Hunter's crimson locks sticking up out of the hole in the ground, a wry smile on her face.

"You said there were still things that needed to be done," she said. "How about you get down here and tell everyone what's needed. Unless you'd rather talk to the wall some more?"

Hunter smiled, then laughed as she slid down the ladder. Moving to the hole, Gameknight stepped onto the ladder and followed her into the darkness, but his mind was still thinking about Herobrine and how he was going to defeat the monster. As he descended, the User-that-is-not-a-user hoped that he'd hear the music of Minecraft—he could have used some encouragement—but all he heard was silence and his own heart pounding in his chest.

CHAPTER 19
MEETING OF KINGS

As Herobrine materialized at the center of a large cave, the light from his glowing eyes illuminating the cavern and casting eerie shadows on the rocky walls. His sudden appearance startled the inhabitants and made the hundreds of bats that clung to the walls and ceiling twitter and squeak nervously.

The evil shadow-crafter turned and surveyed the chamber. It was a standard bat hatchery; a cave fifty to sixty blocks across with a ceiling only a dozen blocks above the floor. The wide expanse made the stony roof feel lower than it was, almost making Herobrine want to stoop . . . but he would never do that in front of any other creature. To stoop would be to show weakness . . . that was something Herobrine would never do.

At one end of the cave, he could see a cool stream of water falling from a hole in the ceiling, filling a wide pool that was only a few blocks deep. As with all bat hatcheries, this pool would be filled with hundreds of eggs . . . maybe a thousand.

Smiling, Herobrine walked toward the pool, his eyes glowing bright. Staring down into the blue waters, his eyes lit up the bottom, revealing hundreds of brown bat eggs lying in the cool liquid, their oval surfaces splashed with tiny black spots.

This was what he came for.

Looking up from the pool, he glanced about the chamber, his glowing eyes painting the walls with a pale, sterile illumination. The light disturbed the bats and made them fly about, trying to get out of the harsh glare, but there was no place to flee other than out of the cave . . . and the bats were not about to leave their unborn children alone with this stranger.

"I have need of your sons and daughters," Herobrine said to the bats, which were just starting to calm down again. "But, first, I must bring more strangers into your midst."

Disappearing for just an instant, Herobrine returned with Xa-Tul.

"Stay here and do nothing," the Maker commanded.

Teleporting again, he returned with the skeleton king, then left and returned with the blaze king, then retrieved the king of the endermen. The flames from Charybdis lit the chamber with a warm orange glow and allowed the four kings to see each other clearly. Instantly, they all took up defensive positions as they stared at the others, unsure if they were friend or foe.

"Be at peace," Herobrine said in a calm voice.

Xa-Tul drew his massive golden sword, causing Reaper to pull out a bow made of bones. Charybdis, unsure what was happening, formed a ball of fire and let it float in front of his flaming body, ready to launch it at the first assailant. Feyd just stood there . . . his eyes glowing bright red, his body surrounded by teleportation particles.

"I SAID BE AT PEACE!" Herobrine shouted.

As his voice thundered throughout the cave, the bats leapt into the air and fluttered about, their shrill voices squeaking like an army of angry mice. With the tiny creatures flying about, Xa-Tul slowly sheathed his sword, but kept a wary eye on the other monsters. Reaper followed suit and put away his bow, while Charybdis extinguished his ball of fire.

"Good," Herobrine said, his eyes glowing bright.

"I brought you all here, my generals—my kings—so that you can know each other before the Last Battle arrives. Events are moving quickly, and we must be ready." He then turned and faced the zombie king, his blazing eyes illuminating the green monster. "Xa-Tul, you have something to report?"

"The User-that-is-not-a-user has been sighted," the zombie said with a growling, animal-like voice. "Xa-Tul's zombie army found the NPCs in a desert village and attacked."

"You did what?" Herobrine exclaimed.

"The zombie army attacked before Xa-Tul could get there," he lied, knowing that Herobrine's wrath for failure would be severe. "The zombie generals thought it would please the Maker to capture the User-that-is-not-a-user. Instead, Gameknight999 and the NPCs escaped through the minecart tunnels."

"The fools," Herobrine spat. "I said to watch them, not attack them! These generals—I want them brought to me."

"That is not possible," Xa-Tul replied.

"Why is that?" Herobrine asked, his eyes glowing brighter with rage.

"They have already been destroyed for their failure," the zombie king lied again.

Herobrine's eyes dimmed a bit as he considered this news.

"I hope they suffered," the shadow-crafter said.

Xa-Tul nodded his huge head. "Terribly," he lied.

"Did any of your generals think to follow the NPCs through the minecart tunnels?" Herobrine asked.

Xa-Tul shook his head.

"The User-that-is-not-a-user destroyed the tunnels during the escape," Xa-Tul answered. "It was impossible to follow."

"So, you don't know where they are?" Herobrine

asked.

Again, the zombie king shook his head.

"But their position must be close to the desert village," Reaper said, his thin, scratchy voice echoing a clattering of bones. "At least we know what they are near."

"That is true," Herobrine said as he paced back and forth, considering the situation. "Maybe the zombies did not completely fail . . . again."

Moving to the edge of the pool, he plunged his already glowing hands into the water. With his eyes blazing like two intense suns, he drove his crafting powers into the waters, accelerating the hatching process. As before, many of the larger eggs hatched healthy creatures, but the smaller eggs did not stand a chance. The minute creatures that came forth from those never made it to the surface, their tiny bodies disappearing as their diminished HP fell to zero.

The bats leapt off the walls and ceiling, flying all about the chamber, their squeaks filled with agitation and distress . . . but Herobrine did not care. All he wanted was to escape this prison so that he could exact his revenge on the users in the physical world, and the lives of a few bats were insignificant.

The surviving newly hatched bats struggled into the air and flew about in the maelstrom of beady eyes and velvety wings, their pained voices adding to the cacophony that echoed off the stone walls. As they swirled around Herobrine, he held his arms out, allowing the pale yellow glow that still hugged his fingers to expand and flow outward into the fluttering storm.

"Here was the last location of my enemy," Herobrine shouted as he projected the image of the desert village into the tiny brains of the flying creatures. "Find him and his friends and report back to me. Failure will be met with the harshest of retributions. *NOW GO!*"

With that, the bats flew toward the dark tunnel that pierced the side of the chamber and led to the surface. As they fluttered through the darkness, Herobrine cackled a maniacal laugh filed with hatred and malice for his enemy. With his eyes burning bright, he turned and faced his four horsemen. They would bring an apocalypse to Minecraft, and everyone, NPC and user, would rue the day that they ever sought to oppose Herobrine.

"Prepare your troops, for the time of the Last Battle draws near," the Maker said to his creations. "Soon, the User-that-is-not-a-user will take the Gateway of Light and free me from this prison."

"But what if he doesn't?" the king of the endermen asked.

"What?" Herobrine asked, turning to glare at the dark red monster.

"What if our enemy refuses to do your bidding," Feyd said, "and chooses death instead of helping you?"

"Then I will destroy him," Herobrine stated. "For there is still another . . . the little girl. I'm sure she can't possibly be as stubborn as this Gameknight999. If he refuses to do as I command, he will be eliminated, and the child will become my servant.

"This Gameknight999 may be too obstinate to do as I wish, but I'm sure the child is more pliable. After the User-that-is-not-a-user's destruction, when the girl is struggling for her last breath, I'm sure she will take the Gateway of Light to save her miserable life . . . then I will exact my revenge on *EVERYONE*! Ha, ha, ha!"

His thunderous laughter echoed off the rocky walls and overwhelmed the four kings, causing them to fall to their knees. And as it diminished, Herobrine reached out with his teleportation powers and sent his four generals back to their respective homes.

Alone in the chamber, Herobrine smiled.

"Everything is proceeding as I have foreseen," he mumbled to himself. "Soon, Gameknight999, we will meet, and you will see the surprise that I have for you. And then you will be mine!"

Gathering his teleportation powers, he disappeared, his glowing eyes leaving behind a shining stain in the air that slowly faded to darkness.

CHAPTER 20

THE OCEAN MONUMENT

Construction of the defenses that Shawny prescribed for the village was going well. Workers were digging holes and trenches everywhere, filling the excavations with redstone-driven contraptions that would surprise Herobrine and the mobs. Gameknight could see that his friend was relying on many slime blocks coupled with pistons to deliver the surprises, but the especially interesting thing was the defensive wall. He couldn't wait to see the look on Herobrine's face when he signaled the first assault.

Around the village, archers were positioned atop the trees on the edge of the birch forest, their watchful eyes scanning for anything hostile, especially bats. Hunter suspected that the bat she missed at the desert village had reported their position to Xa-Tul. She vowed that this would not happen in this location. Positioning the archers so that they had clear fields of fire, they watched carefully for the flying little messengers. If Herobrine arrived before their defenses were ready, it would be a catastrophe.

Holding his boat firmly under his arm, Gameknight999 looked up at the archers in the trees, then glanced throughout the village at the watchful sentinels. They had arrows notched in their bows, ready to fire on any trespasser. This time, the monsters would not arrive until they were ready . . . that was the plan, anyway.

Nodding to the archers, the User-that-is-not-a-user headed down to the water. Everyone else was already waiting for him, so he started to run, but a voice stopped him.

"Gameknight!" his sister yelled.

He paused and turned to see Monet113 running toward him, her neon blue hair flowing behind her. Huge bands of yellow, green, and red adorned her armor, as she had given it a fresh coat of paint recently. The colorful display brought a smile to everyone that looked at it; her art always seemed to affect people on a deep emotional level . . . it was her gift.

"Monet, you should be helping Digger with the defenses," Gameknight said.

"I know," she replied. "I just wanted to say good luck . . . and be careful."

A look of concern . . . and fear came across her boxy face.

"You don't know what's down there," she added. "Who knows what Herobrine crafted to guard the Book of Wisdom?"

"I know . . . don't you think I've thought about that?"

"Just be careful and don't take any unnecessary chances," she said. "I'm not strong and courageous like you; I don't think I could do all this without you being here."

"Don't be ridiculous," Gameknight replied. "First of all, I'll be back soon. Second, Hunter is going with me, and if I did something stupid, like getting hurt, she would never let me hear the end of it. And last, look at the person you've become. You've been in a zombie town and taught them to care about art, you've faced monsters in battle, and you destroyed Shaikulud, the spider queen." He paused for a moment to look deep into his sister's eyes. "Not strong and courageous . . . what a joke. You're stronger and braver than most people I know . . . though still a bit impulsive." He smiled and tussled her blue hair. "Besides, I'll be back soon enough to make sure you don't cause too much trouble."

Monet113 looked up at her big brother, then wrapped her arms around his cracked and chipped diamond armor, squeezing him tight.

"Any time, Gameknight," yelled Hunter from the ocean shore.

They released their hug and looked toward the ocean. Two dozen boats bobbed in the cool water; Hunter stood on the shore, glaring at the brother and sister.

"I need to go," Gameknight said. "Keep everyone working on the defenses. We have to be ready when Herobrine arrives. I'm counting on you to get it done."

"Don't worry—I got this."

She smiled at her brother, then turned and headed back to the construction that was going on all around the village.

Holding his boat under his arm, Gameknight ran to the shoreline. He could feel Hunter's disapproving glare focused on him as he approached.

"Let's get going," Gameknight said with a smile. "What are we waiting for?"

Hunter looked at him and wanted to scream, but instead a smile crept across her square face.

"Yeah . . . right," she replied as she placed her boat in the water.

Gameknight jumped into his boat and pushed off from shore. The group headed toward the location where Gameknight and Stitcher had been attacked before. They spread out so that the guardians of the Ocean Monument couldn't attack two of them at once. The User-that-is-not-a-user was hoping that their numbers would confuse the guardians and make it more difficult for them to defend the underwater temple . . . at least that was his hope. As they neared, Gameknight could start to see squid on the surface flashing bright red.

"Everyone get out your bows and be ready," Gameknight shouted. "Does everyone going into the Monument have doors and boots?"

"You still haven't told us why we need a stack of doors to go underwater," Stonecutter said.

"You'll see when we get down there," Gameknight explained. "Put on your boots now."

"What is this Depth Strider enchantment?" Crafter asked.

"It's something new from the bountiful update to Minecraft," Gameknight said. "It will let you move faster underwater, and I think speed will be important when we get inside the Monument."

"Ahhhh!"

A scream pierced the air and drew Gameknight's attention to one of the NPCs. A beam of light had shot of the water and hit the NPC in the back; a strange buzzing sound filled the air.

"Archers, fire into the water!" Crafter yelled.

Suddenly, the air was alive with arrows streaking into the water. In a second, the guardian was gone, the NPC's screams having stopped.

"Everyone watch the water for the guardians," Gameknight said. "Try to keep out of range of their lasers, but if you see one, shoot it, fast. Those who are going into the Monument with me, come on. The others, we need you to keep the guardians busy and try to thin them out. Stay in pairs, so that one of you can shoot while the other is being attacked. Let's do this!"

Without waiting for any of them to respond, the User-that-is-not-a-user turned his boat and headed straight for the glowing underwater structure in the distance. He veered his boat to the left and right to stay out of range of the lasers, but he had to pull out his bow and fire a few arrows, driving off but not destroying the one-eyed creatures. As he drew over the structure, Gameknight999 turned and spoke to those following him.

"Drink your potion of night vision before you jump in the water. We'll have eight minutes to get in, destroy Herobrine's monster, and get the Book of Wisdom. We then drink the second potion and have eight minutes to fight our way out of the Monument. When the night vision wears off, it will be complete darkness down there, and we'll get lost. So, once we jump in the water, we have to move fast." Gameknight peered over the side of his boat toward the structure underwater. "Remember—keep a door in your hand unless you are fighting," he said.

He pulled a glass bottle out of his inventory and put the potion to his lips, drinking the bitter-tasting liquid in three huge gulps. Gameknight instantly saw his vision change; features that were normally dark on the ocean floor were now clearly visible. He pulled a door out of his inventory, then jumped out of the boat and splashed into the cool water.

Instantly, he began to sink. Looking down, he could see the Ocean Monument clearly. It was built out of some kind of blue-green blocks, some darker, some lighter—prismarine blocks as he remembered. The entire structure stood on thick columns that were at least eight blocks high. The roof of the Monument was built sloping upward, with darker blocks placed at regular intervals along its perimeter. At the top of the building stood an ornate structure, with strange white glowing blocks decorating the tall pillars and open roof. Along the front of the Monument, Gameknight could see glowing arches that spanned an open region, with one side showing a small opening . . . that must be the entrance.

Guiding his descent, he landed softly on the roof of the structure. Behind him he could see his four friends, Crafter, Stonecutter, Hunter, and Builder, slowly settling down as well. Feeling that his air was almost depleted, Gameknight pulled out a door and placed it on the Monument. Instantly, a huge square bubble of air formed around the door. Gameknight stepped next to the door and found air to breathe. The others, seeing what he had done, placed doors themselves to catch a breath of air. Hunter moved next to Gameknight and placed her door so that their bubbles of air merged into one.

"You know, you could have told us this was what the doors were for," Hunter chided.

"But then I'd wouldn't get to see that look of surprise on your face down here," Gameknight explained with a smile.

"You know, you'd think that . . . look out, behind you!"

Gameknight spun, drawing his sword. Directly behind him was a guardian, its one eye filled with anger at their intrusion. Sharp orange quills stood out brightly against its blue-green body as it swished its wide tail. The prickly fish shot quickly through the water, leaving a trail of bubbles in its wake as it circled Gameknight999 warily. Suddenly, the guardian surged forward, trying to impale the User-that-is-not-a-user with its long, deadly spines. Swinging his diamond sword, Gameknight landed a blow on the creature's side, causing it to pull back. Then, drawing his iron sword, he advanced, swinging both weapons at the creature. It disappeared after he landed two more hits. Without stopping to see if the creature dropped anything, he rushed back to his door.

"Did you enjoy that?" Hunter asked as Gameknight gulped down huge breaths of air.

He gave her a frown, then headed across the sloping roof and toward the glowing arches. When he reached the edge of the roof, he jumped off and slowly descended. He could see a door in the side of the structure, and aimed for that. As he neared the opening, he pulled out another door. His lungs were starting to burn as his oxygen level decreased.

A guardian shot out from behind a block and attacked, lunging at him with its orange spines sticking straight out. Gameknight hacked at it with the door that he held. It didn't do much damage, but it drove the monster back. Kicking his legs, he moved himself into the shadowy opening in the side of the building while keeping his eyes on the angry guardian. As soon as he was inside the entrance chamber, he placed a door in the corner of the room and gulped down some air, filling his lungs. He then drew his sword and waited for an attack . . . none came.

Stepping away from his door, Gameknight looked at his surroundings. The entrance chamber was only a dozen blocks across in each direction and three blocks high. Wide doorways trimmed with light green blocks were cut into each wall, the openings leading deeper into the labyrinth of the Ocean Monument. Suddenly, a guardian swam into the chamber, then through one of the three doorways that led from the room. Not wanting to encounter that creature again, Gameknight999 moved across the room to the first doorway. Pulling out blocks of red brick, he sealed up the exit, then moved to the others and sealed them as well, keeping any more of the spiny sentries from entering the chamber. Faint light streamed through the opening on the outer wall, the illumination from the outside sea lanterns barely driving back the darkness of the chamber.

Moving back near the entrance, Gameknight placed doors throughout the room, then drew his sword and readied himself for any more of the spiky fish. As his friends entered, they each ran to the closest door, sucking in precious gulps of air. Gameknight moved to Crafter's door and placed four more doors right next to him so that everyone could be in the same airspace. Motioning for the others to join, he moved next to his friend.

"You see how fast those things are," Builder exclaimed. "They're like thorny missiles shooting through the water."

One of the guardians shot into the entrance and attacked, its laser striking Crafter in the shoulder. Gameknight shot toward the beast and attacked it with one of his swords, but he could only swing his blade at half the normal speed. Pulling out his iron sword, he continued to attack the beast.

The monster lunged toward him, trying to impale him with its long orange spines, but Stonecutter was there, smashing into the creature with his pickaxe. He, too, seemed to be moving in slow motion, but between the two of them, they were able to destroy the beast.

Going back to grab a breath of air, Gameknight closed up the last opening, sealing the group in the room.

"Why were you swinging your sword so slowly?" Crafter asked.

"It's called mining fatigue," Gameknight explained. "I think the guardians do it to us with their lasers. We're going to have trouble digging through the walls."

"Digging won't be a problem," Stonecutter said. "But which way do we go?"

Looking around the room, Gameknight could see the three doorways that he'd sealed up with brick. Each one led in a different direction through the Ocean Monument, but only one would get them to the Elder Guardian . . . but which one?

Go to the right, then up, then straight ahead, a voice said in Gameknight's mind.

It was his friend, Shawny.

What? he thought, imagining his fingers typing in the chat.

It's a maze, Shawny said. *I'm looking at a map online. Apparently most people try to stay on the same level, but they always get lost. Just follow my directions . . . I'll get you to the Elder Guardian.*

The what? Gameknight asked.

The Elder Guardian—that is what's waiting for you . . . have fun.

Gameknight laughed.

"What's so funny?" Hunter asked.

"Nothing . . . just something Shawny said," Gameknight replied. "But he told me which way we have to go."

"And then we'll find your book?" Hunter asked.

"No, but we'll be closer. And with Shawny's help guiding us, we might just have a chance of doing this and surviving."

Moving to the wall of brick across the hallway to the right, Gameknight placed a door so that he could start to dig, but Stonecutter pushed his way past the User-that-is-not-a-user and started to swing his big pickaxe. As he dug, Gameknight placed another door next to the stocky NPC and drew his swords, ready to fight anything that came through the doorway.

CHAPTER 21

THE ELDER GUARDIAN

Moving as quickly as possible, Gameknight led the way through the Ocean Monument, taking directions from his user friend in the physical world, Shawny. Following close behind was the steadfast Stonecutter. The stocky NPC refused to be more than a block or two away from the User-that-is-not-a-user, his pickaxe always at the ready.

Gameknight could see how people could easily get lost within the Monument; every room looked nearly the same. Each one was built from blue-green prismarine blocks, darker ones outlining the room, lighter ones filling in the walls and floor. Every other room had the strange pale glowing blocks called sea lanterns. They cast a dim, harsh light throughout the room but did little to brighten the surroundings. With their night vision potions still working, the team didn't worry about the glowing cubes, but if they didn't get out before the potions wore off, these blocks' light would prove important.

Guardians shot out of the shadows at every

opportunity, charging with spines extended and laser beams firing from their single eye. All of the NPCs took some damage as they wove their way through the structure, but quickly they figured out how to battle the prickly fish.

Working in pairs, they attacked the guardians that came near. Gameknight would act as the bait and charge at the animal, then retreat as Stonecutter moved up next to the monster. With his heavy pick and Gameknight's dual swords, the fish stood little chance. Bringing up the rear, Hunter, Crafter, and Builder were continually assaulted by the swimming beasts as well. Hunter, though, came up with the idea of placing doors across the chamber entrances, blocking the fish from attacking, but allowing them to easily move through the chamber again when it was time to retreat and head to the surface.

Gameknight placed a door in the entrance to an adjacent chamber and peered inside. A strange set of green columns stood at the center of the room, with glowing white sea lanterns connecting the pillars. Moving along the walls, he placed another door and took a gulp of air, then continued, following Shawny's directions.

You're almost there, Shawny said through the chat, the words forming in Gameknight's mind.

Which way do we go now? Gameknight asked.

Around the square thing that's ahead and then to the left, Shawny explained. *You should see an opening that looks out onto a big room that's two stories tall. I'm pretty sure that is the treasure room . . . the Elder Guardian should be there.*

OK, thanks, Gameknight replied, then turned and faced his companions.

Pointing to the next room, Gameknight motioned for them to go around to the left. The others nodded their boxy heads and followed as the User-that-is-not-a-user moved forward.

In the next room was a large square structure built out of dark prismarine blocks. Across the top and bottom, he could see lighter aqua prismarine blocks, with sea lanterns on the corners. The faces of the lanterns glowed brightly, the edges of the blocks outlined with a seafoam green. Under other circumstances, the chamber would have been beautiful and magnificent. But with monsters lurking somewhere in the shadows waiting to destroy Gameknight and his friends, the beauty was hard to appreciate.

Moving around the blocky structure, Gameknight walked down a narrow passage. Suddenly, a single eye was staring at him, the dark pupil filled with rage. As the orange spines of the guardian flared out, the monster charged. With no choice other than to fight, Gameknight rushed forward, both swords slashing with all his strength. His iron sword found the side of the guardian, but not until one of the spines pierced through his armor, stabbing into flesh. Pain radiated down his right arm, and only the strength of his will kept him from dropping his diamond sword.

Turning to protect his right arm, Gameknight prepared to charge again. But before he could move, Stonecutter's hulking form suddenly sailed over his head and landed directly in front of him. Without slowing a step, he charged at the guardian. The spiny fish moved backward, then fired its laser at the NPC. It hit Stonecutter square in the chest, but he did not slow. Swinging his mighty pickaxe with his incredible strength, Stonecutter smashed into the monster and destroyed it with just three blows.

Checking around the next corner to look for more attackers, Stonecutter placed a door and took a breath of air. Moving next to him, Gameknight stuck his head into the volume of air and faced his friend.

"Thanks for that," Gameknight said.

"I won't let anything hurt you," Stonecutter said as he rubbed the spot where the laser has struck.

"Are you OK?" Gameknight asked.

Stonecutter took out an apple and ate it quickly, then nodded to his friend.

"Come on, let's keep going," the stocky NPC said. "Lead on."

Gameknight nodded, then streaked past Stonecutter and continued around the blocky structure. When he reached the other side of the room, he found an opening in the wall that looked down into a huge chamber. Inside stood a large cube made from dark green blocks, glowing white lanterns on every corner. Cubes of prismarine were placed in groups of three throughout the chamber, with pillars stretching up to the ceiling. The floor of the chamber was partially lit but did not illuminate the top of the chamber very much. Anything could be hiding in those deep shadows near the ceiling.

In the darkness, Gameknight could just barely make out something moving. A tail fin swished into the light but quickly disappeared into the shadows. He could see only the faintest impressions of the creature below, but not the whole thing.

He was confused.

He figured it would be the Elder Guardian . . . a fish like the other guardians they'd encountered so far. But from the tantalizing glimpses of the animal below, he could tell that it was gigantic. It was probably twice the size of the fish guarding the Monument's exterior, if not larger. *Was that even possible?* he thought.

A purple spine sparkled in the light of the sea lanterns near the floor of the chamber as the huge monster moved along the perimeter. The razor-sharp spike was easily as long as his sword, maybe even longer.

Hunter moved up next to Gameknight and peered down into the treasure room. She placed a door right behind her so that they could both stand in a bubble of air.

"Did you see that?" Gameknight asked.

"What?" she replied.

Suddenly, something pale streaked past the opening, a long trail of bubbles marking its path. Gameknight saw the faint image of a single eye on the creature's square face, its pupil glowing an angry red. Its body was covered with a dozen of the long pointed spines, each colored a soft lavender, every one of them a lethal weapon.

Hunter took a step back and drew her sword. "What was—"

"That was the Elder Guardian," Gameknight interrupted.

"But the size of that thing—" she stammered.

"I know."

"And all those spines, they're bigger than . . . I mean, they were needle-sharp and as long as . . . me."

"I know," Gameknight said.

"Did you see how fast it moved?" she asked. "How are we going to catch that thing?"

"I don't know."

Suddenly, the creature was floating in front of the opening, staring directly at Gameknight999. His blood turned to ice.

Before he could even move a muscle, a beam of light shot from the creature's angry eye and blasted into Gameknight's chest. Pain enveloped his body as the Elder Guardian's laser carved away at his HP. Looking straight into the creature's eye, he saw hatred radiating from the beast, directed through that laser beam and directly into him.

Gameknight999 was terrified.

Bringing his diamond blade up in front of him, he blocked the blazing shaft of light with the flat of his sword, making it reflect away and melt a glowing scar into the pristine walls. Moving back from the opening, he found a door around the corner and caught his breath.

Crafter moved next to him.

"What was that?" he asked.

"That was the Elder Guardian," Gameknight explained, panting for breath, "and he just blasted me with his laser."

"You OK?" the young NPC asked.

Gameknight nodded.

"I'm not sure how many of those attacks we can take," the User-that-is-not-a-user said.

"Eat something . . . quick," Crafter said as he handed him a melon.

Gameknight took the slice and ate it quickly. He could feel his HP slowly recharge.

"Let's get this done," he said, then glanced around at everyone. "Are all of you ready?"

The other NPCs nodded from their doors.

"OK," Gameknight said as he drew both his swords.

He moved past the edge of the opening and jumped down into the next chamber. As he slowly fell, his night vision potion expired, plunging him into darkness.

"No . . . not now!" he said to no one.

He fell for what seemed forever until he landed gently on the floor of the chamber. The sea lanterns faintly illuminated the corners of the room, but provided little light. Putting his swords away, he reached into his inventory and pulled out his last bottle of night vision potion. As he was about to pull out the stopper, something big streaked past, the turbulent currents and waves that followed the beast knocked the bottle from hand. Slowly, the glass container sank to the ground, disappearing into the darkness that surrounded him.

Oh no! I need that to see, he thought. *It must be somewhere near my feet.*

Quickly, Gameknight knelt to the ground and started feeling around with his hand. As he groped in the darkness, a deadly beam of light shot above his head and slammed into a block of prismarine. The light from the Guardian's laser lit the surroundings just enough for him to see the bottle.

There it is, he thought, *just off to the left.*

Crawling forward, the User-that-is-not-a-user reached out and closed his blocky fingers around the bottle. Pulling the stopper, he quickly drank the dark blue potion, then stood up as his night vision returned. Turning, Gameknight faced the center of the chamber.

A giant eye was just inches from his face, its pupil a bright angry red.

"AHHH!" Gameknight screamed, bubbles floating up out of his mouth.

Before he could reach for his swords, the Elder Guardian slammed into him, its long purple spines smashing into his diamond armor.

And then the monster was gone, streaking into the shadows. A trail of bubbles marked its path, but for some reason they trailed upward . . . that didn't make any sense.

Placing a door, Gameknight took a big breath, then turned and moved out into the large chamber. He scanned the room, trying to find his enemy, but saw only the occasional swish of bubbles here and there. Suddenly, the far side of the chamber lit up.

As Gameknight moved toward the harsh glow, he saw Builder backing up, a bright beam of light hitting him directly in the chest.

"Bring up your sword," Gameknight yelled, but his words did not carry through the water.

Rushing to his friend's side, he reached out with his diamond sword and reflected the laser back toward the giant fish, its own beam striking it next to the great eye. With the swish of its massive tail, the Elder Guardian turned quickly and streaked away, disappearing into the shadows again.

Placing another door, Gameknight dragged Builder into the pocket of air.

"Are you OK?" Gameknight asked.

"I don't know," Builder replied. "I took some serious damage."

"Do you have anything to eat?"

Builder reached into his inventory and pulled out an apple, which he ate quickly. He pulled another one out and ate that one as well.

"You stay here and let your HP rejuvenate."

Builder nodded his head.

Gameknight then took a huge breath of air and charged forward. He had to find this creature and end it before any of his friends were seriously hurt. A swishing sound could be heard above his head as turbulent currents wafted down from above.

Something is moving up there near the ceiling in the darkness, Gameknight thought.

But then the swishing sound settled behind him.

Hot pain suddenly stabbed him in the back. Turning, he brought his sword up and reflected the laser away. He advanced, his iron sword held in his other hand. This time, the monster did not swim away. It waited for Gameknight to get close, but as he neared, the intensity of the laser grew brighter. He could feel the hilt of his diamond sword starting to grow hot. Soon he'd have to drop it. Running forward, he slashed at the mighty beast. But just when he reached the creature, it floated straight upward and out of reach, disappearing in the shadows overhead.

Gameknight moved to a nearby door to catch his breath. On the other side of the chamber, Stonecutter was trying to defend himself as the mighty fish slammed into him from above, its long purple spines sticking straight out. Before the stocky NPC could respond, the fish floated up and moved off to hunt another.

I have to figure out a way to defeat this monster, or it may destroy all my friends.

He moved to a corner, where he placed a door and thought about the problem, hoping the puzzle pieces would show themselves in his mind . . . nothing. But then the music of Minecraft swelled as the Oracle's voice filled his mind.

You can accomplish only what you can imagine, her aged, scratchy voice said. *You are not alone.*

Then the music was gone.

He thought about these words . . . *you are not alone.* Was it a hint . . . a clue? As he contemplated, he saw the Guardian attack Crafter, the young NPC trying to reach the creature with his now-shimmering iron sword, but the creature floated up and out of reach just at the last instant.

"We cannot do this by ourselves; we have to work together," he said to no one. "That's it . . . *you are not alone!*"

He ran to each of the NPCs and spoke quickly, telling them to move back to the chamber where they had entered the Guardian's lair. As Gameknight watched Builder swim to the opening high up on the chamber wall, the Elder Guardian charged. This time, Gameknight was ready. With both swords out, he ran at the monster, ready to block the laser with his diamond sword while he stabbed at the monster with his iron. The fish's purple spines gouged into Gameknight's diamond armor, driving the User-that-is-not-a-user back a step. Feigning injury, Gameknight went to one knee, then brought his iron sword up into the monster's underbelly. He could feel the sword find flesh as the creature flashed red. Before the fish could get away, he slashed at it with his diamond sword, but it floated upward, escaping again. The User-that-is-not-a-user could see a look of overwhelming rage as the one eye looked down on him. But, strangely, the creature's eye didn't radiate with an eerie, evil glow, as all of Herobrine's creations seemed to do. Instead, the eye looked normal, natural . . . pure, the pupil not the color of blood but the color of the clearest ruby.

Gameknight swam up to his friends and floated into the room that overlooked the Guardian's chamber. He placed a door far from the opening, then placed four more for his friends. They all moved into the pockets of air, each breathing heavily.

"How are we going to fight that monster?" Builder asked. "It's too strong . . . this is impossible."

"No it's not . . . we can do this," Gameknight insisted.

"I have to go along with Builder on this one," Hunter said. She pointed to the deep gouges in her iron armor. "Those spines are as hard as diamond and sharper than anything I've ever seen. It attacked me three times, and each time I couldn't even touch it with my sword; it swims away right when you're about to attack."

"That's right; it swims away," Gameknight agreed. "So, we don't let it swim away . . . we block its avenue of escape."

"With what?" Hunter asked.

"With ourselves," Gameknight replied. "Here's what we're going to do."

As he explained his plan, he could see the fear on his friend's faces gradually change to hope . . . and, in Hunter's case, excitement.

"This idea is crazy. It's incredibly dangerous, and has little chance of success," Hunter said. "I like it!"

Gameknight smiled, then moved back to the opening that looked down on the Guardian's lair.

"Let's do this," he said, then jumped into the room. As he fell, his battle cry resonated through the watery chamber: "FOR MINECRAFT!"

CHAPTER 22
THE BOOK OF WISDOM

When Gameknight999 landed on the floor of the Guardian's chamber, he instantly ran to the side of the room and to a door. Gulping in a quick breath, he ran around the large central structure, looking for the beast, but it was nowhere to be seen. He continued to run around the structure and found Builder on the other side. He gestured to the NPC, pointing at his own eyes, then pointing to the room. Builder shook his head; he hadn't seen the creature, either.

Moving out of the room and into the long connecting hallway, Gameknight banged the hilt of his diamond sword on the blue-green prismarine blocks that made up the structure. The noise resonated throughout the Monument like a blacksmith's hammer banging on a hot anvil. Swimming farther out into the corridor, Gameknight999 stopped to listen . . . but he heard only bubbles and the swishing of water.

Suddenly, he saw a bright light off to his right and ran toward the brilliant glare. As he turned the corner, Gameknight caught sight of Builder on his knees, the full intensity of the Guardian's laser blasting into his chest. Running as fast as he could, he tried to reach his friend, but he was just too far away. Builder's chest plate cracked apart and fell to the floor, exposing his flesh to the burning shaft of light. As the NPC flashed red, Gameknight drew his bow and tried to fire an arrow at the monster . . . but he was still too far away, and the arrow flew only two blocks before falling harmlessly to the ground.

Finally, he reached the monster. With his diamond sword, he swung at the creature, but his arm moved more slowly than usual, the Mining Fatigue status effect still acting on him. When his sword hit the Guardian, the monster flashed red, then instantly floated upward out of reach.

But the beam stayed focused on Builder.

Gameknight ran to his friend, extending his sword to block the glaring laser. But before Gameknight could reach his friend, Builder gave the User-that-is-not-a-user one last sad look, then disappeared, his items falling to the chamber floor.

"Nooooo!" Gameknight screamed, but it was too late . . . Builder was gone.

Spinning, the User-that-is-not-a-user glared up at the Elder Guardian, then ran to a nearby door to get a breath of air. Stepping out into the open, he pointed at the spiny giant with his diamond sword, slowly walking backward.

"You can hear me . . . can't you?" Gameknight shouted into the water.

The Guardian looked down at him, the unibrow over his eye furling with anger.

"You killed my friend, and now it's time I punished you!"

Moving backward even faster, Gameknight drew the beast with him.

A blast of searing light shot out of the monster's eye, directed at Gameknight's head, but he was ready. He raised his diamond sword and easily reflected the beam away.

"That's not gonna work on me, monster," Gameknight yelled. "You want me, you're gonna have to come down here and get me!"

The Elder Guardian extinguished its laser, slowly settled to the ground, and approached Gameknight999. Sticking his head inside a pocket of air that surrounded a nearby door, the User-that-is-not-a-user kept backing up, trying to give the appearance that he was afraid. That wasn't hard—he was panicked, but he refused to give up . . . for giving up meant failure.

Gameknight continued to back up but eventually ran out of room and bumped into the chamber wall. Seeing that its prey had nowhere to run, the Elder Guardian swished its gigantic tail and charged forward.

Its long spines tried to poke at Gameknight999, but his iron sword pushed them away as his diamond sword reached for that massive eye. As expected, the creature backed up, but suddenly Hunter was there, her razor-sharp sword cutting into the monster's back. Spinning, it lunged at her, but then Crafter was at her side, his own sword seeking the pale yellow monster's flesh. Seeing that it was surrounded, the Guardian started to float upward.

"*NOW!*" Gameknight shouted.

From above, Stonecutter fell through the water and landed on the monster's back, his mighty pickaxe swinging down and tearing into the monster's spine-covered skin. With the Guardian pinned to the ground, all of them attacked, slashing at the creature's body and seeking revenge for the death of Builder. Not stopping for air, they continued the attack as the monster flashed red over and over again. With its HP nearly consumed, the creature let out a long string of bubbles, then rolled over onto its side, spilling Stonecutter onto the ground.

Gameknight moved to a door to get a quick gulp of air, then approached the creature's eye and spoke.

"You killed my friend, and now it is your turn," Gameknight said. "Your creator, Herobrine, did not make you strong enough to withstand us all . . . his arrogance, and yours, led to your downfall."

"You are mistaken," the Elder Guardian said, his voice filled with the fizzing sound of a million bubbles. "I was not created by Herobrine. That vile creature does not know of my existence. If he did, he would be here trying to destroy me."

Gameknight took a step back, confused.

"If you were not crafted by Herobrine, who created you?"

"The Oracle," the mighty fish replied.

It struggled for a breath, then swiveled its big eye so that it was staring directly at Gameknght999.

"What?" Gameknight asked. "I don't believe it."

"That's what she said you would say," the Guardian replied. "She made me for the purpose of teaching those who come to the Ocean Monument. And for those who learn the lesson, they get the reward."

"What is the reward?"

"Why, the Book of Wisdom, of course," the creature said.

"Where is the book?" Gameknight asked.

"It lies within me. Only through my death can the victor obtain the book," the Elder Guardian said. "You have learned the lesson well, as the Oracle predicted. Gameknight999 is truly worthy and the first to have figured out how to best me in battle. You are indeed the User-that-is-not-a-user."

The Guardian struggled for one last breath.

"Sometimes," the monster rasped, "the lesson is the journey and not the destination." And then the Elder Guardian disappeared, leaving behind many glowing balls of XP and a single, leather-bound book.

Gameknight scooped up the ancient-looking tome as the balls of XP streaked into his body. Moving to the side of the room, he found a door and stepped into the pocket of air. Instantly, he found Crafter, Hunter, and Stonecutter at his side.

"Well," Crafter asked. "What does it say?"

"I haven't opened it yet," Gameknight replied.

"What are you waiting for?" Hunter asked. "Read it quickly so that we can get out of here."

Stonecutter moved to his side, but said nothing, his stocky frame lending silent support.

This book is going to show me where to find the wisdom and courage to face Herobrine and use the weapon from the Oracle, he thought. *Without it, we'd be lost, but now I'll know where to find what I need to save Minecraft and all my friends.*

Breathing a sigh of relief, he carefully opened the book. Staring into the ancient volume, he couldn't believe what he saw. Flipping to the next page, he saw the same thing. Turning from page to page, Gameknight saw the same thing over and over.

"What is this . . . some kind of joke?" Gameknight yelled, his eyes filled with anger and frustration.

"What's wrong?" Crafter asked. "What does it

say? Where can you find what you need to defeat Herobrine?"

Gameknight999 looked down at the book in disbelief. Every page was a mirrored sheet, reflecting his own image back to him.

"I needed to know where to find bravery and wisdom to defeat Herobrine and all I get is my own reflection," Gameknight said, his voice filled with anger.

Handing the book to Crafter, Gameknight turned around and stared at the wall, furious.

We fought that monster, and Builder had to die for this cruel joke, he thought. *Who knows how many NPCs are getting hurt battling the guardians up on the ocean surface? And we did all that just for a mirror . . . ORACLE!!!*

But the music of Minecraft was silent.

Taking the book back from Crafter, he looked up at the ceiling.

"We have to get out of here before the night vision potion runs out," Gameknight said.

Looking at the spot where Builder's items still floated, Gameknight sighed. He felt betrayed and defeated.

"Come on," he said. "Let's go."

He swam upward, then moved to the chamber high on the wall. But instead of following the twisting corridors that snaked through the Monument, Gameknight floated upward. Taking out his diamond pickaxe, he cut through the ceiling. Instantly, the group was in open water with blue spiny guardians all swimming about, chasing squid. Before any of the one-eyed fish noticed them, they reached the surface and climbed into their boats. Looking about the ocean, he could see NPCs in boats, but, sadly, some of the boats were empty. Sighing again, Gameknight steered his boat for shore.

"Come on, everyone, we have to get back to the village," Gameknight shouted.

As they headed for shore, Crafter moved his boat up next to Gameknight's.

"What do you think that book meant?" the young NPC asked.

Gameknight sighed.

"I don't know . . . maybe it means nothing . . . maybe the Oracle is just a mean, spoiled child like Herobrine, and she played this trick on us just for fun."

"I can't believe that," Crafter said. "It has to mean something."

"All I needed was to know how to defeat Herobrine," Gameknight complained, then sighed. "Maybe she was trying to tell me that the courage and wisdom that I need is already within me."

"That's possible," Crafter replied.

"Well, she could have just told me," Gameknight said angrily. "Builder and many others had to sacrifice their lives for me to learn this . . . it's not fair." He then looked straight up into the blue sky and screamed. "YOU HEAR ME ORACLE! *IT'S NOT FAIR!*"

The music of Minecraft was silent.

"Perhaps you wouldn't have truly believed the lesson if it had just been handed to you," Crafter mused.

Gameknight sighed again as he nodded his head.

"I know I can be courageous when I have to be," the User-that-is-not-a-user said. "And I'm not an idiot . . . I have some wisdom within this thick skull of mine, but I don't feel that this is enough. There's something here that I'm missing." He pulled out the Book of Wisdom and stared into its shiny pages. "Looking at my own reflection isn't really helping me find what I need . . . there's something else here that

I was supposed to learn—but what?"

He looked out across the calm blue waters; the splashes of squid playing nearby added to the beautiful scene. He could see the shoreline approaching, the village just becoming visible in the distance. A feeling of dread began to fill Gameknight as he saw the village getting closer. He knew that soon Herobrine would be here, and he still didn't know what to do. Everyone was relying on him to save them, and he didn't even know how to save himself.

Anger began to bubble up within his soul.

"I don't know what to do, Crafter. I'm afraid I'm going to fail everyone."

"Do not despair, User-that-is-not-a-user," Crafter said. "You will find a way . . . you always do."

"You don't get it, Crafter!" Gameknight snapped. "That was my last chance. I have to face Herobrine in battle, and I know that I can't defeat him. This book was supposed to tell me how to stand up to him, but it gave me nothing. What am I supposed to do now? He's coming . . . I can feel it, and he's coming for me. And you know what I have to stop him? NOTHING!"

Crafter grew silent. Gameknight felt bad for yelling at his friend, but he was so frustrated and angry that he didn't know what to do. As he rowed for shore, he tried to imagine himself defeating Herobrine. But in his imagination he could see only himself lying on the ground and Herobrine standing over him, a malicious smile on his square face.

CHAPTER 23

THE FOUR HORSEMEN OF THE APOCALYPSE

As Gameknight stepped out of his boat and moved onto the shore, he could tell that something was wrong. Everything was eerily silent. He couldn't see anything moving, neither NPC nor animal. Glancing to the pens that held the livestock, Gameknight999 could see the pigs and cows all looking toward the forest. The animals were motionless, standing perfectly still, as if some terrible predator were there waiting for them, and any movement would draw its attention . . . and its wrath.

"Come on," Gameknight whispered to the others.

Drawing his sword, he ran to the village. As he sprinted, he glanced up at the watchtower. There was nobody standing guard . . . how could that be? Running even faster, he headed for the cobblestone building, but before he could reach the structure, he heard a maniacal laugh percolate out of the nearby forest. Moving to the nearby Baker's house, the User-that-is-not-a-user pressed his back against the wall, then motioned for the others to find cover. Crafter and Stonecutter ran quickly to his side. Moving to the edge of the wooden structure, Gameknight cautiously peered around the corner toward the tree line.

In the distance far off to the right, he thought he could see a figure standing on a grassy hill, watching. It looked like a zombie, but how could that be? It was daytime. Again, the distant zombie looked to have something drawn across its chest. This time, a lavender field of flowers seemed to traverse the zombie's chest, with rows of yellow sunflowers adorning its arms, its legs painted grass-green.

How can that be . . . a painted zombie . . . in the daylight?

It reminded Gameknight of something, but he couldn't quite place it. But that painted creature was not the source of that evil laugh; it had come from the nearby tree line, not that grassy knoll. Still, he felt that he should recognize the zombie. As he searched his memory, a figure emerged from the forest shadows before him. It looked to be a woodcutter by the color of its smock, but Gameknight could tell by the glowing eyes that it was not.

It was Herobrine.

A cold wave of fear crashed down on him, driving away the last vestige of courage.

"So, User-that-is-not-a-user, we meet again."

Gameknight drew his iron sword with his left hand and tried to ready himself for battle. He could feel the Book of Wisdom in his inventory, its shiny pages still mocking him with his own image. Behind him he could hear the rest of the NPCs approaching his hiding place.

"He knows we're here," Gameknight said to Crafter.

"Then there is no reason to hide," the young NPC replied.

Drawing his diamond sword with his right, Gameknight stepped out from behind the baker's home and faced the monster; the other NPCs lined up behind him, Stonecutter at his side.

"Ah . . . I see you brought your army with you," Herobrine mocked. "What do you have there, fifteen villagers? Ooo . . . I'm so scared. Well, let me show you what I brought with me."

Moving with lightning speed, Herobrine crafted

four portals from obsidian, each with a pale yellow field inside the dark stony ring.

Out of the first portal came a skeleton king riding a skeleton horse. This bony creature was the biggest monster Gameknight had ever seen. Both rider and mount were colored a pale white, as if they'd be left in the desert sun for years. Gameknight could see their ribs curving out from jagged spines, their arms and legs clattering as they moved forward. Atop the rider's boxy skull sat a shining metal helmet that looked to be made of golden bones. The helm encircled the monster's head and kept it from bursting into flame because of exposure to the sun's lethal rays. In its hand, the monster held a bow that looked to be formed from the bones of some long-deceased creature, a massive arrow notched into its string. The skeleton king, eyes glowing blood-red, stared at Gameknight999 with an utter hatred for his very existence.

Out of the second portal came a massive blaze riding a horse composed of glowing blaze rods and flame. The heat from the duo singed the grass at their feet, instantly charring it until the once-green blades crumbled to ash. Blaze rods revolved quickly through the center of the monster, its flaming body holding the glowing staffs together somehow. Those that formed the horse, however, did not revolve. Rather, the smoldering blaze rods formed the bones of the creature, so that it looked much like the skeleton horse, though the blaze horse's body and skin were composed of flame. But the most unsettling thing were the blaze king's eyes; they stared straight at the User-that-is-not-a-user, but instead of being black, the eyes were like red-hot coals, burned a hungry, angry red.

From the third portal stepped Xa-Tul, the zombie king. He rode a zombie horse whose eyes were smoldering with hatred, as were its rider's. Xa-Tul looked as he did during their encounter in the desert, though this time he wore his crown of claws. The horse he rode had the look of a zombie creature, with rotting flaps of skin hanging off here and there, bones visible through decaying sections. When Xa-Tul saw the User-that-is-not-a-user, he drew his massive golden sword, then sneered and gave him a hateful glare as his eyes shone bright red.

"These are my three horsemen," Herobrine said. "I believe you have already met Xa-Tul, but let me introduce Reaper, the skeleton king, and Charybdis, the blaze king. But, more importantly, I want you to meet my fourth horseman."

Out of the fourth portal stepped a black horse that was covered with purple teleportation particles. Sitting atop the dark mount sat an enderman far bigger than any other Gameknight had ever seen.

Can it be? Gameknight lamented to himself.

The dark creature's arms rippled with strength; his legs looked strong as iron. He sat atop the terrible ender-horse and looked down on Gameknight and the villagers with hateful superiority as if the NPCs before this monster were too insignificant to live.

No . . . it can't be, Gameknight pleaded to himself

The enderman's skin stood out from that of his mount. The ender-horse's flesh was the typical pitch black, as all endermen were shaded . . . except for one. Gameknight could see teleportation particles dancing about the horse's flesh; it could likely disappear with just a thought. But the rider . . .

It can't be . . . I killed him on the steps of the Source.

The rider was shaded a dark, dark red . . . the color of dried blood. And the monster's eyes glowed with an evil blood-red color that turned Gameknight's courage to ice.

Was it him . . . back from the dead? Was it Erebus?

Fear rippled down his spine as he thought of all the battles he'd faced with that creature.

"Allow me to introduce the new king of the endermen, Feyd," Herobrine said. "These are the Four Horsemen of the Apocalypse, and they are here to bring doom to Minecraft."

How am I going to face four of them, and then face Herobrine? Gameknight thought.

Herobrine held up a hand and snapped his finger. The sound resonated through the landscape like a hammer hitting a piece of hot steel. Instantly, monsters poured out of the portals and gathered behind their respective kings.

A burning field of blazes stood behind Charybdis, their flaming bodies filling the air with ash and smoke. Many of the trees in the forest burst into flame at the touch of the fiery monsters, but right now, nobody cared. Behind Feyd marched hundreds of endermen, each showing eyes filled with hatred for the NPCs of the Overworld, their bodies cloaked in a mist of tiny purple teleportation particles. But most shocking were the zombies and skeletons in broad daylight. Each wore a cap of leather that protected them from the burning rays of the sun. Their ranks swelled as they emerged from their portals, the green monsters growling and moaning, the white skeletons clattering as they jostled for position behind their leader.

Before Gameknight stood at least two thousand monsters, more than had ever been assembled together in the history of Minecraft. And glancing behind him, Gameknight could see fifteen NPCs, all with their weapons out and a look of overwhelming fear on their blocky faces.

"Prepare to meet your doom!" Herobrine said as he held up a hand, ready to signal the charge.

CHAPTER 24

TWIN VOICES OF COURAGE

Just before Herobrine could move his arm, a rumbling sound echoed through the ground. Huge sections of sand were falling away, revealing wide steps that led deep underground. As the landscape transformed, a loud, angry yell erupted.

"FOR MINECRAFT!" came the battle cry. Hundreds of NPCs charged out of the stairway, forming a wall of bodies between the User-that-is-not-a-user and Herobrine. Gameknight could see Digger at the head of the column while Monet and Stitcher ran for the watchtower, their enchanted bows in their hands.

NPCs from all across Minecraft must have come to this village. Likely Smithy's riders had found recruits to help with the defense of Minecraft, and by the looks of their numbers, everyone had answered the call to battle. Gameknight could see villagers from every occupation ready to stand up against the horde of monsters that wanted to destroy Minecraft.

"Ooo . . . impressive," Herobrine said. "But where are your walls, Gameknight999? You always seem to like trapping yourself behind walls. All I see are holes in the ground. I hope you don't think we're going to be dumb enough to fall in those holes."

Herobrine chuckled, causing the entire monster army to burst into laughter.

"If this NPC rabble is all you have to stand against

us, this is going to be a quick battle indeed."

The evil shadow-crafter raised his hand and prepared to signal the charge, but before he could issue the command, a loud popping sound echoed across the landscape. Suddenly, a lone user appeared standing off to the left of the village, a shining server thread stretching up into the sky, the name SHAWNY floating over his head.

Instantly, all the NPCs dropped their weapons and linked their hands across their chests. This made the monsters laugh even harder.

"Shawny . . . what are you doing?" Gameknight screamed.

"Wait for it," he replied.

"But you can't—"

"Wait for it," he said again.

Suddenly six hundred users appeared around him, each with diamond armor and enchanted weapons. Instantly, they started to build TNT cannons while the archers and swordsmen took up defensive positions around the artillery.

"Ha, ha, ha," Herobrine laughed. "Your NPCs are so foolish. You can have users at your side or NPCs, but you can't have both. You have lost, Gameknight999, even before the battle has begun."

The User-that-is-not-user could see that the NPCs wanted to help, wanted to pick up their weapons and fight, but if they did, they would be excommunicated from every village . . . they'd become the Lost. He couldn't ask anyone for that kind of sacrifice. But without them, Herobrine was right. Without the NPCs, they stood no chance of winning.

"Your own NPCs have abandoned you, Gameknight999," Herobrine yelled, an eerie smile on his face. "This is better than I expected. The feeling of rejection must be terrible . . . this is fantastic. Look at them—the cowardly NPCs abandoned you at their first opportunity. They aren't a community; they are heartless cowards. Ha, ha, ha!"

Suddenly, someone was standing next to Gameknight, nudging him. Looking down, he found Topper gazing up at him, Filler right behind.

"It's OK, kids, you can't help it," Gameknight said. "Herobrine's right; you can't help me . . . I'm alone in this and on my own."

The twins looked at each other and frowned, then looked up at their friend. Gameknight could see the internal struggle that was going on, but knew that they couldn't help . . . they'd have to give up everything, and he wouldn't ask them to do that. Stepping forward, he pushed through the stiff bodies of NPCs and stood at the front of the crowd.

"These NPCs are not part of this, Herobrine; you leave them alone," Gameknight said.

"Ha . . . sure, I'll leave them alone," Herobrine said, "if you take the Gateway of Light."

"NEVER!"

"Your friends have abandoned you, and all you have is a pathetic collection of users at your side," Herobrine said. "Soon you will be totally alone!"

"No, he won't," squeaked a voice from behind the NPCs.

"That's right," said another.

Moving through the crowd of stationary NPCs came Topper and Filler, each holding toy wooden swords.

"We don't care if we become Lost," Filler said, her voice filled with confidence and strength. "We don't abandon family."

"That's right!" shouted Topper in a young, high-pitched voice.

This made the monsters laugh even more, but the snickering stopped when Hunter stepped forward, her bow in her hands, arrow notched.

"I guess I'm with them," she said.

"Me, too," said Digger as he moved to stand at his children's side.

"And me . . ."

"And me . . ."

In an avalanche of courage, triggered by two small voices, the entire NPC army bent down and picked up their weapons. They banged their swords and bows against their armored chests, creating a sound of pounding thunder that echoed across the land.

Gameknight looked about at his friends . . . his family, and was so proud. They were indeed a community, and the brave looks on their faces told the User-that-is-not-a-user that this battle was not lost yet.

"So be it," yelled Herobrine.

He raised his hand again and brought it down.

"*CHARGE!*" Herobrine yelled.

And the flood of hatred and violence was released as the Last Battle for Minecraft finally began.

CHAPTER 25

PAINTED THUNDER

The monsters charged straight toward the NPCs, their growls filling the air. But before they could reach the defenders, Digger stepped forward. He turned and looked at a small structure with thick cobblestone walls and iron bars across all the windows. Gameknight could see that there was an NPC inside the small building facing a wall of buttons and levers.

Instantly, he knew what it was.

"Redstone 1!" Digger yelled.

The NPC in the control room flicked a lever.

Instantly, the sound of pistons could be heard as holes appeared in the ground. Blinking cubes of TNT popped into the air, launched by slime block pistons. The red and white cubes exploded when they were one block in the air, tearing into the monsters but leaving the mechanism unharmed. More holes appeared on the ground as TNT cubes leapt into the air, tearing more HP from monster bodies. It was like watching a destructive popcorn popper at work. The cubes burst out of the ground and detonated all across the field of battle, appearing where they were least expected. The mechanisms then reset themselves, only to launch another explosive block into the air.

The User-that-is-not-a-user turned and looked toward Shawny. He could see his friend smiling, and knew that this was his design; Gameknight knew that his friend's ingenuity would come in handy.

But the monsters did not slow. They charged right into the blinking cubes, unaware that the bombs were even there. There were simply too many of them.

"Redstone 2 . . . now!" Digger yelled.

More pistons sounded as underground mechanisms moved and shifted. Suddenly, stacked pistons raised a stone wall three blocks high into the air, right in front of the charging monsters. As the monsters smashed into the barricade, NPCs quickly built steps to get on top of the wall. They poured a lethal rain of arrows down on the onslaught of advancing creatures.

The monsters retaliated. Blazes shot flaming balls of death at the defenders on the stone wall, forcing them off the fortification. Endermen teleported forward and tried to remove underground blocks that supported the redstone circuits, but the wall still held. Zombies charged the walls and started climbing over their own comrades, standing on their blinking bodies so that they could gain access to the top of the wall. Warriors tried to stand on the barrier and hack at the decaying monsters, but the blazes took a terrible toll on any who climbed atop the ramparts.

The users fired their TNT cannons into the mass of blazes, but quickly drew a fiery response. Prepared for this, the warriors put away their bows and swords and instead pulled out snowballs. They ran forward, throwing the icy spheres at the flaming creatures. The balls of snow extinguished many of the monsters, but there were too many of them to have much effect. Charging onward, the users smashed into the ranks of blazes while the TNT cannons turned their fiery breath upon the skeletons.

Standing atop a block of dirt, Gameknight watched the battle and could tell that they were completely outnumbered. They were exchanging a defender for each monster, life for life . . . it was a losing battle. They needed more warriors . . . but where would they come from?

Then, out of the corner of his eye, he saw that lone painted zombie again, its chest of purple flowers standing out against the rolling green knoll on which they stood. Suddenly, there were two painted zombies, both with leather caps, then another and another. With a roar, hundreds of zombies came running over the hill, headed straight for the battle.

But, to his shock, Gameknight could see Monet113 running directly toward the creatures. She had no weapon in her hands . . . in fact, she had her hands outstretched, ready to give one a hug.

Leaping off the wall, he sprinted toward his sister. But as he ran, Gameknight saw her embraced by one of the zombies.

Is she being attacked? Gameknight thought. *I have to hurry . . . I can't let anything happen to her!*

And then he met the first of the painted zombies. Readying his weapons for battle, he stopped to stand his ground. But instead of attacking, the monsters ran right past him and headed for the endermen that were just beginning to get into the battle. Confused, Gameknight continued to sprint toward his sister, dodging painted zombies as he ran. When he reached her, he found that Monet was in tears . . . and so was the zombie.

What's going on?

"Gameknight, you remember Ba-Jin," Monet said.

He looked at his sister, confused.

"You remember . . . from the zombie-town?" she added.

Gameknight999 looked at the zombie and saw a huge purple flower painted on her shirt and colorful dots running down her arms and legs—and then he remembered her. Monet had taught this zombie how to paint and express herself. This was the zombie who, with her colorful friends, had stood up to Xa-Tul and refused to kill for no reason. This was the zombie into whom Monet had planted the seed of self-respect and pride, and the refusal to simply follow orders and put the clan above the individual. Here was where the trouble had begun to brew in zombie-town, boiling over into this army of painted monsters; a violent group of vicious creatures now transformed into a caring community. This zombie was living proof of the effect Monet had on those around her; her joyous, colorful view of life had infected the green child.

"Gameknight999, ah . . . I . . . was looking forward to meeting you again," Ba-Jin said.

"What is happening here?" Gameknight asked as he turned and looked at the battle.

The painted zombies were locked in battle with the

endermen, keeping the lanky creatures from attacking the NPCs.

"The Free Zombies, as we call ourselves, are here to help," Ba-Jin said. "It is time for the violence to stop and everyone to live together in peace."

"That's right!" Monet added.

Suddenly, the ground started to shake as the sound of thunder filled the air. The noise was so loud that they had to cup their boxy hands over their ears. Looking toward the source, Gameknight could see the forest trees shake and fall, as if some kind of gigantic beast were pushing through the woods, snapping the birch trees as if they were sticks. Then the sound of metal grinding on metal filled his ears, and the User-that-is-not-a-user knew what was causing all the commotion.

Out of the forest came a silvery wall of arms and legs, with dark eyes glaring at the monsters before them and vine-covered chests shining bright in the sunlight. They were iron golems—hundreds of them—and at the front was a metal giant whose head was ringed with a crown of vines: the king of the golems.

Gameknight sprinted to the king's side.

"Thank you for coming," Gameknight said. "I fear that without you, we would have lost the battle. Now, with you here, we may yet turn the tide."

"I did not come here for you, User-that-is-not-a-user," the golem king said. "I came for them."

The metallic creature pointed at the villagers who fought behind the stone wall.

"We protect NPCs whenever we can," the metal giant said. "We do not care about your struggle with the virus. We are here for the villagers, and that is all."

"Well," Gameknight said. "I'm just glad you're here."

The iron wave lumbered past the

User-that-is-not-a-user and smashed into the monster horde. Flinging their arms up quickly, the golems sent monsters flying into the blue sky, their bodies flashing red when they crashed to the ground. They were like a massive juggernaut of fists and feet as they pushed through the multitude of zombies trying to climb over the defensive walls. Seeing the mass of angry metal approaching, the zombies retreated, running back to their leader, Xa-Tul.

With the golems, the painted zombies, the users, and the NPCs, they might just have a chance at defeating this army of monsters. But looking across the battlefield, Gameknight could tell that a lot of creatures were going to die on both sides of the battle lines . . . and that was not good.

There must be a way to stop all this violence . . . but how?

Suddenly, Monet113 screamed.

Turning around, Gameknight found Herobrine standing next to his sister, his evil hand on her shoulder. Before Gameknight could move, the vile shadow-crafter disappeared, taking his sister with him. He could see Herobrine materialize behind all his troops, right next to the new king of the endermen, Feyd. Shoving Monet into the dark red creature's arms, Herobrine disappeared, then reappeared atop the tallest tree in the line. He cupped his hands around his mouth to make his voice project, then let loose a bloodcurdling scream that pierced through the sound of battle and made all the combatants take a step back. For a brief moment, the fighting stopped, which allowed the four horsemen to screech out commands, causing the army of monsters to withdraw and move back to the tree line, regrouping behind their leaders.

The painted zombies, unsure what to do, moved

back to their leader, Ba-Jin, while the iron golems stopped in place and glared at Herobrine, a vile loathing in their dark eyes. The users, suspicious of anything the monsters did, moved back to their TNT cannons, repairing and rearming as needed.

Gameknight sprinted back to the village and mounted the barricade while the NPCs tended to their wounded. Standing on the top of the wall, he watched as Herobrine teleported back to Feyd. Pulling Monet from the enderman's icy grip, he teleported to the center of the field of battle with his prisoner, then drew his sword.

"Come out and face me," Herobrine yelled, "or she dies!"

Herobrine put his sword right next to Monet's head. His eyes flared bright as he stared directly at the User-that-is-not-a-user.

"Gameknight, you can't go out there," Hunter said. "It's a trap, and you know it!"

"She's right," Crafter added. "You'll just be playing into his hands."

Gameknight looked at his friends, then turned and looked back at his sister. He could see the look of terror in her eyes as she stared up at the diamond sword that was pressing against her forehead.

"I don't have a choice," Gameknight said. "She's my sister—my responsibility—and I won't let anything happen to her, not if I can stop it."

The User-that-is-not-a-user then jumped off the wall and walked straight toward Herobrine. Reaching into his inventory, he could feel both his weapon and the Book of Wisdom, but he didn't know how either was useful. Regardless, he had to face the evil shadow-crafter, even if it meant his doom.

CHAPTER 26

THE LAST BATTLE

As Gameknight walked toward Herobrine, he was suddenly knocked to the ground, hitting his head, hard. It took a moment to figure out what had happened.

Was I attacked? Did Herobrine do something? What's happening?

Confusion slowly faded away as he realized that he was not hurt . . . just stunned and surprised. But as he stood, he saw a stocky figure running toward Herobrine with an iron pickaxe in his hands.

"You aren't going to hurt Gameknight999—I won't allow it!" the NPC said.

And then Gameknight realized who it was . . . Stonecutter.

"Nooooo!" Gameknight yelled . . . but it was too late.

Stonecutter crashed into Herobrine, the shadow-crafter in a woodcutter's smock simply staring at the attacking NPC in disbelief. Herobrine crashed to the ground and lost his grip on Monet, who started to run back to the NPC army. Feyd moved quickly, teleporting directly in front of her. The tall enderman wrapped his clammy arms around her, then teleported back to the monster army, his captive held tight.

Frozen with panic, all Gameknight could do was watch . . . and pray.

"So, you wish to test yourself against the great Herobrine," the evil shadow-crafter said. "As you wish."

Herobrine charged at the stocky NPC, his diamond sword seeking flesh. But Stonecutter was faster than Herobrine expected. Stepping to the side, he let the razor-sharp blade just barely miss his shoulder, then spun and brought his mighty pickaxe down onto the Maker's back. Herobrine flashed red, and a look of surprise came across his vile face. Turning, he attacked Stonecutter again, charging straight at the NPC, but just as he reached his adversary, he disappeared, then materialized behind him. Slashing with his sword, Herobrine tore at the NPC's HP, gouging armor and tearing flesh.

Stonecutter screamed, then lunged at his adversary, swinging his pickaxe with all his might. Ducking under the attack, Herobrine teleported to an unprotected side and slashed at his enemy's exposed skin. As Stonecutter yelled out in pain, he flashed red again and again.

Turning to face the attack, the stocky NPC found nobody there. Herobrine had teleported again. Looking to his left and right, Stonecutter readied his pickaxe, then glanced to Gameknight999, who was slowly standing to his feet. The User-that-is-not-a-user started to run to his friend.

"I'm sorry; I couldn't stop him," Stonecutter yelled to the User-that-is-not-a-user. "I've failed."

"No, you haven't failed," Gameknight screamed. "Just run away."

Stonecutter shook his head, refusing to give up, then spun around just as Herobrine's sword came down on him, claiming the last of his HP. As Herobrine laughed, Stonecutter disappeared with a pop, his items falling to the ground. Three glowing balls of XP bobbed near his pickaxe. Herobrine, looking at the approaching User-that-is-not-a-user, smiled as he stepped forward. The XP flowed into Herobrine's body, and instantly his appearance changed from that of some unknown woodcutter to that of Gameknight's friend, Stonecutter.

"NOOO!" the User-that-is-not-a-user screamed as he approached his enemy.

"Why, hello, Gameknight999," Herobrine said using Stonecutter's deep voice. "You like my new look?"

"I hate you," Gameknight spat.

"Oh, my . . . are we angry?" Herobrine mocked.

Gameknight stared at the monster before him. He looked identical to Stonecutter, with his stocky build, dark hair with a sprinkling of gray, and the numerous scars on his arms and hands.

How am I supposed to battle my friend? Gameknight thought.

This was the exact replica of his friend, save for one thing . . . the eyes. They still had the evil glow of Herobrine, and that was what Gameknight had to concentrate on . . . the eyes.

"What's wrong, Gameknight? You look a little pale," Herobrine said. "Maybe I should build another wall and let all my friends and family perish again."

Herobrine laughed.

"Shut up!" Gameknight yelled. "Leave his memories alone!"

"This is truly wonderful. I get to torture you using your friend's body." Herobrine smiled. "If only you could feel your friend in here." Herobrine pointed to his head with a boxy finger. "What's his name? Oh, yeah, Stonecutter. If you could only feel Stonecutter's torment for failing to protect you . . . it's just delicious."

Screaming, Gameknight charged at his enemy, his diamond sword in his right hand, his iron sword in his left. They clashed at the center of the battlefield like two titans, their swords creating a shower of sparks when they met.

Spinning to the side, Gameknight slashed out at Herobrine's legs with his iron sword as he stabbed with his diamond blade . . . but Herobrine wasn't there. Rolling across the ground, Gameknight narrowly avoided Herobrine's attack as a diamond sword whizzed past his ear.

He knew he couldn't stand toe-to-toe with Herobrine . . . he needed some help. He could see a lanky young NPC standing on the fortified wall, his dark hair matted down with sweat. Taking a step back, he shouted to the boy.

"Herder . . . NOW!"

The NPC nodded his head, then disappeared. In seconds, a growling, howling sound filled the air as a hundred wolves came bounding over the defensive wall and headed straight for Herobrine.

"Was this your plan?" the shadow-crafter asked. "You're siccing a bunch of dogs on me? Ha, ha, ha!"

Herobrine laughed as he brought out a light brown egg that had dark brown spots all across its surface. He threw it to the ground, and a rabbit suddenly appeared, the black and white bunny hopping around playfully. Herobrine pulled out more of the spawn eggs and tossed them, more and more, until the ground was covered with the fluffy creatures.

As the wolves approached, they were completely distracted from their task, chasing the rabbits instead of attacking Herobrine.

"You see, fool, wolves have no choice but to chase a rabbit," Herobrine explained. "Your little friend, the Oracle, created the wolves with this flaw in them. She was as careless as she was weak. When I destroyed her, she begged for her life on her hands and knees like one of her pathetic little pets there."

"That's not true," Gameknight yelled as he charged again.

His diamond sword slashed out at Herobrine, but the shadow-crafter disappeared. Instinctively, Gameknight brought his iron sword over his back. It blocked an attack that would have done some damage. He then spun and charged at the monster, trying to get to Herobrine before he disappeared . . . but the shadow-crafter was just too fast.

Pain shot through Gameknight's arm as the diamond blade found his flesh. He could feel his HP decrease.

Turning, he charged, slashing, at the monster. Herobrine brought up his diamond blade and blocked the attack, but he was not fast enough to stop Gameknight's iron sword. The metal point found the shadow-crafter's ribs, making him flash red.

Herobrine screamed out, more in frustration than in pain, as he teleported four blocks away. His eyes now blazed with an intensity that made Gameknight look away.

"I'm done playing with you, User-that-is-not-a-user," Herobrine screamed, his voice filled with rage. "It is time that I show you what I can really do."

Charging forward, Herobrine slashed at Gameknight999 with his blade. The shadow crafter was moving it faster than ever. Backing up, Gameknight blocked the advance. He tried to use his other sword to counterattack, but the shadow-crafter was still too fast.

Suddenly, Herobrine disappeared, then materialized on Gameknight's side. Stabbing at Gameknight, he disappeared again, then reappeared, his sword driving into Gameknight's shoulder. Over and over this happened, all in just a single second, Herobrine attacking from what seemed like multiple places, nearly simultaneously. Gameknight tried to block the attacks, but they were happening all around him; he could not be everywhere at once.

Pain shot through his body as he was wounded repeatedly. Bringing up his sword to block an attack, Gameknight saw his arm flash red as Herobrine's blade tore into his back, destroying the last of his diamond armor. As the protective coating fell to the ground, Gameknight was overwhelmed with pain and fear as Herobrine pressed the attack. He slashed at him until he barely had any HP left. And as Gameknight's legs failed him, he fell to the ground with Herobrine standing over him.

Some of the items in his inventory spilled out. Right next to him, he could see the Book of Wisdom lying on the ground, open. The reflective page was facing him . . . his own reflection mocking him.

Desperation surged through him.

Was this the end? Gameknight thought. *Is this the end of my life?*

He knew that the digitizer was still fried, but he wouldn't use it anyway, for that would unleash Herobrine on the physical world. Gameknight999 wasn't going to do that, no matter what.

"Well, you seem to be in a difficult predicament," Herobrine mocked as he stared down with glowing eyes.

Glancing to the fortified wall and the NPCs, Gameknight could see Herder standing on the barricade, a look of panic and fear on the lanky youth's face. At that moment, a calm realization filled his mind. This was the moment . . . the time to act and use what the Oracle had given . . . he knew it! As he reached into his inventory to draw out the weapon, he could hear the music of Minecraft swell and grow in volume.

"You can't help him with your pitiful music, Oracle," Herobrine spat as he raised his sword. "He is mine!"

Gameknight pulled out the pink egg, its dark pink spots almost glowing with anticipation. With all his strength, he threw it at his enemy. Stepping back quickly, Herobrine watch the egg hit the ground and crack open, his sword held ready. But what stepped out shocked them both. A pig . . . a little harmless pig, probably the lowest and most insignificant of creatures.

This is supposed to defeat Herobrine? Gameknight thought.

The dark shadow-crafter laughed as Gameknight's hope fell to nothing. Moving next to the pig, Herobrine held his sword up high, ready to destroy the innocent creature. But, instead, he lowered his weapon and picked up the insignificant little pig. Herobrine threw it as far as he could, sending it sailing through the air like a pink missile. When it hit the ground, the pig flashed red and disappeared. Where it landed remained only pieces of pork and three balls of XP.

A pig . . . how was a pig supposed to help?

Gameknight wanted to scream at the Oracle for this betrayal, but before he could even move, Herobrine was standing over him again, an evil smile on his face. And at that moment, Gameknight999 knew that this was truly the end.

CHAPTER 27

MONET113

"It is time for you to choose," Herobrine said with a slow, methodical voice. "Either take the Gateway of Light . . . or die."

Gameknight glared up at the vile monster, but was overcome with a sense of defeat. He hadn't been smart enough, or strong enough, or good enough to defeat Herobrine. The bitter taste of failure filled his entire being as he stared up at his enemy. But there was still one thing he could do.

"I will never help you escape these servers," Gameknight said, trying to make his voice sound strong, though it cracked with fear. "I would rather die than use the Gateway and let you get into the physical world."

"As you wish," Herobrine said with a sigh.

The vile monster glanced at Monet113 and smiled, then turned back to stare down at Gameknight999.

"I would have preferred that you were the instrument that let me loose on the world, but no matter." Herobrine glanced at Monet again. "I'm sure the little girl with be less stubborn than you."

Gameknight laughed.

"You have no idea," the User-that-is-a-user said with a smile.

"Goodbye, Gameknight999," Herobrine said as he raised his sword.

Just then, a wave of glass bottles flew through the air, some of them directed at Gameknight999, others aimed at Feyd. Turning his head, Gameknight could see that Shawny had built a tall tower of wood with a line of dispensers sitting on top. Redstone could be seen flashing atop the tower, triggering the dispensers to fire ammunition as fast as possible.

Bottles began hitting the ground near Gameknight and Herobrine, the red liquid within splashing all over the pair. But Gameknight was ignoring the healing potion that was coating his body. He was instead watching the bottles of blue liquid landing amid the sea of endermen. Instantly, the dark creatures started to sizzle and smoke as the water within the bottles splashed over their clammy skin. Feyd released his prisoner as water sprayed across him.

As soon as the king of the endermen released his grip, Monet113 bolted toward her brother. As she ran, she pulled out her bow and fired at Herobrine. With the shadow-crafter's back turned, he did not see her shots as the first arrow sank into his shoulder. When Herobrine turned to identify his attacker, Gameknight rolled onto his side, then kicked Herobrine hard in the stomach, sending him flying backward.

Standing, Gameknight faced his enemy, his mind filled with anger. Monet ran to her brother's side and drew her own sword.

"I thought I might give you some help," she said.

But Gameknight did not hear. His mind was overwhelmed with rage, but not at Herobrine . . . at the Oracle.

You said that the Book of Wisdom was supposed to show me where to find the wisdom and courage to face Herobrine, but all it showed me was myself.

Suddenly, images of their past adventures flashed through his head: rescuing Monet from the zombie-town, defeating the spider queen, escaping Herobrine's trap at the jungle temple, escaping Xa-Tul at the desert village, defeating the Elder Guardian . . . all these things required courage and wisdom. And

Gameknight had found these traits within himself . . . they'd been there all along. He *could* do this!

But then something that the Elder Guardian had said echoed within his mind.

Sometimes, the lesson is the journey and not the destination.

Defeating the Guardian hadn't been the important thing in the Ocean Monument; it had been figuring out how to defeat him with the help of his friends. The real lesson was that working together with others makes a person stronger than himself, alone . . . and that was the secret that he needed.

"HUNTER, FIRE ARROWS ALL AROUND US!" Gameknight screamed. "ALL ARCHERS, FIRE AROUND US . . . KEEP HEROBRINE CLOSE TO US."

Suddenly, the air was alive with pointed shafts as arrows fell from the sky. This forced Herobrine to keep his teleportation close to the brother and sister.

Gameknight moved next to Monet. But instead of attacking Herobrine, he focused on defending himself and his sister. Monet saw this and instantly went on the offensive. When Herobrine moved to block Monet's attack, Gameknight slashed his blade against the shadow-crafter's armor, causing it to crack.

Together, they pushed back Herobrine's attacks, but he was still too fast, and was doing damage to both Gameknight and his sister. As they circled each other, the User-that-is-not-a-user saw the spot where the pig had landed, the three balls of XP still glowing bright . . . and then Gameknight started to laugh.

He'd figured out the weapon that the Oracle had given him, that pig-spawn-egg . . . and it was brilliant.

"HERDER . . . I NEED YOU!" Gameknight yelled.

"I don't have any more wolves," the boy screamed from the walls.

"Not wolves . . . pigs," Gameknight shouted.

"Attack with pigs!"

He could hear shouts of confusion from the village walls, but he knew that Herder would not question him . . . he would just follow orders.

Suddenly, the oinks of fifty pigs filled the air. Deflecting one of Herobrine's attacks, Gameknight dared a glance. He could see Herder charging forward, sitting on a saddled pit, a long fishing pole out in front of him. A carrot hung from the end of the fishing line, causing the pig to sprint. Behind him, a massive cluster of pigs followed close behind, all of them after the elusive vegetable.

As Herder neared, he started throwing the carrots at Herobrine, the orange vegetables raining down on him. Soon, Gameknight could hear howls of laughter from the village as the pigs surged forward, trying to get to the carrots. Herobrine was having difficulty attacking Gameknight and Monet with the pigs in the way, and was getting frustrated.

"Stonecutter, if you can hear me . . . I need you," Gameknight shouted to Herobrine.

The vile shadow-crafter turned to face Gameknight999 and started to say something, but then paused as his eyes faded a bit. Then Herobrine stopped fighting and just stood there. The User-that-is-not-a-user could see that some kind of internal battle was taking place within Herobrine, his eyes glowing bright, then fading, then glowing again. But, finally, the internal light of Herobrine's evil presence finally faded to the background, his eyes turning to a stone gray.

"Stonecutter, attack the pigs . . . quick."

Stonecutter looked at Gameknight, confused.

"JUST DO IT!"

Raising his sword, Stonecutter brought Herobrine's blade down on a pig. It squealed, but it was not fast enough to escape the second strike. It disappeared with a pop as its HP was consumed, leaving behind pork chops and three glowing balls of XP.

Suddenly, Stonecutter's eyes started to glow as Herobrine took back control of the body, but it was too late. The balls of XP were moving toward the shadow-crafter. Gameknight pushed through the pigs and moved behind Herobrine, then gave him a shove, pushing him into the balls of XP.

Instantly, the evil shadow-crafter started to shriek as the XP flowed into his body.

"*NOOOOOO!*" Herobrine screamed as his body started to change, morphing into the XP of his last victim. This time it wasn't an NPC—this time it was the lowliest and most insignificant of creatures . . . a pig.

Herobrine dropped his sword as he fell to the ground, landing on his hands and knees.

"No . . . no . . . noooooo!" the evil shadow-crafter screamed. "Someone help me!"

But as he yelled, his voice became higher and higher in pitch, until it sounded like the squealing of a . . .

His body shrank down as the gray smock of Stonecutter changed into a soft pink. Muscular arms and legs shortened as they became stubby little pig-legs, his head shrinking to a small rosy cube.

And then it was done . . . Herobrine had been captured within the body of a pig.

Before he could move, Digger was there, placing blocks of cobblestone around the pig. The animal's eyes glowed bright, each filled with a venomous hatred for Gameknight999, but Digger ignored the animal and focused on the enclosure. In seconds, the pig was completely surrounded with stone.

Herobrine had been captured.

CHAPTER 28

COMMON GROUND

The capture of Herobrine caused a panic among the monsters. Zombies gave off sorrowful moans as the skeletons clattered nervously. The flames of the blazes flickered with uncertainty as their labored wheezing became louder and louder. The only creatures that seemed unmoved were the endermen, their dark forms staring at the stone enclosure with hatred in their eyes.

At that moment, the painted zombies moved out onto the battlefield again and surrounded Gameknight, Digger, and Monet. They glared at the other monsters as the iron golems moved forward to show their support, their lumbering forms making the ground shake.

As the users moved next to the iron golems, Ba-Jin stepped forward and faced the four horsemen. Gameknight looked through the group of users, trying to find Shawny. He saw Honey-Don't and Zefos, their weapons still in their hands, looks of grim determination painted on their square faces. Moving next to Gameknight was Lowpixel, the great mapmaker; his old friend, AttackMoose52; and Disko42, the redstone master. He could see friends who had been there on the steps of the Source during the previous battle . . . and now they were here again. He felt truly blessed to have all these friends. Who would have thought that Gameknight999, once the self-proclaimed king of the griefers, would have so many users willing to help him? He was humbled and was about to say something, but suddenly a young voice cut through the uneasy silence.

"Herobrine used you so that he could escape from Minecraft," Ba-Jin shouted to the monsters that stood before them. "He wasn't going to change anything in Minecraft." She pointed up at the sun. "The sun would still burn, and we would still have to stay near our HP fountains. All would have stayed the same, except for the lives that would be lost in this battle."

She stepped forward so that she was closer to Xa-Tul than she was to her own forces. Running forward, Gameknight stood next to her, both swords held ready.

"No one benefits from this battle continuing," she said to the king of the zombies. She then turned and addressed all the monsters. "Go home, take care of your children, take care of your communities, and be at peace. The Last Battle is over." She looked around and could see items strewn all across the battlefield, balls of XP from the deceased floating in the air. "No one has won here today, but we all have lost. Look at all the lives that were ended because of Herobrine's hate-filled insanity."

Slowly Ba-Jin raised her hand high into the air, claws extended. She then shouted in a loud, high-pitched voice.

"To those who died for the clan, the salute of sacrifice is given."

Many of the zombies behind Xa-Tul looked at the young girl, then glanced across the battlefield at all the items and pieces of zombie flesh. Slowly, green zombie hands began to sprout out of the sea of decaying bodies, clawed fingers spread wide.

Many of the NPCs saw this and also raised their

hands, fingers extended.

Then the zombies leaned back their heads as one and howled such a sorrowful moan that tears came to Gameknight's eyes. Looking across the zombie army, he could see that many of the decaying monsters were also weeping for the friends and family who had died. Turning back to look at the NPCs, he could see similar emotions playing on their faces.

"For the good of the clan," one of the zombies shouted, but this time it was not echoed. Nothing had happened this day for the good of the clan . . . it had only been for the good of Herobrine, and they all now realized it.

As the zombies slowly brought down their hands, they looked about the battlefield in disbelief, then glared up at their king. Gameknight could see that they hated Xa-Tul for bringing them to this place and letting all these monsters die for nothing. A few of the decaying monsters broke formation and moved through the portal, leaving the battlefield.

"NO!" barked Xa-Tul. "The war has not ended!"

Ba-Jin then took a step forward and looked directly at the zombie king, challenging him. Gameknight moved directly behind her.

"It's over!" the young zombie said, then turned her back on the zombie king and the other horsemen, showing her lack of fear.

"NO!" screamed Xa-Tul, but none of the zombies listened.

This display of bravery triggered something in the zombies that they hadn't felt for a long time . . . respect. Abandoning the battle, they started to move through the portal in pairs . . . then in groups . . . then in mass, taking the shimmering gateway back to their zombie-towns.

The skeletons could see countless white bones

scattered across the battlefield. There were so many that they couldn't even count them. Many grumbled questions to their leader, but Reaper ignored the complaints and shouted orders.

"Get ready to attack," the skeleton king shouted in his raspy, clattering voice. "We will fight to the end!"

The bony monsters looked up at their king with a look of hatred, then followed the zombies' example. Moving through the pale yellow gateway in large groups, the skeletons ignored the glaring stare of Reaper, abandoning the Last Battle.

Once the monsters of the Overworld left the field of battle, the blazes could tell that the balance of power had significantly changed. They were now completely outnumbered, and had no desire to face the users with their snowballs while at the same time having to confront the iron golems. Ignoring the growling commands of Charybdis, they too moved through their portal and went back to the beautifully warm and smoky Nether.

Last to leave were the endermen. Their hateful stares were focused on the User-that-is-not-a-user, but he did not return their gaze. In fact, everyone was careful to not stare back at the dark monsters, for it could enrage them. The shadowy monsters could fight only if something enraged them . . . if left alone, they could not join the fighting. It was how they were programmed.

Knowing that there was no battle here for them, then endermen used their teleportation powers and disappeared back to their home, The End. In seconds, all that remained of the enderman army was a cloud of purple teleportation particles.

And in minutes, triggered by the bravery of Ba-Jin, all that remained of Herobrine's massive army were the four horsemen, the apocalypse that they sought to bring to Minecraft having evaporated into peace. The four evil creations all glared down at Gameknight999, but he did not shrink back. Instead, he stared back at them, unafraid, for now he knew the secret to accomplishing great deeds and shouldering impossible responsibilities: let those around you help, for no one is truly alone.

"Your armies have abandoned you," Gameknight said. "Your leader, Herobrine, lied to you, and has been defeated. You now have two choices before you. Either go away, now and forever, or fight all of us and be destroyed."

Charybdis did not even pause to think. He pulled his flaming horse around and rode into his portal, going back to the Nether. Reaper then did the same, guiding his horse through the pale yellow portal and back to his skeleton-town.

That left only Xa-Tul and Feyd.

Gameknight took a step forward and glared at the king of the zombies.

"What will it be, zombie?" the User-that-is-not-a-user asked. "Will you leave, or will we dance again?"

Suddenly, a user named Sky came to his side, AntPoison standing directly behind. Their diamond swords sparkled in the sunlight, reflecting shafts of light on the ground at Xa-Tul's feet.

The zombie king growled, then guided his zombie horse to the portal. But before he stepped through, the monster turned his massive head and glared at the User-that-is-not-a-user one last time, his dark eyes filled with hatred and a thirst for revenge.

"Xa-Tul and Gameknight999 will meet again," the zombie king growled. He then guided his zombie horse through the portal and disappeared.

"That leaves only you, enderman," Gameknight said.

"You killed my predecessor, Erebus, and now you insult all endermen with your presence in Minecraft," Feyd screeched in a high-pitched voice. "This is not over, User-that-is-not-a-user. Your time will come!" The king of the endermen then pointed his long black arm at all the users and NPCs. "All of you will rue the day that you tangled with Feyd, king of the endermen. We will exact our revenge, and then you all will suffer."

One of the users named GeneralSprinkles laughed, causing others to snicker, mocking the monster's screechy speech. With his eyes glowing bright red, Feyd glared at Sprinkles, then disappeared, leaving behind a cloud of purple teleportation particles that quickly evaporated.

Another user, Mumbo, sprinted forward and quickly broke a block on each of the portals, causing the shimmering fields that were held within the obsidian rings to grow dark and disappear. The user turned and waved at Gameknight999, then disappeared as he disconnected from the server, the rest of the users following his lead.

Sighing with relief, the User-that-is-not-a-user looked down at Ba-Jin and found the zombie looking up at him, smiling. Gameknight marveled at her bravery and wisdom. She had turned back the tide and stopped all the killing with her tenacity and refusal to be violent . . . she was remarkable. And the seed that had been planted within the young zombie to cause this change had come from a delicate flower being painted on her shirt. Gameknight's sister had ignited this fire with the spark of her art and love of beauty in all its forms. Monet had truly caused trouble in zombie-town, for her actions had changed the entire species.

Suddenly, Monet's arms were wrapped around Gameknight's chest, squeezing him tight.

"I knew you could do it," Monet said excitedly, wiping tears from her cheeks.

"I didn't do it . . . we did it . . . all of us," Gameknight said as he gestured to the NPCs, painted zombies, and iron golems. "That's what the Oracle was trying to teach me. Alone we are weak, but together we are strong."

The Oracle sounds like a wise person, a line of text said in Gameknight's mind.

Shawny, is that you? Gameknight thought, his words appearing in the chat window.

Nope—it's me, your dad.

"Dad?!" Gameknight said aloud.

"DAD!?" Monet shouted. "He's back?"

Gameknight nodded. *What are you doing on the chat?* he asked.

I came home early and found Shawny in the basement, his father explained. *Shawny explained about the digitizer, and I fixed it. I'm disappointed that you messed with it.*

It wasn't my fault; it was Jenny's! Gameknight explained. *I was just doing what you told me to do . . . watch after my sister.*

Well, we'll discuss this when you get home. Are you ready?

Just a moment, OK? There are some things I need to do first, Gameknight said.

His father waited for a moment, then replied.

OK.

"Great," Gameknight said.

The others looked at him, confused, but he didn't care.

Gameknight moved to the king of the golems. The mighty giant looked down at him with his dark eyes, an angry scowl on his iron face.

"Thank you again," Gameknight said, bowing his

head. "The iron golems helped save Minecraft once more. All will hear of your bravery and might."

"We are always here to protect villagers," the metal giant said, then turned and led the other golems back into the forest, the rumbling thunder of their metal feet slowly fading away.

Moving back to the painted zombies, Gameknight found Ba-Jin being congratulated by her fellow monsters. Nearby, he saw Hunter standing next to Crafter, her eyes cautiously darting to the green creatures. Moving to her side, Gameknight grabbed her hand and pulled her toward Ba-Jin.

"Ba-Jin, thank you for your help," Gameknight said. "But the challenges are not over. We must find a way for NPCs and zombies to live in peace."

Ba-Jin looked up and found Hunter staring down at her.

"You gave the Salute for the Dead?" Hunter said, a sound of surprise in her voice.

"We call it the Salute of Sacrifice," Ba-Jin answered.

"None of our people should have to sacrifice or die because of hatred," a voice said from behind.

Turning, Gameknight found Stitcher approaching, pushing her way through the users and zombies.

"There is much in common between our people," Stitcher said, her voice echoing with strength. "But we must learn more about each other so that we can find more common ground. It's not necessary for us to always be killing each other . . . we can live in peace."

Hunter looked down at Ba-Jin, then glanced across the army of painted zombies. Bringing her gaze back to Ba-Jin, she nodded her head, her crimson curls bouncing like coiled springs. Ba-Jin reached out with her clawed hand, touched Hunter's red hair, and smiled.

"Your hair is beautiful," the young zombie said as

her dark claws caressed Hunter's shining locks. "I'm going to paint a picture of it when I get back to our zombie-town."

"Maybe I could see it, someday," Hunter replied.

Ba-Jin smiled and nodded her head.

"It is time we went back home," the zombie said as she turned to face Monet113. "Will I see you again?"

"Absolutely," Monet answered.

Ba-Jin smiled again, showing her sharp, jagged teeth. Raising her hand over her head, she led the painted zombie army back into the forest and toward the caves that led to their portal.

Turning away from the painted zombies, Gameknight found Crafter and Digger standing before him.

"I knew that the User-that-is-not-a-user would not fail us," Crafter said in a loud voice.

A jubilant cheer rang out from the NPCs as they moved out from behind the defensive wall, many of them holding a block of dirt or stone. They moved to the cobblestone cube that held Herobrine and placed the blocks on top of the prison, each wanting to contribute to the enclosure.

"What do we do with him?" Gameknight asked, pointing to the growing pile of blocks.

"Every year, we will have a celebration in this village," Crafter explained. "NPCs will come from all around to place a block onto the tomb of the evil Herobrine, and all will help keep him trapped here in his pig-body, forever."

Gameknight moved to the mound that was already four blocks high and placed a hand on the cool stone. He thought about Stonecutter, and the sacrifice he'd made to protect him. Likely, Herobrine would have defeated Gameknight if it hadn't been for the stocky NPC's strength when he was trapped within the vile shadow-crafter's mind. Stonecutter had finally protected those who were relying on him. In fact, he had protected everyone.

"I won't forget you, Stonecutter," Gameknight said to the pile of stones, then turned and faced his sister.

"OK, Jenny, it's time to go home."

CHAPTER 29
GOING HOME

Gameknight put an arm around Monet113 and gave her a hug.

"Believe it or not, I'm glad I had to chase you into Minecraft," Gameknight999 said. "If we hadn't been here, I don't know what would have happened."

"Likely, Herobrine would have taken over Minecraft and destroyed us all," Crafter said. "We needed the symbol of the User-that-is-not-a-user to bring us all together and stand up against his evil plans."

"And if Monet113 hadn't come into Minecraft, the painted zombies wouldn't have helped us," Stitcher added. "Her art allowed NPCs and zombies to work together for the first time . . . maybe it will lead to a lasting peace between our people."

"I hope so," Monet113 said. "But next time, I will—"

Suddenly, a circle of light enveloped Monet113. Its intensity made Gameknight feel as if he were staring into the sun, forcing him to step back and look away. When the glare faded, she was gone.

Dad, is she OK?

Right as rain, his father replied. *Now it's your turn.*

Gameknight looked at his friends and could feel small square tears running down his face. He felt incredibly sad. These were his friends—his family—and he hated to leave them. But he knew that he was from the physical world, and that was where his physical family lived . . . his home. He had to go.

"I'm going to miss all of you," Gameknight said, his voice choked with emotion. "But I will be back to visit . . . this time sooner than the last time."

"You promise?" Stitcher asked with a scowl.

Gameknight nodded his head, causing the young NPC to smile. Running forward, Stitcher gave him a gigantic, bone-crushing hug, then stepped back, wiping tears from her eyes. Suddenly, a pair of bodies slammed into Gameknight, knocking him to the ground. Looking up, he found Topper and Filler wrapping their small arms around him, hugging him with all their strength.

"You can't go," Topper said.

"Yeah, you have to stay," Filler said, her eyes filled with tears.

"I'm sorry, kids, but my world is out there, in the physical world. But I *will* come back and visit . . . I promise."

"You promise . . . for real?" Filler asked.

Gameknight nodded his head as he stood, helping the twins to their feet.

"I'll be back," the User-that-is-not-a-user said. "Besides, someone has to keep you two out of trouble, and since I'm the biggest rule-breaker in Minecraft, I know just what you'll be planning."

The twins giggled, then ran to their father, Digger, who was approaching. The big NPC walked up to Gameknight999 and placed a muscular hand on his shoulder.

"We started out as enemies, Gameknight999,"

Digger said, making Gameknight lower his head. Reaching out, Digger lifted his chin so that they were looking eye-to-eye. "But now we are like brothers . . . we are family . . . and family always takes care of family, right?"

"Right," Gameknight answered.

Turning, he faced Hunter. He could see that there were tears in her eyes, and that made him smile.

"Shut up," Hunter snapped as she wiped her cheeks dry.

"I hope you have found peace, Hunter," he said.

She looked up at him and smiled, then nodded his head.

"Maybe," she replied. "These new zombies . . . maybe there are things in common between them and us . . . I don't think they need to be exterminated. Maybe I can put aside the need for revenge and just live my life."

Gameknight smiled, causing her to smile back, nodding her head.

The User-that-is-not-a-user then turned to his oldest friend in Minecraft, Crafter.

"Are you going to be OK?" Gameknight asked.

"I think so," Crafter replied. "We'll take the minecart network back to our village. It may take a while, but since we don't have armies of monsters chasing us, we can take our time getting back home . . . for a change."

The young NPC placed a hand on Gameknight's shoulder and looked up at him with his big blue eyes.

"Be at peace, User-that-is-not-a-user."

"And you, Crafter," Gameknight replied.

A warm glow started to surround Gameknight, making Crafter step back and wave, triggering all the NPCs to wave and say goodbye. As the glow grew brighter, Gameknight could hear the music of Minecraft build within his mind. Suddenly, the ancient voice of the Oracle rose up.

Take what you've learned here in Minecraft back to the physical world, the Oracle said as the music of Minecraft swelled. *You have grown a great deal, but still have much to learn.*

Thank you for everything, Oracle, Gameknight thought. *I will carry your lessons with me.*

That is all I can hope for, she replied.

As the music of Minecraft grew louder and louder, the Oracle left Gameknight999 with one last message, her words echoing in his mind as he disappeared from Minecraft:

Imagine what you can accomplish . . . then do it!

READ AN EXCERPT
FROM THE NEXT
GAMEKNIGHT999
ADVENTURE!

SAVING CRAFTER

CHAPTER 1

CRAFTER

Looking down on the battlefield, Crafter watched as the last of the zombie horde disappeared into the woods, their fallen comrades leaving behind glowing balls of XP and the occasional sword. Piles of zombie flesh floated about across the grassy plain.

"They almost made it to the village gates that time," Stitcher said.

She paced nervously along the battlement, her eyes probing the forest for any sign they might return.

Crafter grunted his agreement.

"If they didn't have all those leather caps, they'd be forced to attack at night," Digger said. "Then at least we'd know when to expect them."

"The zombie king is driving them harder and harder," Hunter added as she put away her bow and wiped her square forehead with a green sleeve. "Did you hear the zombies during the battle? They blame us for the defeat of their king's master, Herobrine."

"Yes, I heard them," Crafter snapped. "Everybody heard them. The zombie commander screamed it loud enough for all of Minecraft to hear him."

"We need to do something. We need . . . you know . . . *him*," Hunter said.

"He's done enough for us," Crafter said as he walked across the top of the wall and took the stairs down to the ground level. "We need to learn to defeat these monsters on our own."

He stopped at the foot of the stairs and looked back up at Hunter. The noon sun shown down on her curly red hair, causing it to glow with a crimson aura.

"Besides, the decision by the Council of Crafters still holds; we cannot interact with users for any reason—no matter what," Crafter explained. "Would you be asking him to risk his life again and come back *into* Minecraft? Are we that desperate?"

"Well . . . I don't think . . ." she stammered.

"We will let Gameknight999 live his life in the physical world while we live ours in the digital world," Crafter explained. "Is that understood?"

Hunter nodded her head as she moved down the stairway, her curls bouncing like little scarlet springs.

Crafter gave her a smile, then moved out through the iron doors to examine the battlefield closer. The lanky form of Herder followed close behind.

"Baker, collect all that XP," Crafter ordered one of the NPCs. "Give it to Smithy; we need some more enchanted armor. Gather it quickly before it disappears. Digger, we need some archer towers on either side of the bridge that crosses the moat. When Xa-Tul returns with a bigger zombie army, he'll be able to cross the bridge and reach the iron doors. With that huge golden sword of his, he'd smash them to bits within seconds and open the village to his horde. We have to protect it."

Digger nodded.

"Herder," Crafter continued, "we need your wolves to . . ."

Stopping in mid-sentence, the young NPC looked at the grassy plain before him, his bright blue eyes open wide with surprise. Zigzagging across the grassy plain was what looked like a dark, shadowy bolt of lightning. No, not a lightning bolt—the shadow of a lightning bolt, for it was all black, a diseased stain on the surface of the Overworld. It moved erratically, zipped forward in one direction, then abruptly turned and moved in another. Like a hound sniffing after a wild rabbit, the jagged shadow shot about the plain, stalking something. In a second, it had reached Baker and touched his foot. Instantly, the NPC yelled out in pain as black shafts of . . . something . . . stabbed at his foot.

"Baker, are you alright?" Crafter asked.

The dark stain seemed to hear Crafter's voice. It moved away from Baker and headed toward the young NPC. Herder stepped in front of his friend and looked down at the shadowy presence. When it touched the tip of the lanky boy's foot, he jumped into the air like he'd stepped on burning coals. Suddenly, the jagged stain turned when it had found the scent of its prey and shot straight for Crafter. As he took a step back, Crafter felt an evil presence emanate from the jagged shadow; hateful spite rose from it like steam from a boiling pot. Turning to run away, Crafter took a single step, but the shadowy form had found its target. It jolted forward with lightning speed, enveloping the ground under the young NPC's feet.

Crafter screamed out in agony as the shadow of evil attacked him from the ground. Dark shapes shot from the diseased patch like shadowy jagged blades. They stabbed at Crafter over and over again, causing his body to flash red, signifying the consumption of his HP. Hunter ran to Crafter's side and shot an arrow into the shadowy stain, but the barbed projectile just sank into the sandy ground, having done nothing.

Crafter moaned as he fell to the ground. Dropping her bow, Hunter caught the young boy. She held him above the ground and away from the darkness. It tried to reach Crafter, slicing the air with slivers of darkness, but could not. Hunter jumped from here to there, playing a deadly game of keep-away. As she held her friend high over her head, the shadow of evil evaporated, leaving behind a scarred patch of ground where it had killed the grass and flowers. Eventually, satisfied the threat was gone, she slowly lowered him to the ground.

"Crafter, are you alright?" she said softly.

NPCs ran out of the village gates to help their leader. A group of horsemen rode quickly across the bridge that spanned the moat and streaked past their fallen leader. Taking up defensive position, the cavalry readied themselves for battle in case the zombies were preparing an attack.

"Hun . . . ter," Crafter said weakly.

She looked down at him and could see that his skin was pale. He was cold to the touch. His normally bright blue eyes were dim and faded, as if the life had been sucked out of them. A worried look came across her face.

"Crafter, are you OK?"

He shook his head slightly, then tried to speak, but he was too weak to be heard.

"What was that?" she asked in a low voice.

He shook his head again. Leaning down, Hunter brought her ear to Crafter's lips.

His voice was so weak. Terrified thoughts of Crafter dying shot through her mind and chilled her to the bone.

Taking a strained breath, Crafter tried to speak again. "Bring Gameknight99—"

And then he fell unconscious, his breathing labored

"What did he say?" Digger asked.

Looking up, Hunter was surprised. She hadn't noticed the big NPC next to her.

"He said to bring . . . *him*," she said. "It must be serious."

Standing, she scooped the young NPC into her

arms and handed him to Digger.

"Take him to Healer," she said. "I will handle the rest."

"You should take others with you," Digger said, motioning for the cavalry to approach.

"No, I can move faster alone," she said and asked for two of the warriors to dismount. Jumping into the saddle, she took the lead to the second horse. Turning, she looked down at Digger. "Take care of him. I'll be back as quickly as I can."

"We will do what is needed."

"I know you will." She then turned her horse, pointed toward the dark forest, and patted the horse on the neck. "I need every ounce of speed you can give me, horse, for we ride to save Crafter."

Sprinting away, she disappeared into the woods.

But where will I find Gameknight999? she thought as she galloped across the Overworld.

CHAPTER 2
GAMEKNIGHT999

Gameknight999 swung his sword at his adversary's head, stopping just short of actually striking a blow.

"You're supposed to block," he sighed. "I told you—don't just focus on attack; block as well."

"I don't see what this has to do with playing Minecraft," his opponent complained.

"There are monsters out there who will try to kill you," Gameknight explained. "You have to know how to defend yourself or you'll just die right away. Now come on, Dad, concentrate!"

Bringing up his wooden sword, Gameknight pointed it at his father.

"Are you ready?" he asked.

His father, Monkeypants271, nodded his head. His appearance was that of a monkey dressed in a Superman outfit, complete with red boots and a large "S" painted on his chest. Gameknight looked at his father and just shook his head.

"Why did you have to choose that ridiculous skin?" he asked his father.

"All the other skins looked like warriors or ninjas or monsters," Monkeypants explained. "I wanted something that would stand out and people would remember."

"Well, if that was your goal, you nailed it." Gameknight said.

Monkeypants grinned.

"And what about that name? Really, Monkeypants?"

"I like it, don't you?" his father asked.

Gameknight shook his head, embarrassed.

A ridiculous name and a ridiculous skin, Gameknight thought. *What was I thinking, trying to teach my dad how to play Minecraft?*

At least his father was home instead of away on one of his many trips. Gameknight was glad his dad was back, though having to teach him how to play Minecraft wasn't what he had planned for their time together. He wanted him here, at home, just not down here in the basement or in Minecraft . . . in *Gameknight's* domain. What could he say? His father knew how rough it was on the family when he was gone. But was this how he was trying to make up for it, all in one day? By playing Minecraft?

"Come on, let's try this PnP thing again," Monkeypants said, raising his own wooden sword, ready for battle.

Gameknight sighed.

"I told you a hundred times, *Monkeypants*. It's not PnP, it's PvP."

"Oh yeah," his father answered. "PnP is a transistor junction in computer chips, me bad."

"Not me bad, *my* bad!" Gameknight shouted, exasperated.

"There's a difference?"

Gameknight shook his head again, frustration boiling just beneath the surface. Looking past his father, he could see a tall outcropping that stood some twenty blocks in the air, a long stream of water falling from its height and flowing into a deep underground chamber. That was their next destination: the underground tunnels where zombies would be lurking. But first he had to teach his father how to fight or it would be a quick trip.

Sighing, he readied another lame attack to demonstrate fighting in Minecraft.

Why is he doing this? Gameknight thought. *Why is he pretending that he wants to learn how to fight? I know he hates this. All he ever wants to do is build and invent . . . and the funny thing is, that's all I want to do with him. Why doesn't he realize that?*

Gameknight could remember the countless hours he'd spent with his father, building invention after invention in their basement. He loved those times, but his father was never home anymore and those invention sessions had happened so long ago.

It's unfair. Jenny has her art, that's her thing. But my thing is helping my dad build new creations, and I can't do that when he's always gone. Gameknight was getting angry. *He's never home, and now that he is, we're wasting time in Minecraft!*

Gripping his wooden sword firmly, he danced from

foot to foot as he allowed his anger to slowly dissolve, then sprang forward, his blade streaking through the air. As he neared, Monkeypants just dropped his sword and stared over his son's shoulder. Gameknight stopped the attack and started to yell at his father, but Monkeypants raised a hand and pointed to the edge of the basin where they were practicing.

Looking in the direction his father was pointing, Gameknight999 was surprised to see Hunter approaching on horseback, a riderless horse trailing behind. She rode to the edge of the falling water, then dismounted right where Gameknight had battled that spider on his first day trapped inside Minecraft. As soon as her feet hit the ground, her hands slid into her sleeves, arms linked across her chest.

Gameknight signed.

"The Council of Crafters has decided that users and NPCs must stay separate?" Gameknight asked.

Hunter nodded her head, her red hair appearing to be painted to the side of her head rather than the flowing curls that Gameknight had become accustomed to seeing. He wasn't *in* the game now, as he had been before.

In the past, Gameknight had used his father's invention, the digitizer, to actually enter the game and live it for real. While he was *in* Minecraft, everything looked so vivid, with more detail than he'd ever seen on the screen. But right now, everything was flat and just looked painted on the surface—like Hunter's curls. Gameknight and Monkeypants weren't really *in* the game, they were just playing it; a pair of users practicing their PvP skills.

Hunter glanced above Gameknight's head, then looked back down at him. He figured she was looking at the shining white server thread that stretched up from his head and high into the sky, connecting him to the servers. Only NPCs could see the server threads; that was how they knew who was a user and who was an NPC. Well, that and the letters that floated above his head.

"Why are you here?" Gameknight asked.

She did not respond. Instead, she glanced at the horses, leaning her square face toward him and then toward the horse.

"I think she wants you to go with her," Monkeypants said.

Gameknight looked at his father. Monkeypants stepped forward as he put away his wooden sword and moved to his son's side. Turning back to Hunter, Gameknight saw that she had mounted her horse again. The riderless mount leaned its head down into the pool of water and took a drink.

"What's wrong? Is everyone alright?" Gameknight asked.

She shook her head.

"Is it Stitcher?" he asked.

She shook her head again.

"Herder? Digger?"

She said no.

"Crafter?"

She nodded.

"Oh no, not Crafter! What's wrong?"

Hunter looked at the riderless horse and looked back down at Gameknight.

"I understand," he replied.

After he leapt up onto the horse, Gameknight999 turned and looked back at his dad.

"Oh, no you don't," his father complained. "I'm going with you."

Monkeypants ran toward the horse and leapt up into the saddle behind his son.

"Let's go," Gameknight said as he turned to face

Hunter, but she was already riding away toward the village.

Urging the horse to a gallop, he followed his friend toward the village that lay hidden behind the horizon. Glancing at the sun overhead, Gameknight knew it would only be up for a few more hours; they would barely make it to the village before sundown, and only if there were no delays.

"Monkeypants, take out your bow and get ready to use it," Gameknight said as they galloped across the landscape. "There will be more monsters as it gets closer to sundown, and we can't afford to let any of them slow us down. If you see any monsters, shoot them. Don't wait for an invitation. Do you understand?"

"That seems pretty . . . violent," Monkeypants said. "You know, sometimes there's a better way other than the sword."

"Yeah? You tell the monsters that when they attack," Gameknight replied.

"Son, you will have to make choices in life when faced with challenges," his father lectured. "You will have to decide if you're going to do the *right* thing that will help the most people, or take the easy path and do the wrong thing. Violence is almost always the wrong path, for it just leads to more violence. Maybe we need to think of another way."

"Dad, you still don't understand Minecraft. Any monster you see will want to attack you over and over until all of your HP is gone. For us right now, we'd just respawn back near our hidey-hole, but for the NPCs, it means death. So we have to look out for them and make sure that they're safe, and the only way we can do that is if we're alive . . . you understand?"

"Well . . . yeah, I guess so," Monkeypants answered.

"So if you see a monster, like that spider over

there," Gameknight said, pointing to the top of an oak tree. "You attack it before it can attack you. That's how you stay alive in Minecraft."

Monkeypants nodded his head, but Gameknight999 could tell that he still didn't get it.

Hunter veered to the right; she'd seen the monster hiding in the tree branches. As they skirted around it, Gameknight kept a watchful eye on the creature. The spider sat atop the leafy canopy, glaring at them with its multiple red eyes, a look of anger in those tiny glowing orbs. Monkeypants drew an arrow back and aimed it at the monster but did not fire. Instead, he only watched it as they passed.

Spurring his horse forward, Gameknight followed Hunter's stead, moving from a trot to a gallop. As he rode, his thoughts went to his friend in trouble. *I won't let anything happen to you, Crafter,* he thought. *I'll take care of everything.*

He tried to make his thoughts sound confident and strong, but he knew that things must be dire to warrant Hunter looking for him. Driving his horse even faster, he thought about all of his friends while his soul filled with dread.

CHAPTER 3
THE VILLAGE

The trio rode across the landscape in silence, pushing the horses as fast as they could go. Glancing nervously at the square sun overhead, Gameknight followed its progress as it slowly crept down toward the horizon. They had to make it to the village before sundown or they were in trouble; in Minecraft, nighttime was monster-time.

Shifting his eyes from left to right, Gameknight was on high alert. He could hear the clicking of spiders echoing across the land, but he didn't see any of the fearsome creatures.

"What is that sound?" Monkeypants asked.

"Giant spiders," Gameknight answered.

"I'm sorry I asked. Where are they?"

"They're hiding. Usually they would attack anyone found on the surface of the Overworld, but that was before."

"Before what?" Monkeypants asked.

Gameknight brought his horse up next to Hunter's and looked at his friend. She turned her head and gave him a knowing smile, then turned and looked forward.

"Before we killed their queen, Shaikulud," Gameknight said proudly.

"You killed their queen?" his father asked. "Why?"

"Well, she was trying to kill all of us," Gameknight999 explained. "The spider queen was leading a massive army against everyone in Crafter's village. I did what I had to so that my friends would be safe."

Monkeypants nodded his head and said nothing. Gameknight couldn't see the look of pride on his father's face.

"So what do you think is going on now?" Monkeypants asked.

"I don't know. Hunter said it was something about Crafter," Gameknight said as he turned his head so that he could look at his father over his shoulder. "He's my best friend, Dad, not just in Minecraft, but . . . in the whole world. I have to help him."

"Well, I guess we will found out soon," Monkeypants

said as he pointed a stubby square finger forward.

Gameknight turned and could see the village in the distance. A tall cobblestone wall ringed the collection of wooden buildings, a watery moat surrounding the fortification. A narrow wooden bridge spanned the moat, stretching across to the iron gates embedded in the barricade. The orange light from the setting sun reflected off the metallic doors, making them appear to glow as though heated from within. It was beautiful. Tall archer towers loomed high up in the air, positioned near the bridge to give the warriors a clear field of fire upon those foolish enough to cross the walkway uninvited.

"We have to hurry," Gameknight said as the sky darkened, the bright orange slowly blushing to red.

As they approached the village, they could hear the sad growling moans of zombies in the nearby forest. Glancing at the dark collection of trees, Gameknight could see the decaying creatures gathering near the tree line. Those with leather caps stood out in the sunlight, their head-covering keeping them safe from the burning rays of the sun. Those without were hiding in the ever-darkening shade.

"Are those real zombies?" Monkeypants asked, his voice filled with excitement.

"Yes."

"Let's go closer. I want to see them."

"This isn't a game for these villagers, Dad. The zombies are going to try to break into the village and destroy everything. We need to do what we can to help them, and that means getting inside the village as quickly as we can."

Spurring their horses into a sprint, they headed straight for the wooden bridge that led into the village. When they neared, Gameknight jumped off and landed gracefully on the ground.

"Monkeypants, go into the village!" Gameknight shouted as he ran toward the zombie mob. "I'll be there in a few minutes."

"But what about—"

"Just trust me and follow Hunter. I'll be right behind you."

Not waiting to see if his father listened, Gameknight ran straight toward the tree line. Looking up, he smiled as the sparkling faces of stars emerged on the darkening sky. He stopped at a place he knew was still within range of the archer towers and pulled out blocks of TNT. He placed them on the ground in plain sight and spread them out across the battlefield. Running toward the bridge, he placed more of the striped blocks on the ground. As he crossed the wooden overpass, he placed four explosive blocks right in the middle and then ran for the iron doors. When he passed through the entrance, he looked for the person who he knew would be nearby—Stitcher. He found her on the top of the cobblestone wall. Her bow was likely tucked away in her inventory, her arms linked across her chest.

"Stitcher, shoot the TNT if you need to drive the zombies back," he yelled to her. "Destroy the bridge if you must. It would be better to rebuild it rather than let the monsters reach the doors."

He knew she wouldn't respond, so he turned and sprinted for the cobblestone tower that stood at the center of the village. He found Hunter standing near the entrance, Monkeypants at her side. As soon as she saw him, she walked through the open doorway and moved into the building.

"Come on, Monkeypants," Gameknight said as he streaked past his father.

Moving to the far side of the room, he pulled out

his pickaxe and dug into the corner block. After three strong blows, the cobblestone shattered, revealing a dark vertical shaft, a ladder clinging to one wall. Without waiting, Hunter stepped onto the ladder and disappeared into the darkness.

"Follow me," Gameknight explained. "We're heading for the crafting chamber. That must be where Crafter is."

Gameknight stepped onto the ladder and began his climb down. He could hear the footsteps of his father above him, though he could see little in the darkness of the tunnel. As he descended, Gameknight looked down and could see a faint circle of light in the distance—a torch marking the end of the vertical descent. Slowly, the tunnel grew brighter as he drew near the end. Jumping off the ladder, he found Hunter waiting for him, a look of annoyed impatience on her face. Gesturing him to follow, she sprinted down the horizontal passage. After running a dozen blocks, she stopped and placed blocks of stone in front of her, closing off the tunnel ahead. She then turned and closed off the passage behind them, enclosing her and Gameknight in darkness and blocking out his father...